THE

RAILWAYMAN'S DAUGHTER

W. E. MORELAND

PublishAmerica
Baltimore

ISBN: 1-4137-4049-9
PUBLISHED BY PUBLISHAMERICA, LLLP
www.publishamerica.com
Baltimore

Printed in the United States of America

For
Allen
with love

THE
RAILWAYMAN'S
DAUGHTER

———

CHAPTER ONE

Dorothy, still drowsy from the long anaesthetic, took her daughter's hand and squeezed it.

"I'm sorry to have given you all such a fright. I don't know how I came to fall like that."

"It was an accident, Mum, these things happen. You mustn't fret about it, just concentrate on getting better." Elizabeth's heart ached for her mother who looked so small and vulnerable in between the crisp white sheets of her hospital bed. Her hair needed brushing, and she still had blood behind her fingernails from the fall.

"What a way to spend your eightieth birthday, Mum. Never mind I'll be in tomorrow and we'll make the most of it. I'll bring in a nail file and your hairbrush."

The following day Elizabeth cancelled the family birthday celebrations. She bought a large, iced cake, collected a photograph from her mother's flat, and a few essential items, and went in to visit her. Her mother was sitting up in bed looking quite perky. Several large balloons were tied to the bed rail. Her table was covered in birthday and get-well cards. Baskets of flowers festooned the windowsills. Elizabeth was amazed at the difference in her mother.

"Gosh, you look better today. How are you feeling? Everyone has made an effort to get all these cards here so quickly, Mum."

"Haven't they, dear? I had to get help opening them, there were so many and my hand is very sore." Dorothy's hands were a bit shaky and she needed assistance to open Elizabeth's present. It was a pretty silk dressing gown and nightdress.

"How lovely, dear, it's perfect for in here, it's so warm. Thank you for thinking of the photo." She hugged it to her chest and slipped it in the drawer beside her bed.

Mother and daughter were very close. Life had not been easy for Dorothy, and the two had shared many difficulties over the years. Elizabeth's happy and successful marriage to Tom had not weakened the bond between them, indeed in many ways it had strengthened it. Her mother loved him, and he had soon become like a son to her.

Although the surgery had gone well, there were medical complications. Dorothy was not as quick to get back on her feet as everyone hoped she would. She was dismayed at this, but accepted that it would be necessary for her to spend some time in a rehabilitation centre. She needed intensive physiotherapy, to get her walking again.

"It's not just the hip replacement giving your mother problems. It is her ongoing cardio-vascular disease." The consultant, a sympathetic man, liked the spirit of the old lady. "We'll get her right, but it is going to take some time I'm afraid. I think she will do well in rehab. She has the right attitude."

A geriatric nurse before retiring, Dorothy felt a mixture of emotions at becoming a patient herself. Her wonderful sense of humour came to the fore and she soon became popular with the nurses and physiotherapists in her new placement. She had the liveliness of one twenty years younger, and was still a fine-looking woman. Her white hair was as shiny as her brown bob had been years before. Her eyes were forget-me-not blue, and if her eyesight had faded a little, the colour certainly had not. She had always seemed taller than her five feet four inches. This was due to the way she carried herself, her back straight, and her head held high. She had passed this discipline on to her sons and daughter, all of whom had overtaken her height by many inches.

The long days were filled with physiotherapy, stretches of boredom and daily visits by Elizabeth. Friends visited too, but her close relations were scattered far and wide and visits were not made easily.

Her daughter was now her contact with the real world.

"Have the bills been paid, dear?"

"Yes, Mum, all of them. Richard is fine. He is learning how to cook and shop. He can even use the washing machine." Dorothy's youngest son still lived at home, and was not allowed to do anything in the house in spite of his mother's age.

The weather was unusually hot during her forced confinement indoors. Elizabeth would arrive, dressed coolly to combat the heat. She was far taller than her mother, taking after her father's family for looks. Her two brothers resembled their mother. Elizabeth was the sensible one of the family, the one they all ran to for help. It had always been like that. She was, however, quite sensitive beneath her capable exterior, and inclined to worry. Her dark hair, prematurely greying, was due to a family trait rather than worry. For the time being her days were filled with getting her mother fit to get home as soon as possible.

"I hate being cooped up like this, Elizabeth. I can't walk far normally, but at least I can get fresh air when I feel like it."

The long hot days dragged slowly by. Although often exhausted by her treatment and learning to walk again, Dorothy found it difficult to sleep. It was too hot for comfort. The mattress and pillows had plastic covers beneath the normal sheets and pillowcases. These were obviously necessary, but did not make for comfort. She perspired profusely and longed for her poly-cotton covered duvet and her own small bed. A light was left on all night for the nurses' benefit. It happened to be above her bed. This also ensured her lack of sleep.

As she lay there, hour after hour, her thoughts drifted down the years to her two marriages and back to her childhood. How vivid the memories were. It was as if it were yesterday.

* * *

Little Dottie Fisher bounced up and down on the end of her bed. Florence, her grandmother, was busy doing the weekly wash downstairs. She had lit the boiler earlier and when the water was hot enough, she had put the washing in to soak. Dottie could hear the activity downstairs and knew that before long Grandma would come and get her, and the day would begin. She chewed on the bread and jam she had been given to keep her going until things quietened down a bit. Then Grandma had time to wash and dress her. Dottie had lived here in the small two-up and two-down terraced house in Garston, a suburb of Liverpool for two years now.

"I'll be up soon, Dottie," Grandma called upstairs.

In 1915 Dottie's mother Emily had died tragically in childbirth; the baby was stillborn. Her distraught father had tried to keep Dottie with him and carry on his job with the railways as an engine driver. Eventually he realised that even with the best will in the world, and the unstinting help of neighbours, he could carry on no longer. Shift work meant many hours away from home, and so, reluctantly, he took up Emily's mother's offer of more permanent help. Dottie was totally happy with her grandma. She saw her dad as often as possible and she was mercifully too young to miss her mother. She had been barely one year old when the tragedy occurred. Today was to be another turning point in her short life. Happily eating her hunk of bread and jam, she was blissfully unaware of how her life was about to change.

Chapter Two

Archie Fisher jumped off the tram as it slowed down at the corner of his mother-in-law's street. He had something very important to tell her, and he knew it was going to be difficult. He had just finished a long, hard shift. The Great War had not been over by Christmas, as everyone had said, but he had been exempted from the armed forces because of the nature of his work. He did more than his fair share as a civilian. His engines pulled coal and munitions, and often troops. He regularly did double shifts because of the shortage of labour. A man of modest height, but handsome, he was blessed with a mop of thick brown hair. His clear blue eyes twinkled with good humour. Dorothy had inherited both his sweet nature and his beautiful eyes.

He pushed open the back door of the little house, and there was Flo, enveloped in steam. She looked hot and dishevelled as she turned and spoke.

"Hello, Archie. I didn't expect you here this morning."

"I have something to tell you, Ma," he replied quietly. The tone of his voice made Flo's stomach flutter.

"You'd better come in the other room and sit down. You look all in lad. I'll put the kettle on, I could do with a cup of tea myself."

Archie walked through to the living room. It was clean and bright. The furniture was old, but well polished and comfortable. He sank down into an armchair by the window, which was open slightly. A gentle breeze moved the net curtain, and it brushed against the aspidistra that sat on the sill.

"Tea won't be long." Florence Truman came into the room, glad of a respite from the washing. She was a thin woman with a pale face that showed a lifetime of hard work and worry. A life she had somehow risen above, and found joy in family and friends, and the occasional good things that happened.

11

"Now then, Archie, what's this all about? You seem a bit bothered to me."

"It's good news really, Flo." Then, the words came tumbling out. "I'm getting married again. She is a wonderful woman. I still can't believe she said yes. You know her, she's Olivia Markham. Her dad is the manager at the mill. She works in the office there." Archie stopped for breath. He was relieved to have told Flo about Olivia. It would, after all, affect her life considerably. She had been a mother to Dorothy for two years now and loved her grandchild dearly. Florence sat down in stunned silence. She had no idea that Archie was seeing anyone on a casual basis, never mind planning to get married, and to Olivia Markham of all people.

"Yes I know her, Archie, and her reputation. How in the name of heaven did you get involved with her?" Flo stared questioningly at her son-in-law. She was shaking with shock and disbelief.

Archie was taken aback at Flo's tone of voice. He had expected her to be upset, but not to this degree.

"She is a lovely woman, Flo. I can't believe that she has agreed to marry me, of all the men in Garston, a widower, with a child at that. She could have any man she wanted."

"She probably has," replied Flo tartly. "She has had her family heartbroken with her goings on. Her father is at his wits end trying to keep her under control. She's man mad and that's all there is to say about her."

Archie was speechless. He had been so thrilled when Olivia had agreed to walk out with him. He had looked at no one since Emily had died. He had grieved quietly and privately, losing himself in his job. Then recently, he and Olivia had started catching the same tram when he was on his morning shift, and casual conversation had quickly become a looked-for treat when the stint next came round. One thing led to another and before long he had fallen totally under her spell.

"She is getting her claws in you, Archie, because most eligible men are away in the army, and her father is trying to keep her on a tight rein. You must bide your time on this wedding idea, give yourself a chance to get to know her better. She certainly won't want Dorothy and I wouldn't let Dorothy go to her if she did."

Archie listened to Flo's outburst quietly. He did not know how to cope with it. However, he knew that nothing anyone could say would make him change his mind. Flo would come round, and he would set up home with Olivia. Perhaps Dorothy could come for weekends at first, and gradually get used to her new mother. She would still see lots of her grandma, as she would not be far away.

"Don't spoil it for me, Ma. I love the woman and that is that. I can never repay you for taking Dottie in the way you did. You gave her a good and loving home for little or no reward."

"I didn't do it for reward." Flo was shocked at the mere suggestion. "She is my flesh and blood. It will break my heart to lose her. Can't you leave her here with me? I could adopt her. I am not too old to bring her up, and you wouldn't be far away." Flo began to weep, silently at first, then with loud sobs that racked her slight frame. The enormity of what was happening began to sink in.

Dottie could remain upstairs no longer. She heard the voices of the two people she loved best in all her small world getting louder and louder. Grandma was crying. She clambered down the steep staircase, her bare feet sticking to the linoleum as she stepped onto the hall floor. She walked into the living room, her eyes wide with fear. Flo turned and saw her. She jumped up and flung her arms round the frightened child. She hugged her tightly.

"Dottie, Dottie, Grandma is here, everything is fine. Come on, let us make some cocoa, you like that, and you can sit and drink it with Dad."

"You were crying, Grandma, are you hurt?" The little girl peered anxiously into her grandmother's face.

"I'm better now, dear. Go and sit with Dad. I will be back in a minute." Flo left the room, glad of an excuse to be alone and compose herself. Her mind was racing and she sought to get control of her thoughts as she put the milk on the stove to make a drink for Dottie.

Flo calmed down as she busied herself in the kitchen. She must not let Dottie see her like that again. When Archie had gone she would be able to think more clearly. If he went ahead with this marriage she must see to it that Olivia never had charge of his daughter. The woman was selfish and conceited, and Flo knew that Archie would regret the day he fell for her. She was beside herself with worry, and yet her heart ached for her son-in-law. She remembered how happy he and her daughter Emily had been during their short time together. The arrival of Dorothy had completed their happiness. She poured the milk into Dottie's special mug, stirring in the cocoa and sugar as she did so. Then she took a deep breath and went back into the other room.

CHAPTER THREE

Over the next twelve months, Flo did all she could to persuade Archie not to marry Olivia. She knew that this woman was not the one for him, but Archie was besotted with her. She was an exceptionally beautiful young woman. She wore her black hair rolled up high around her head in the fashion of the day. Her eyes were a curious tawny gold. She was a little on the plump side for her short stature, but knew how to make the most of her assets.

Flo's attitude towards Olivia saddened Archie. He knew that his fiancée's past history was not what he would have chosen, but it was all behind her now, and she was to be his wife.

"We have fixed the date for the wedding, Flo," he said one day. "You are going to come, aren't you? Mrs Roberts says she will look after Dottie."

Mrs Roberts was the sort of neighbour everyone should have, always ready and willing to help.

"Dottie isn't going?" Flo was taken aback. "She will feel very left out. I don't think that is a good idea."

"Olivia believes weddings are not the place for children."

"This is your daughter, Archie!" exclaimed Flo. "She is not just some distant relation who might be a nuisance on the day."

Archie mumbled something about not wanting to upset Olivia, and the conversation was closed. He could have added that he was not happy about the decision himself. He and Olivia had almost rowed about it, but she had talked him round.

A few days before the wedding, which was to be a quiet one, Archie and Olivia took Dottie into Liverpool on the tram to buy her a new coat. It was to be a consolation present for not going to the wedding. Dottie was excited. Due

14

to the war, new clothes were a rarity. Olivia certainly had a flair for fashion within the limits of what was available. She chose Dottie an emerald green, woollen coat with a matching bonnet, and the little girl was delighted. Her soon-to-be stepmother picked her up to show Archie how good they looked together. As she did so she pinched Dottie's plump little thigh as hard as she could.

"Archie, see how pretty she looks. Doesn't she suit green?"

The pain that made her leg ache shocked Dottie. She looked into Olivia's face ready to cry out, but something in those golden eyes, so close to hers, made her bite her tongue. It was the first incident of cruelty that Dorothy experienced at the woman's hands. It was a sign of how things could be, and the fulfilment of Flo's fears for Archie and the child.

Shopping completed, the couple returned Dottie to her grandmother, where she stayed until the wedding, two days later. These were the last truly happy days of her childhood.

Archie and Olivia set up home in the Railway house, which went with Archie's job. Her dad told Dottie that Olivia was now her new mother. She would still see Grandma from time to time, but must realise that things were different now.

"Do I call you Grandma too?" asked the child of Olivia, who was standing at Archie's side. The new Mrs Fisher drew herself up to her modest five feet two, and turned furiously on Dottie.

"You most certainly will not. You will call me Olivia, not Grandma, Mother, or anything else."

Archie was taken aback.

"Surely, Olivia, she can call you Mum, I'd really like that. It would make us a proper family, which is what we are now," said Archie quietly. He was very upset at this unexpected turn of events, and surprised at Olivia's attitude.

"People would think that I am years older than I actually am," she replied. "No, I have made my mind up, and that is the end of the matter." She turned on her heels and stalked out of the room. Archie was flummoxed. However, on reflection he decided to let the matter go. After all, as long as she was good to Dottie, what did it matter what she was called? Flo felt that Archie was losing his integrity and that he was too weak to stand up to Olivia. She tried to tell him, "Archie, I know you love Olivia but you must not let her rule you. Remember Dottie is your child and she needs you now more than ever. You must look out for her. Olivia is inclined to be a little jealous, you know?" It was difficult for Flo to say more as she did not want to fall out with him.

So Archie and Olivia began their new life together. The war came to a close, and Dottie started school. There she became known as Dot, Dorothy being too grand, and Dottie too childish for a girl at St John's Church School. She did not like going there, largely because Olivia would send her dressed in unsuitable clothes and shoes. These were hand-me-downs from various sources. Olivia preferred to spend any spare money on her own back. The other children teased her, and she had a tough time coping with them. The first few months, at Archie's insistence, Olivia would meet her from school. She would get her own back for this inconvenience, by threatening Dot on the way home.

"I'll give you such a whipping when we get back. You won't be able to sit down." Sometimes she did, and sometimes she did not, leaving the terrified girl not knowing what was going to happen. If her father was home she knew she was safe. Olivia would be sweetness and light, or just ignore her.

One evening, early that first winter of their marriage, Archie said goodbye to the two girls in his life, and left for work. Olivia pushed Dottie towards the back kitchen door, saying as she did so, "Lock the door and then get off to bed."

Dottie walked the short distance to the door, her bare feet cold on the stone surface, and tried to turn the key. She could not move it. It was a heavy old-fashioned lock, which was badly worn, making it difficult to place the key in it correctly. Like so many things there was a knack to it, but it also required a strong hand. Dottie turned to Olivia.

"I can't do it," she said fearfully, waiting for her stepmother to shout at her, or worse.

"No such thing as can't," the woman said coldly. "You will stay there until you do as you are told. I will punish you if you move without doing it."

Olivia left the forlorn child and went upstairs to lie down. She was feeling unusually tired these days. She only meant to rest for a while, but fell into a deep sleep. It was morning when she woke. She looked at the old brass clock on the chest of drawers. Archie would be home soon. She went downstairs to put the kettle on, to find Dottie still standing by the back door. The girl was stiff with cold, her lips blue. She was shaking with fear. She tried to speak, but Olivia bundled her up the stairs. Archie would be back any minute, and this could be difficult to explain.

"You stupid child, fancy staying there all night. Have you no brains at all? Don't say anything to your father, because he will think you are an idiot. I will bring you a hot drink. You stay there until you are warm again."

Dottie curled up beneath the blankets. She heard Olivia telling Archie as he came through the door that Dottie was not too well this morning.

"Don't worry though, dear, I'll look after her. Children are down one minute and up the next. She will be fine. I would not go up just now, let her rest."

Archie sank down into his armchair, weary after a long shift. It was good to know his daughter was in such capable hands.

Upstairs, Dottie waited in vain for her father to come and see her. She quietly cried herself to sleep. When Archie went up to bed himself, he looked in on her. She was hidden, deep down under the blankets, and he could not see her tear-stained face, or hold her cold, little hands.

CHAPTER FOUR

Dottie never forgot that night. For all her tender years, she had Olivia weighed up, and from then on she began to fight back as best she could. Sometimes, simply by avoiding her, at other times by getting her father in between them. She soon discovered that Archie would not listen to tales of Olivia's unkindness, dismissing them as childish jealousy of the new person in his life. Olivia was, of course, the doting mother whenever her husband was around.

The reason for Olivia's tiredness of late soon became apparent. She realised that she was pregnant.

"Archie, dear, I have such wonderful news for you. I am expecting a baby at the end of the summer." She came to a halt, waiting for his re-action. Thinking to herself that if nothing else it would get his wretched daughter out of the limelight.

"That's wonderful news, Olivia!" He was delighted, but for a fleeting moment a shadow of doubt moved across his mind. He remembered how his darling Emily had lost her life, as their dead son had been delivered. He kept these thoughts to himself, and in the event he had no cause to worry. Edward was delivered safely. Two years later Joan was born. Margaret, who was always known as Meg, was born on Joan's second birthday.

Flo came into her own at the time of Olivia's confinements. She had Dottie to stay for a month at a time. Olivia would not let her own children go to her, but Mrs Roberts, the kindly neighbour, practically lived with them until Olivia was fit again.

"Where shall we go today?" Flo asked early one morning during nine-year-old Dottie's latest stay with her.

"Can we go on the boat?" She jumped up and down with excitement. "Please, please, Grandma, let's go on the boat."

"Get your coat," Flo said, having already anticipated the child's reply. "We'll catch the next tram if we hurry." They ran to the corner of the road, arriving just as the tram appeared. The vehicle rattled off, shaking them about on the hard wooden seats, laughing and joking as they went.

Flo was concerned about Dottie. She looked rather pale to her, and far too thin. She had tried to talk to Archie about her, more than once, but he would not listen.

"She's fine," he had said, "probably outgrowing her strength. She is shooting up like a weed."

The tram arrived at the Pier Head, and Flo and Dottie boarded the waiting ferry for the crossing to Birkenhead. It was a beautiful day. The Mersey was unusually calm, reflecting the deep blue of the sky in its quiet waters. Puffs of white cloud moved overhead, billowing like pillows that had been newly plumped. They disembarked after the short trip, full of fresh air and sunshine. Dottie had colour in her thin cheeks. Her eyes twinkled like her father's as she laughed along with Flo at the antics of two small boys showing off to their mother. They were playing leapfrog over the bollards on the edge of the landing stage.

They went into a small café for a cup of tea and a scone. They watched the world go by through the clear spaces they rubbed in the steamed-up windows. The warmth inside was welcome after the crossing, in spite of the sunshine. Dottie thought that Birkenhead was wonderful, much better than Garston. She was so happy today. All too soon it was time to catch the ferry back to Liverpool, and the last few precious days together, before she was due to return home.

Olivia's stepdaughter had become a very useful person to have around. Olivia had stopped physically hurting her, but continued to make Dot's life a misery in other ways. She took great delight in stopping simple pleasures like a trip to the pictures on a Saturday morning. At the last minute she would insist that Dot must take Edward out for some fresh air.

"I can take him when I get back," Dot said on one occasion, courageously facing Olivia on the donkey-stoned doorstep. This was as far as she had got when Olivia had grabbed her thin arm.

"Not without money you can't, my girl," and with this she tore the pennies from Dot's hand. They were precious pennies that Grandma had given her for a little treat when she went home. She was near to tears. She knew she would never see the money again.

Edward sat in his black go-chair. Four years old, plump and smiling, he adored Dot. She looked down at him resignedly.

"Come on then, we'll go to the park and you can have a go on the swings. No use taking it out on you, is it?" Dot smiled at him. She loved her half-brother so much, as she did Joan, and would doubtless love Margaret too. There was not a jealous bone in her body. Nothing Olivia could dream up to torment her would stop her loving the little ones, as she called them to herself.

It was about this time that Dot resolved to leave home as soon as she could. She was nine years old and had no idea how she was to achieve this, but achieve it she would.

After Margaret was born, life at the Railway house began to change. Olivia turned her attentions to other men. Dot became more of a mother to the little ones than Olivia herself. No one knew better than Dorothy that nothing short of her father taking his head out of the sand could change her life.

CHAPTER FIVE

Olivia was a strong, healthy young woman. She soon recovered from the births of her children. She had Dot to help in their upbringing, and after five or six years of marriage to Archie she began to tire of him. She had been faithful to her doting husband up to now, but it was the advent of a new constable on the beat that gave her thoughts of straying.

One evening, after Archie left for work, Olivia crossed the living room floor to look out of the window. Bored with her life of domesticity, she spotted a diversion in the person of the young policeman. She hurried to the front door, opening it just as he reached the house.

"It is a bitterly cold night, officer," she purred in her soft voice. "Would you like a cup of tea?" She stood on the front doorstep, pretending to polish the doorknocker with her handkerchief. She wore a thin, cotton housecoat, with very little underneath. It was hardly the attire for polishing brass outside.

George Brownlow was a little taken aback. People in those days did, of course, have good relationships with their local bobby on the beat. The attitude and attire of this woman suggested more than a cup of tea was on offer here.

"That would be very nice, madam." He stepped inside, cautiously. He stood awkwardly in the hallway. Olivia smiled, beckoning him into the living room.

Dot was curled up in her father's armchair reading a comic. She was an avid reader, devouring anything that came her way. A smoky fire burned in the black-leaded grate. Olivia touched her gently on the shoulder.

"Time for bed, dear, school in the morning. We can't have rings under your eyes, can we?" Olivia turned to her guest, trying to give the impression of a devoted mother, and at the same time signal her interest in him. Archie was forgotten in the excitement of re-discovering her interest in men, and remembering the thrill of the chase during the years before her marriage.

I wonder why that policeman is here, Dot thought. *There doesn't seem to be anything wrong, or Olivia would be upset.* She went upstairs as slowly as she dared, hoping to hear something that would explain what was going on. Her tactics were to no avail. Olivia closed the door to the living room and only muffled conversation could be heard.

Dot undressed quickly in the cold bedroom that she shared with the others. It was too dark to read, so she settled down to sleep.

"Sh! You'll wake the children," Olivia hissed, sometime later, as she and George reached the top of the stairs. She stifled a giggle, and with much whispering, they went into the big bedroom and closed the door.

"Is that Dad?" Edward, roused from his sleep, asked of Dot.

"I don't know who it is," replied Dot. "Go to sleep, Ed, there's a good boy." Dot had no idea what was going on, but she knew it was something wrong. However, her well-developed sense of self-preservation told her not to tell anyone.

George appeared regularly after that night, and Dot was suddenly forbidden to see Flo anymore.

Olivia hated Dot's grandmother for a variety of reasons. She knew the girl confided in her, and she was scared that something might be said about her nocturnal visitor.

"She is a bad influence on the child, Archie, and fills her head with all sorts of rubbish. She also undermines my authority and it is difficult enough coping with a stepchild without a grandmother's interference." Olivia's voice was loud and determined. She stood with her hands on her hips, her head held to one side.

Archie was dismayed at this outburst. Flo's warnings came echoing down the years.

"That's a bit hard, dear. Flo has been wonderful with Dot. I do not know where I would have been without her when Emily died. Look how good she was when you had the children too." Then he added quietly, "It would break her heart not to see the girl anymore. She is all she has left now."

"For heaven's sake, Archie, don't be so dramatic. Anyway you don't know what it is like for me, coping with these children. You are always at work, away from it all."

He stood silently, listening to her shouting. He almost hated her when she was like this. He knew that it was no use arguing with her. She was being unkind and unreasonable, but she was right about his never being there. He was on the Lime

Street to Euston run regularly now, and the shifts were long. He sighed and slowly nodded.

"All right then, if you think it is for the best."

Olivia smiled her thanks and kissed his cheek.

"It is all for the best, dear, you'll see." Inside she heaved a sigh of relief. She knew that Dot would talk to no one but Flo about George staying the night at the Railway house. Her secret diversion was safe, and she had that bitch Flo out of their lives at last.

Dot was shattered on being told of the decision.

"Please," she begged. "Oh! Please let me see Grandma." Then angrily, without waiting for a reply, she asked, "Why can't I see her?"

She looked into Olivia's eyes. They gleamed with pleasure at the girl's distress, and Dot knew she was beaten.

"It is your father's decision. He knows what's best for you I'm sure. You have no say in the matter anyway."

Dot knew that to argue was futile. She was powerless against this woman who had her father wrapped round her little finger. She did not believe for a minute that this was her father's idea. She also knew that Grandma would be heartbroken about it all.

Flo was devastated, but she had to accept the situation. Olivia would make Dot suffer if the two of them managed to meet. She sent her grandchild cards on her birthday, which she never received. Olivia always intercepted the mail, and not just Dot's. Archie's letters were regularly steamed open and vetted, before being carefully re-sealed and dropped on the hall floor the next day, as if just delivered.

Flo was not one to give up without a fight all the same. She must somehow let Dot know that she understood what was happening. She decided to see if she could enlist the help of Dot's head teacher. One Friday afternoon, she sat in a small dusty office, waiting to speak to Mrs Morris, the principal of the school. She looked around at the shelves lined with old box files and much used reference books. The air smelt of old paper and mildew. She felt nervous and told herself to calm down and gather her wits.

Mrs Morris came briskly into the room.

"What can I do for you, Mrs Truman? I gather it is something to do with your granddaughter." Flo explained about Olivia's ban on Dot seeing her, and how desperate she was not to lose touch.

"Could you tell Dot that I am thinking about her and love her very much?" asked Flo. "I understand that you can't let me see her here, but at least she would know that I haven't given up on her."

"That's all I can do," replied the head, "but I'll do it willingly." She was concerned about Dot herself, but didn't tell Flo. The girl had a good brain and did well in class when she was there. She was, however, frequently absent from school, and there was no continuity in her education. Occasionally the school board followed up the absences, but were usually satisfied with Olivia's excuses, either of her own indispositions or the child's.

"I must leave you now, Mrs Truman, I have a class to take, but I will get someone to bring you in a cup of tea before you go." She felt guilty as she hurried out of the room. Perhaps she should look into Dot's welfare a little more thoroughly. Flo was left amongst the books and papers.

How did I come to be in this position? She did not wait for the tea. She picked up her bag and hurried out of the building as fast as she could.

Knowing nothing of her grandmother's concern, Dot continued her dreary life of skivvying for Olivia and minding the children. She snatched what education she could and dreamed of how things would be when she finally broke free from the woman who made her life a misery.

Every now and then, at night, beneath the thin blankets on her shared bed, she would weep a silent tear for Flo.

"One day, Grandma, it will be all right," she whispered into her hard pillow.

CHAPTER SIX

One beautiful September morning, a few days before Dot's thirteenth birthday, Flo attempted to see her granddaughter. It was Saturday and she knew that Dot was likely to be in the park looking after the children. Olivia, of all people, had joined the Salvation Army. It did no good for the Salvationists' reputation, but provided endless cover for her extra-marital activities. Saturday morning was a genuine Army meeting time to discuss their evening collection arrangements.

"Now I have heard everything," had been Flo's comment when she had been told by a mutual acquaintance about Olivia's enrolment. She had refrained from adding anything further.

Today, Dot had the three little ones with her. Edward was almost eight now. He helped with Joan and Meg, pushing them on the swings, and taking turns with them on the seesaw. Dot sat on the grass reading Jane Austin. It was a library book from school. There were no books at home, and if there had been, she would not have been allowed to read them. Olivia permitted her no time for herself.

Flo walked the mile and a half to the park. She arrived at the swings very warm and puffed.

"You are not getting any younger," she told herself, then seeing Dot and the children, she called out to them.

"Hello there."

"Gran!" shouted Dot delightedly, jumping up off the grass and running over to Flo. "I can't believe it's you." She flung her arms around her grandmother and hugged her tightly. Flo hugged her back, weeping with emotion.

"I have missed you so much, Dottie, but it won't be forever, love. You will be left school soon, won't you?"

"Another year, Gran, that's all," Dot replied, thinking what a long time a year was.

Flo was thinking much the same, but for different reasons. She was now in her sixties and beginning to feel her age. Who knew how long she would live?

"I have something for your birthday, Dottie." She handed over a small white envelope. "It is money I have saved for you. It will give you a start when you leave school. I couldn't get you a present because Olivia would ask questions. There is no point in looking for trouble." She looked around as she spoke. She was uneasy and angry at the ridiculous position Olivia had put them both in.

"I won't stay, Dottie, in case someone sees us and tells your stepmother. You know I'll always love you, and I'm thinking of you, dear."

"Who is that lady?" asked Edward, pointing at Flo, as she and Dot said their good-byes. He was too young to remember her, before Olivia had stopped Flo's visits to the family home.

"Just someone I used to know, Ed." She brushed the tears from her eyes with the back of her hand. *I hate you, Olivia*, she thought. She pushed the envelope into her cardigan pocket, thinking to herself how much older her grandmother looked.

Flo retraced her steps slowly. She too was thoughtful. *The child was painfully thin. In fact she looked half-starved. What was the matter with Archie that he had let things come to this?*

The Fisher children finished their visit to the park, knowing that the Salvation Army meeting would be over by now, and their mother home again. As they arrived at the Railway house, Olivia opened the front door. She was on her way to the shop for a loaf, but Dot could go now instead.

"Get me a large tin from the baker's," she said. "I need it right away, so don't dawdle." She handed Dot a sixpence. The girl tucked the small coin away, drawing Olivia's attention to the envelope.

"What's that?" she demanded of her stepdaughter. "There, in your pocket, that envelope."

"Nothing," replied Dot hopelessly, knowing that this was the last she would see of Grandma's money. "It is just an envelope."

Olivia leaned forward and snatched it roughly. She opened it and stared at the pound notes inside. It was an absolute fortune.

"Where in the name of heaven did you get this?" Olivia screamed at her, not caring who might hear. She slapped Dot across her face, and pushed her indoors.

Dot stood, stubbornly silent. Olivia took her by the shoulders and shook her until her teeth rattled. Edward was horrified at what was going on. Anxious to save his sister, he shouted to his mother.

"The lady gave it to her, in the park. Honest, Mum, she did."

At this point, Joan and Meg began to cry. Olivia, fuming at Dot for seeing Flo and irritated by the crying children, stormed out. It had to be Flo, who else? She slammed the front door behind her, nearly knocking Mrs Roberts over as she stepped outside. Ignoring her neighbour, Olivia continued her flight down the road.

Back at the Railway house, the three younger children sat on the stairs. They huddled together for comfort.

"It is nothing to worry about," said Dot quietly, trying to calm them. "She is mad at me. She will get over it. Come on, I'll get you something to eat, and then I'll tell you a story."

There was a knock at the door just then. Dot gently pushed the children into the living room, and answered it.

"Hello, are you all right?" Mrs Roberts asked kindly. She saw the red weal on Dot's face, and knew that she did not need an answer. A lot went on in this house that she did not approve of, but the treatment of this young girl worried her most.

"I have come to tell you, Dot, that I am moving from Garston. I am going to live over the water in Birkenhead, to be near my sister. I have nobody here now." She had lost her husband two years before. She handed Dot a scrap of paper with her new address on it.

"I'll miss you, Mrs Roberts, I really will." The motherly woman had been kind to Dot over the years. She had filled the gap that Flo's absence had left, bringing a little warmth into the girl's life. Dot gave her a hug and the woman moved to leave, saying, "I will keep in touch, let you know how I am doing." Dot started to say that Olivia would fix that, but changed her mind.

"I would like that," she said. "Maybe I will come and see you when I am working." The thought of leaving school and becoming independent gave her heart a lift.

"It is only a year now until I finish. It will soon go." The latter was to convince herself, as much as Mrs Roberts.

An hour later, Olivia returned home. Nothing was said about the incident and Dot was left to wonder what had happened to the money.

CHAPTER SEVEN

That winter, Archie began to have trouble with his chest. He had two bouts of bronchitis, which really laid him low. This of course meant no wages, and somehow money had to be found to pay the doctor's bills. The family struggled through the cold months, and Archie juggled with their slender savings.

There was a good side to all this. Dot saw more of her father that winter than she had ever done. Olivia had to moderate her attitude towards her in front of Archie. She spent more and more time working with the Army, as she called it.

"How are you feeling today?" Dot asked her father one December morning, anxiously waiting for his reply.

"Better, love, much better. I'll be back at work before long."

"I wish you could do something else, Dad. That coal dust and smoke is bad for your lungs."

"I know, I know, but what else could I do? Anyway, jobs are hard to come by these days. We will have to start thinking about you starting work soon."

"I would like to go into nursing, Dad." She had given a lot of thought to what she was going to do when she left school. Archie was not impressed with the idea.

"No daughter of mine is going to work in a hospital. It is a terrible life, long hours, hard conditions, and poor wages. No, a nice little office job, that's what you want."

Dot did not bother to tell him that she had no hope of that. She was miles behind at school. She really needed to stay on another year to catch up. Her head mistress had discussed this with her, and wanted to talk to her father about the possibility.

"Oh no, Mrs Morris," Dot had pleaded. "I have to start work as soon as I can. We need the money." This was true, but not the real reason for Dot's protest.

Mrs Morris took the easy way out as usual and said nothing more about the subject.

It was New Year's Eve, but there were no celebrations in the Fisher household. Archie was still off work, but just about fit to go back. Olivia was out collecting with the Army. The children all went to bed early. It was warmer there.

Midnight struck. Throughout the town people sang "Auld Lang Syne" and welcomed in nineteen twenty-eight. It was the year that Dot left school, and she slowly began to take control of her life.

She finished in July. Although not fourteen until September, it was not necessary for her to stay on until Christmas.

Olivia had a job sorted out for her in good time. She went to work at the bobbin mill, starting the week after she left school. Her day began at six o'clock, with a scratch breakfast followed by a half-hour walk to Greenaway Brothers. It was not a bad place to work. The women were good fun and immediately took Dot under their wings.

"God help us, girl, don't you get fed at home?" When they saw the bread and dripping she took in to eat at break time, they were horrified.

"Aye, lass, what you need is a good beef sandwich to put some meat on your bones." Dot grinned.

She proved to be very nimble fingered and quickly got used to the machine she had been allotted. She eagerly anticipated Saturday, her first payday.

Olivia was waiting when she arrived home at one o'clock.

"Pay packet, Dot," she demanded, her hand stretched out. She snatched the proffered envelope and emptied its pathetic contents on the table. "Just about what you are worth, my girl." Olivia snorted ungraciously and threw a sixpence across at Dot. "That is to keep yourself in bits and bobs. Don't come running to your father or me for money. Those days are over."

What days? When did I ever ask, or get money from you? She kept a still tongue though, knowing the futility of arguing with Olivia. *How am I ever to escape from here without money?* Sixpence a week, it would take forever.

Olivia's cash flow was improving by the minute. On top of Dot's slender earnings, she was making money through the Army. She had a collection tin for them and one for herself. Then she had another bright idea.

"Dot," she said one evening, "would you like to come along with me to collect for the Army tonight? Edward can look after the girls." The boy was nine now and considered to be responsible enough to take care of his sisters. Dot was not so available, now that she was working.

Dot was surprised by Olivia's question, even more by the smile bestowed upon her. Olivia was not given to smiling in her direction. She hesitated, trying to work out the reason for the invitation. It soon became apparent.

"You can carry one of my collection boxes. The public might be generous to a girl like you." She might have said a waif-like girl, but that could have reflected on her as a mother.

"All right," said Dot briefly, thinking that it would make a change. It did too. It was fun seeing all the jolly people in the pubs. How happy they all seemed, and how generous. Olivia was delighted at the weight of Dot's box, but neglected to tell her stepdaughter.

The girl's pleasure disappeared, when on reaching home Olivia took her box from her and emptied the coins onto the living-room floor. She proceeded to count them into piles, and then swept them into her handbag.

"A very good night, Dot. We will do that again."

Dot was horrified. Enough was enough. It was time to go, to escape from this dreadful woman and the misery she caused.

The following Monday morning, she got up at six o'clock as usual. She dressed quickly. Then she put her few possessions in a brown paper carrier bag and blew a kiss to the sleeping children. She went downstairs. As usual at that time, there was no one else about. She picked up Olivia's handbag from the kitchen table and removed seven shillings from a brown leather purse.

She has taken far more than that from me since I started work. Nobody can say I stole what was not mine. The purse was bulging with the charity money, but it did not cross Dot's mind to take more than she believed to be hers. She left by the back door as usual.

"Bye, Dad. I will be in touch when I am settled," she said aloud as she set off down the road. She did not once look back. The first tram of the morning rumbled to a stop, and she jumped on board. "Pier Head, please," and handing over the necessary coins, she went and sat down on the hard seat.

CHAPTER EIGHT

Dot gazed out of the window, watching houses and shops go past. It was still dark, but daylight was beginning to show. The bone-shaking tram journey reminded her of the day she and Gran had gone over to Birkenhead. She felt a twinge of sadness as she thought of Flo. She alighted from the tram at the Pier Head. A ferry was almost ready to sail. She hurried on board, fingering the coins she would need to pay her fare on the other side.

The Mersey was in a very different mood that morning. The crossing with Flo, all those years before, had been idyllic. Darkness gave way to a heavy, grey sky. The wind blew against the tide, turning the strong currents into unpleasantly choppy water. Dot, however, had the resilience of youth, and was not bothered by the motion.

I can't believe I am here. After all these years of waiting, I am free of Olivia. Her heart gave a lurch at the mere thought of the woman. *She won't realise that I am missing until tonight. By then I will be lost somewhere over the other side, and she will never find me.* She looked sideways at her fellow passengers. *I wonder if they are all happy at home?* she thought, and mused about them each in turn. The tall, thin man with the ginger hair turned up his collar and pulled his head down into his coat, like a hibernating tortoise. The plump lady, who looked as if she might be with him, scrabbled in her bottomless handbag. There was no one near her own age on board. She supposed it was too early for them to be out and about. A man in some sort of uniform paced up and down, whistling tunelessly to himself.

He might be in the Sally Army. I wonder if he has two collecting boxes? Her reverie was interrupted by the arrival of the boat at Woodside.

She disembarked, walked up the ramp to the ticket booth, and paid her fare. She had arrived in Birkenhead. Elation suddenly gave way to a moment of fear. She realised that for the first time in her life, she was on her own.

Remembering the café where Gran had taken her, she decided to see if it was still there. It was, and more importantly, it was open. Men who worked at Cammell Laird, the great shipyard just along the dock road, were in the habit of getting breakfast there, or maybe a cup of tea.

Dot pushed open the door and went inside. The place was empty. It was too near clocking on time for any workmen to still be there.

"A cup of tea and a round of toast, please." The miserable woman behind the counter nodded and waved in the vague direction of a table.

"I'll bring it over."

"Thank you," said Dot, walking over to a table by the window. She sat down and rubbed the condensation off the glass with the back of her hand. Dozens of men were hurrying past. They all wore overalls, underneath a variety of jackets and overcoats. The older ones wore flat tweed caps. The canvas bags over their shoulders probably contained their sandwiches and tin mugs.

All these people have a home somewhere, thought Dot. *Where on earth am I going to be when it goes dark?* She felt her stomach churning with apprehension. The woman brought her order over.

"You look as if you need that," she mumbled kindly. Dot immediately felt mean for thinking she looked a misery. She smiled in reply, and then fishing a crumpled piece of paper out of her pocket, she asked, "Can you tell me where this is?"

The woman looked thoughtful for a minute then replied, "Yes, love, it's not far from here. I'll show you when you are ready to go." She went back behind her counter and began to wipe the top down with a clean cloth. Dot munched the toast hungrily. The hot tea was wonderful and her spirits rose.

What a good job Mrs Roberts left me her new address before moving. If she is home, she'll know what I should do next. It was an encouraging thought and she brightened up.

"That was very nice, thank you," she said politely as she paid for her breakfast, thinking how quickly the seven shillings were disappearing. The woman accompanied her to the door and directed her to Mrs Roberts' street. "Thanks again," she said, setting off at a brisk pace to find her old friend.

"I don't believe it. Dottie Fisher, where did you spring from, and at this time of day? Come in, come in, let's shut the cold out." She pushed Dot gently into the cosy living room, shutting the door behind her. "Now tell me how you got to be over here." She gestured Dot to sit down by the fire. "Warm your toes, you look half frozen."

The sight of her old friend's familiar smile was just what Dot needed to give her courage.

"I hope you don't mind me coming here, Mrs Roberts. The fact is I have left home. I have got to get a job as soon as possible. I have no money and nowhere to stay. I am hoping that you can tell me what to do next, but I don't want to be a nuisance." The kindly woman looked at Dot, thinking, *You poor little devil, I'm surprised you waited this long.* Then she spoke thoughtfully.

"What you need is a live-in job. You know, go into service or something, where you will get your bed and keep, and a small wage as well." Dot's eyes lit up.

"Mrs Roberts, you are a genius. I knew you would be able to help."

"Don't get too excited yet. It is only an idea, but I think it is a good one, if only for a start. There is an employment bureau in town. We will go there later and see what we can find out. Meanwhile we will get you tidied up a bit and find you something warmer to wear." She boiled some water on the hob, for Dot to have a wash.

Luxuriating in the unaccustomed kindness and attention, the runaway began to relax.

"It is going to be all right," she murmured, "it really is." She pulled on the jumper Mrs Roberts had found for her. It looked quite smart over her old dress. She put on her coat. A little pull-down hat, also produced by her benefactor, completed the outfit. The hat made her look older, and Dot was rather pleased by her reflection in the mirror by the front door. Mrs Roberts looked at her approvingly.

"You'll do," she said. "Let's go and see what we can find for you."

They stepped out into the street. A cold wind was blowing straight into their faces as they set off for the Employment Bureau. It was only a short walk away, and they arrived, rosy cheeked and excited. They pushed open the door and went into the welcome warmth. A pleasant middle-aged woman, who said she would be with them in a minute, greeted them. She shuffled some papers into a tray.

"Now I am all yours, what can I do for you?"

"This young lady is looking for a live-in job. She is very experienced with children of all ages, and not afraid of hard work."

"How soon could you start?" the woman said directly to Dot.

"Right away," she replied, without hesitation, turning to Mrs Roberts with a big grin.

"Well, I think you might be in luck, young lady. I have someone here desperate for a nursery maid. It is ten shillings a week plus your keep. The house is in Bidston, a very nice area."

Dot's eyes were like saucers. She could not believe this was really happening. She cleared her throat.

"It is just what I am looking for by the sound of it." Dot's voice was as grown up as she could make it, but she could not disguise her delighted grin.

"Fine. I will just take some details then, and try to organise for you to see Mrs Fergus tomorrow."

"Tomorrow!" exclaimed Dot. She still had to sort out where she would stay that night.

"That is fine," interrupted Mrs Roberts. "You give us a time and we will be here."

Shortly after, they were on their way.

"Come on, Dottie Fisher, let's go home. We will have a bit of dinner and make up a bed for you for tonight. Then you can bring me up to date on the news from Garston this afternoon." They did just that. Followed, for Dot, by an early night. She was exhausted.

Could it only be this morning that I left home? She thought about her dad and the children. She would have been missed by now. She climbed into Mrs Roberts' feather bed and snuggled down. Her head touched the pillow and with that sweet gift of youth she was asleep in an instant.

CHAPTER NINE

Jean Fergus arrived in good time for her appointment. She was a tall, elegant woman, well dressed, as befitted the wife of a ship owner. Her short hair just peeping from under the narrow brim of her hat was nut brown in colour.

She watched the arrival of Dot and Mrs Roberts. She liked the girl's open face and neat appearance.

"There you are," said the employment agent. "Let me introduce you to Mrs Fergus, then we can sit down and get on with the interview."

Her prospective employer impressed Dot. No one she knew wore clothes like that, and what beautiful shoes! Jean Fergus proceeded to ask Dot a lot of questions about childcare, and rather tricky ones about what she would do in certain situations. Dot answered queries about her family and home life, with a directness that impressed Mrs Fergus, and she was satisfied that the girl was suitable for the post.

"You understand, Dorothy, that you will be working under Nanny? She has complete charge of the nursery and all that goes on there. Mr Fergus and I have three children. Two boys of eight and six, and baby Alice who is six months old." Dot nodded her understanding.

"You will be expected to live in, and you will have one day off a month. I am sure that you have been told about the wages. They are paid weekly."

Dot could hardly contain her excitement. Mrs Fergus smoothed down her skirt with her perfectly manicured hands, then continued. "I will of course require two character references, will that be a problem?" Dot and Mrs Roberts exchanged glances. They should have anticipated this.

"I can supply one, Mrs Fergus. I have known the girl since she was born and I would stake my life on her honesty, and she is not frightened of hard work."

Mrs Roberts spoke with such conviction that she caused Jean Fergus to smile broadly.

"Well, that it is a good start, Dorothy, now what about a second one?" Dot was suddenly afraid that this opportunity was going to slip away. *Whose name can I give? Certainly not the manager at the bobbin mill, after all I left there without any warning.* Mrs Fergus watched the girl's face sympathetically. She had taken an instant liking to the young applicant. She was a good judge of character and felt that this girl was right for the job. She was sure that Nanny would like her.

"How about your school? Would anyone there give you a reference?"

Dot heaved a sigh of relief. Mrs Morris of course, her old head mistress. She would be glad to help, Dot was sure of that. Mrs Fergus was as relieved as any of them.

"Right, Dorothy, that sounds excellent. We will assume that the reference is forthcoming, and get you started right away. Of course if it fails to appear, then I will have to let you go. You understand that?" Dot nodded. "Well, we can collect your things and then we will drive home to The Moorings.

Mrs Fergus shook hands with the agent and walked gracefully to the door. Dot and Mrs Roberts followed close behind. A shiny black car moved forward as they left the bureau, stopping alongside them. A uniformed chauffeur stepped out, saluting Mrs Fergus as he did so.

"Thomas, we are going to collect this young woman's belongings and then we are returning home. Dorothy is to be our new nursery maid. I am sure that you and the others will make her welcome. It is her first job away from home, so she will feel a little strange for a while." Mrs Roberts directed Thomas to her house, and the three of them got in the car. Thomas closed the doors, having tucked a tartan rug around Mrs Fergus's knees. He started the engine and drove off.

Dot's face was flushed with excitement. Her dream had come true. At last the future was in her own hands. If this job did not work out, she would regard it as a stepping-stone to something better. She leaned back in the soft leather, thinking that only yesterday she had been sitting on a tram with hard wooden seats. She knew well enough that servants did not travel by car as a rule, but that did not diminish her pleasure in doing so now.

The car covered the short distance to Mrs Roberts' house within minutes. Its arrival caused some excitement in the street. Net curtains twitched at several windows. The more curious found excuses to open their front doors. Jean Fergus waited in the car for Dot to collect her things, and to say good-bye to her old friend once again.

"How can I ever thank you, Mrs Roberts? None of this would have happened without your help. I had no plan you know. I just ran."

"You don't have to tell me, love. I know you have been to hell and back since your father married that woman." She flung her arms round the thin, little body and hugged her tightly. "Take care, young Dot, keep in touch. I am always here if you need me."

Dot kissed her on the cheek, turned and hurried out to the car. Mrs Fergus told her that she could get in the front with Thomas and Dot was thrilled to do so. She waved to Mrs Roberts as the car moved off, and they were on their way.

It was less than three miles to Bidston, but the change in the landscape was quite dramatic. Rows of tiny back-to-back houses gave way to bigger ones with gardens. Dot became aware of more and more trees. They reached Bidston Hill and left Birkenhead behind. The houses were now becoming quite grand and were set in large grounds. Dot squealed with delight, as she spotted several red squirrels darting across the road in front.

Then the car turned into a long circular drive. The gravel surface crunched beneath the wheels. It came to a halt at the front door.

"We are home, Dorothy," said Mrs Fergus, turning to Thomas as she spoke. "You may take the young lady to the nursery and introduce her to Nanny. Tell her I will be up shortly. You may use the front entrance on this occasion."

Dot scrambled out of the car clutching the carrier bag she had brought from home. It all seemed like a dream. Everything had happened so quickly that it was hard to take it in. She stood in the hall of the lovely house and looked around. The walls were panelled in oak, and hung with several portraits. These were lit from above. There were several high-backed chairs scattered about. Dot's gaze fell upon an elegant small table on which was placed a silver tray. Another table held a formal arrangement of fresh flowers. She felt as if she was in one of the pictures she went to see at the cinema.

Oh Dad, if you could see all this. You could live in this hall!

Thomas came in and accompanied her to Nanny's quarters. As they reached the landing he called out, "Hello, Nanny, can we come in?" He pushed open the door to the nursery, beckoning Dot to follow. "Nanny, this is Dorothy, your new assistant, just arrived. Madam will be up to see you shortly."

"Thank you, Thomas. Come in, dear, don't be shy. I am just having a cup of tea, would you like one?" Nanny was sitting by the nursery fire, which had a guard around it. She smiled warmly at Dot and held out her hand. The high mantelpiece was covered in bric-a-brac. Ornaments that her young charges had given her over the years. Post cards from faraway places, and letters waiting to be answered. A lovely, old, chiming clock had pride of place in the centre. Dot felt as if she had come home. Nanny poured her some tea without waiting for a reply.

"Tell me all about yourself, Dorothy. Is this your first job? You look very young." Dot took the cup and saucer and sat down on the other side of the fire. The chintz-covered chair was well worn but comfortable nevertheless. She felt at ease as she told Nanny about leaving home and why she had left. How she had got this job, and could hardly believe that she was here.

"I feel that I am going to wake up any minute and find I am still in Garston."

Dot's honesty impressed Nanny. She felt she could make something of the girl, and, given the chance, she would.

"You must write and tell your father that you are all right, Dorothy. He will be very worried you know." Dot was ashamed to admit that she had not thought about that. In her desperate run for freedom, it had simply not crossed her mind that her father might be worried.

"I can't let them know where I am, or Olivia will make me go back. You have no idea what she is like. I could write to Gran though. She would let Dad know that I am safe and well, but she would not give anyone this address."

Nanny was disturbed by the girl's distress.

"Don't worry any more about it, dear. We will get you settled in here first. Tomorrow I will help you with a letter to your grandmother. Then you can relax."

Dot was grateful for this kindness, and thought how incredibly lucky she had been to end up here with all these wonderful people. They drank their tea and Nanny took Dot to meet baby Alice. She was a delightful child, a blue-eyed, rosy-cheeked, good-natured, little bundle. Her hair was a mass of blonde curls that framed her face. Nanny picked her up and gave her to Dot to hold. Alice looked into her face and beamed, then chuckled her approval.

At this point Mrs Fergus put in a brief appearance. Seeing Nanny and Dot getting on so well together, after a few words she left them to it.

"I will explain your duties to you as we go along, Dorothy," said Nanny. "I usually take Alice out in her pram at this time. Today you can come with me. I can tell you about Robert and Hal. They are both at day school at the moment, although Robert will be going to boarding school next term."

The day flew by. Ten o'clock found Dot once more ready for an early night, although she could not believe she would sleep. There was so much going around in her head. She looked at the tiny bedroom. It was her very own, situated in the nursery wing and next door to Nanny's. Hanging on the wardrobe door was her uniform. It consisted of a simple candy-striped dress and a white apron and cap. Another set lay ready in a drawer. Mrs Fergus was to take her to buy suitable shoes the next day. Dot planned to buy new underwear on her day off.

Tomorrow her duties would begin in earnest. She would supervise the boys' morning wash, clean their shoes, and then take breakfast with them in the nursery. Thomas drove them to school each morning. She climbed into bed thankfully. It had been a long day. The thoughts, tumbling around in her brain, gave way to dreamless sleep.

CHAPTER TEN

Mrs Morris did not let Dot down. The request for a reference was supplied by return of post. It proved to be generous, but honest, and so Dot's employment became secure.

Nanny, set to making something of the girl, as she put it, and Dot settled down to her new life with pleasure and anticipation. As promised, Nanny had helped her with a letter to Flo. Its purpose, to re-assure her of her grandchild's safety and happiness, without giving any clue as to her whereabouts. Thomas offered to post the letter in Liverpool on his day off, thus making sure the postmark gave no clues.

The day after her arrival, Dot met the rest of the staff. They were not large in number, for the size of the house. There was Evans, the butler-cum-valet, who ruled the staff, Mrs Jennings, the cook, and two maids Norah and Peggy. Norah was the scullery maid, while Peggy was the more glamorous, upstairs maid. A gardener and an odd job man completed the team.

Dot did not see much of the others, nor indeed of her employers, Mr and Mrs Fergus. The nursery suite was her world, and Nanny her companion. Alice was no trouble at all. She was a pleasure to look after. As for the boys they were Edward all over again. Dear Edward, she did miss him, and the girls.

One bright morning, about ten days after Dot's arrival, Nanny said, "Dorothy, I have some mending to do. Would you take Alice for a breath of air before lunch?" She had soon discovered that needlework was not Dorothy's strong point. This she would address later, but for the time being it was better for Alice to get used to the girl.

"Yes, of course, Nanny. I'll get her coat and hat. The pram is all ready." Dot loved taking Alice out. At the moment the roads were covered in crisp, brown leaves. They looked so pretty in the great piles the wind had made of them. The antics of the squirrels delighted both Dot and Alice. Some of them were quite tame and would sit on the lower branches of the big oaks, munching away, not moving, even when the big black pram came near.

A robin sang his sweet song as he eyed a patch of newly dug ground. It was magic to Dot. There had been the park at home, but nothing like this, acres of private gardens, full of shrubs and trees. The air smelt of damp grass and wood.

It was barely two weeks since she had left Garston, and arrived on Mrs Roberts' doorstep. Already she had put on weight, doing justice to the good food served in the nursery. Her skin had a healthy glow, and she had colour in her cheeks. She walked with a spring in her step.

"Alice," she said as they turned for home, "it's a wonderful world!" Alice smiled her ready smile, which Dot took to be a sign of agreement. They reached the great gates to the drive and turned in. It was not easy pushing the pram on the gravel, but at the side of the house it was easier. Here the pathway was concreted and the wheels moved smoothly over it. As they reached the side door, which led to where the pram was kept, it suddenly opened. Thomas stood there.

"The mistress is in the drawing room, Dorothy. She wants to see you right away."

That is strange, thought Dot.

"I'll take Alice up to Nanny first, Thomas. Do you think that will be all right?"

"I should think so. Nanny may be able to tell you what the mistress wants. Don't worry. It can't be much. You have only been here five minutes." Dot laughed and picked up Alice and climbed the stairs to the nursery.

Nanny was still sewing. On seeing Dot, she said anxiously, "I don't know what you are needed for, but it seems important. You had better go down right away. Make sure you knock before you go in."

Dot ran down the servants' stairs, slowing down as she reached the bottom. She ran her fingers through her hair and smoothed her apron. Reaching the drawing room door, she knocked gently and waited quietly for a response.

"Come in." Mrs Fergus' voice was different somehow. "Dorothy, you are back. There is someone waiting to see you." Dot turned and saw her stepmother, standing by the bay window. She was dressed in her Salvation Army uniform, trying to smile sweetly for Mrs Fergus' benefit, but not quite succeeding. Fear flooded through Dot's body in waves.

"Olivia." The girl's voice faltered as she voiced the name.

"Indeed, Dorothy, and I am here to take you home."

"No. I am not going anywhere with you. I am staying here. I have a good job. I am happy. You don't want me at home, why would you make me go back?"

"Shall I leave you two alone for a while?" Mrs Fergus was at somewhat of a loss as to how to deal with the situation. Dorothy looked devastated by this woman's arrival.

"That will not be necessary, Mrs Fergus. The girl is coming home with me. I need her there. She is an ungrateful brat who cares for no one but herself."

"I am not leaving." Dot was adamant. "You can't make me."

Olivia turned to Mrs Fergus, saying, "You do realise that she is under age? She can't legally leave home, without our permission, until she is sixteen."

Mrs Fergus wished that her husband was at home. She was one of the few people who saw right through Olivia from the word go. However, she knew that without the parents' consent there was no possible way she could keep the girl on.

"I am sorry, Dorothy. You do see that there is nothing I can do to help you at the moment?" Dot looked directly into Mrs Fergus' face.

"I understand, but thank you for giving me a chance. I am so sorry for all this trouble. It is the last thing I wanted, or expected." Mrs Fergus shook her hand warmly.

"Good luck," she said, and they were dismissed.

Olivia and Dot went into the hall.

"Wait here. I'll go and get my things." Dot did not so much as look at her stepmother. She went up to the nursery where Nanny was waiting.

"They have found me, Nanny. I have to go home." Only then did she let the tears come. "I will miss you and the children. Thank you for all your kindness. I won't forget what you taught me. I will write." She went into her little room, changed into her own clothes, collected her few belongings and closed the door behind her.

Downstairs, Olivia waited impatiently. There was a bus due at the top of the road in ten minutes. It would take them to Woodside for the ferry. As Dot appeared at the top of the stairs she shrieked at her to hurry up. For a moment, she forgot to be the gentle Salvationist bringing home her errant child. In the drawing room Mrs Fergus cringed.

Olivia hustled the girl to the bus stop, and they were soon on their way to the ferry. Neither of them spoke. Once they were on board and seated in a quiet corner, Olivia started.

"You ungrateful little bitch. You don't give a damn about anyone but yourself. Your father has been nearly out of his mind with worry. If it had not been for Mrs Morris we would never have known if you were alive or dead. When we get home my girl, I'll—"

"You'll what, Olivia?" Dot stared coolly at the furious woman. Olivia was taken aback at the interruption.

"I'll—"

"You'll do nothing. You will never do anything to me again. I won't stay. As soon as I am sixteen I shall go, and there is nothing you can do about it."

Olivia stared open mouthed at Dot. She hardly recognised the girl. Two weeks had turned her into a stranger. Dot, herself, was surprised at the confidence she displayed. Her fear of this woman had simply dissolved. All the years of abuse were behind her. She knew instinctively that she had somehow crossed a line, and that Olivia could touch her no more.

The ferry reached the Pier Head and they went to catch a tram. Nothing more was said until they reached the door of the Railway house. Then Dot turned to Olivia, saying, "You won't keep me here, believe me." Then she went inside calling the children's names. "I'm back," she shouted, adding quietly to herself, "for now."

However, the children were not yet home from school, and she spoke to an empty house.

CHAPTER ELEVEN

Archie stepped off the tram and set off slowly for home. He was overjoyed that Dot had been tracked down, and that she was unharmed. It had been the longest two weeks of his life. His imagination had run riot as to what the outcome of her disappearance might be. His emotions had ranged from guilt that his daughter had been so unhappy as to run away from home, to anger that she could have been so inconsiderate as to leave no indication of her plans.

He opened the front door slowly, trying to compose himself for the reunion with his daughter. Suddenly she was there in front of him. She looked so well, different too, in a way he could not put his finger on.

"Hello, Dad," she said softly, "how are you?" Then she ran the short distance up the hall and flung her arms around him. "I did not mean to worry you, Dad, but I had to go, and I had to go then, while I had the courage." She felt his slight frame tremble in her arms. She released him, and as she kissed him on his cheek, she noticed the silent tears slipping down his crumpled face.

"Now you will get the punishment you deserve, upsetting your dad like that." Olivia had appeared in the kitchen doorway. Her voice was harsh with triumph at bringing the girl home. She could not wait for this showdown. She could scarcely hide her glee.

"Leave us alone, Olivia, will you please? Dot and I have a lot to talk about and we need to be on our own for a while." Archie's voice was strong and firm. He straightened himself up, took a blue handkerchief from his pocket and wiped his eyes. Olivia was taken aback at Archie's tone. He was usually so quiet and manageable. She decided that it would be prudent to leave them to it, without argument, and retired to the kitchen. As the door closed behind her, Archie took

Dot's hand and led her into the living room. They sat down together on the old sofa. He was still holding her hand.

"Dot, I blame myself as much as anyone for what has happened. I have known for years how unhappy you have been. I don't suppose I have any idea of what Olivia has put you through. By the time the light dawned and I realised you were being badly treated, the others were born and I had to keep the family together for their sake." Archie sighed. Another tear slipped down his cheek and he brushed it away.

Dot could hardly believe what she was hearing. She did not know whether to be happy or sad. Her father had known for years about Olivia's ill treatment and said nothing. She was glad the truth was out, but disappointed in her father's lack of courage. He had failed to deal with the situation. At the same time her heart ached for him. He looked so small and vulnerable sitting there beside her. She did not want to hurt him, but now was the time for honesty.

"I won't stay, Dad. You do realise that? As soon as I am sixteen I'm off. I promise that I will do it differently next time. There will be no more running away."

"Running away was the best thing you ever did, Dottie, remember that. You are like a different person in two short weeks. It is wonderful! We will make the next year as good as possible, and when the time comes we will give you a proper send off." He pulled her close and hugged her tightly. "You look so like your mother now. It is as if I have got you both back at once, but don't tell Olivia that, will you?" They both laughed and went into the kitchen together.

Olivia, hearing the laughter as they walked in, could hardly believe her ears. She turned from the stove and saw them standing, arm in arm, their eyes alight with love and relief. For once, she was speechless. This was a new situation and she would have to tread carefully for a while. She was confident, however, that she would soon take control again. Once Archie was over this affair, she would have him under her thumb once more. As for Dot, well, she was only a child still, and no match for Olivia. She smiled benignly at the pair.

"I'll make us all a nice cup of tea and get on with the meal. The children will be home from school before we know where we are. They will be so pleased to see you, Dot." She could not resist adding, "It was very hard for them you disappearing like that you know."

Archie squeezed Dot's hand.

"They won't mind all that now, Olivia. The girl is back and we will put the last few weeks behind us. Now what about this tea?"

Shortly after the welcome drink, Dot heard Edward's voice as he opened the front door. He burst into the kitchen, shouting, "Anything to eat, I'm starving?" He stopped in his tracks as his eyes fell on Dot sitting at the table with his parents. "Oh, Dot, you're back, you're back. I am so glad to see you! Joan, Meg, look who is here. It's our Dot."

The girls came dashing in. They flung their arms around their big sister, squealing with delight. Olivia, not pleased with all the attention Dot was getting, shooed them all out of the kitchen. For all her instinctive caution to go easy on Dot for the time being, as she pushed them through the door, she said, "You had better get down to Greenaways, first thing tomorrow, and see if they will take you back." Before Dot could reply, Archie said, quite sharply for him, "Give the girl a chance to settle in again, Olivia. There is plenty of time for Greenaways. Let her get over all this for a day or two." Olivia turned away and said no more. She could bide her time. That little bitch was going to pay for what she had done.

Chapter Twelve

Dot did go back to Greenaways. She had proved herself to be a good little worker during the time she had been there, and they always had vacancies to fill.

She soon settled back into life at the Railway house, but now there were subtle differences. Olivia never physically ill-treated her again. She tended to ignore her when possible, although she made good use of her stepdaughter when it suited her. When Dot was not at work she usually had the children in tow. This, she did not really mind. She loved them all, as they did her. They were delighted to have her back, and never tired of hearing about her adventure. Over and over again they asked to be told about the big house, and the people who lived there.

At work she was a bit of a heroine.

"Weren't you scared, Dot, going off on your own like that?"

If you only knew, Dot thought, but simply shrugged her shoulders in reply. It was a nine days' wonder of course and soon forgotten.

Shortly after Dot's return, Olivia tired of the Salvation Army. There were a few mumblings about her collections. She thought it prudent to quit while she was winning. She decided to become a nurse, which she did, quite literally. She acquired a second hand uniform from a pawnbroker, complete with a sister's badge and a watch pinned to it. She began to take the *Nursing News*, and advertised her services in the window of the local corner shop. "Care of the elderly and infirm, nursing mothers, etc. Qualified, nursing sister, reasonable terms." These words were accompanied by a box number. So Olivia's new career began. She wrote a letter of recommendation, praising herself and her abilities. Strangely, no one ever asked for references. Her indefinable charm won each prospective employer over within minutes. She had new and more vulnerable people to exploit now, and Dot was of no further interest to her.

"Dad, what is Olivia up to?" Dot was intrigued by her stepmother's goings on. Her father seemed unaware, as usual, of most of what went on around him. He and Olivia simply co-existed nowadays. When he was home, she was out.

"I don't know, Dot, I really don't know. Perhaps it is best that way."

Dot never knew if he was aware of Olivia's philandering. She certainly was not going to tell him. What good would it do? George Brownlow had long since disappeared off the scene. Others had replaced him, but none of them stayed around for long. One great benefit from her adventure was being able to see Flo again. There was no argument when she said she was going to see Gran on her first Saturday home. Flo had no idea that the girl had been brought back. She had passed on the message posted so carefully by Thomas in Liverpool. She had been relieved to know that Dottie was safe and suitably employed. She walked arthritically to answer the knock at the front door, to find Dottie standing on the step.

"My dear girl, it's you. You are home." She flung her arms around her and hugged her tightly. "I can't believe that you are here in my house again, after all these years."

"I'll be here often now, Gran, as often as you wish. I will bring the others to see you, if you like." She thought her grandmother looked older and smaller somehow, but it was so good to see her. Flo looked at her, smiling her pleasure, thinking how poised and mature Dot seemed, so in control of herself.

"Are you too grown up these days for cocoa?"

"No one makes cocoa like you do, Gran. Have you still got the blue and white mugs?" Gran nodded, and they went together into the kitchen, arm in arm. They had a lot of catching up to do.

* * *

"Tea or coffee, Dorothy?" The orderly brought the trolley to a halt at the foot of Dorothy's bed. "You were miles away, dear. Are you ready for a drink?" Dorothy roused herself from her reveries, rubbed her eyes and pulled her aching limbs up the bed. She must get staff to help her into her chair. Lying in bed was no good at all.

"Tea, please, Vera, strong as you can. You know how I like it." She took the polystyrene cup from Vera's hand and took a sip. She was always thirsty. The heat of the ward was not helped by the continuing Indian summer, which had taken the outside temperatures up to the high seventies. Dorothy, a fresh air fiend at the best of times, was nowhere near a window. The other patients complained about draughts when a breeze blew on them anyway.

48

When will I get out of here? she thought. It was nearly the end of September now, three weeks since her fall. Her recovery was slow, but the physiotherapists were wonderful. Working on her, several times a day, they encouraged her all the time.

"It will come," they said. "Patience is the name of the game." Drinking the tea from the disposable container, she thought how much better it would taste in a decent cup. "Never mind, Elizabeth will be here after lunch," she told herself and she brightened up visibly.

Elizabeth continued to visit each day. She brought with her little treats for tea, bits of news from home, and magazines and weekend papers, which did not demand too much concentration, in the general bustle of the ward.

"Have you ordered what you want for lunch, Dorothy?" Vera stopped to collect the empty drink container and threw it into the black bin liner with the rest.

"I was spoiled for choice," replied Dorothy, with a touch of sarcasm. She was not enamoured with the hospital food. "Yes, thanks," she added more politely. She settled back against the pillows, the protective plastic, crackling behind her shoulders. She watched Vera collect the rest of the cups and remembered Flo's lovely blue and white mugs. In her mind's eye she could see the cocoa in them. Wisps of steam rising from creamy froth that swirled around after sugar had been stirred in.

* * *

Dot took the mug from Flo. They sat opposite one another at the well-scrubbed table in the small kitchen. She sipped the sweet, chocolate drink, relishing its rich flavour. Flo reached forward and put her hand on Dot's encouragingly.

"Now then, love, tell me all about it. Right from the beginning." She settled back in her chair, her head tilted to one side, expectantly.

CHAPTER THIRTEEN

Dot took another sip of the cocoa. She savoured the moment. Here, in Gran's kitchen again, after all these years, she felt comfortable, warm and secure. Relaxing in the homely atmosphere, Dot began to relate her story.

"I caught the early morning tram to the Pier Head, Gran. Just like we did the last time I stayed with you. I went to the same café. It was open, at that time of day, imagine." She stopped. The memory of how she had felt, excited, scared and not a little lonely, came flooding back. *There had been the kindly woman, behind the counter. Then Mrs Roberts, what would I have done without her?*

Flo misunderstood her hesitation.

"You don't have to talk about it if you don't want to, Dottie. It will keep, love."

"Oh, I do want to tell you, and not just about running away. I want you to know why I did it, what's been going on all these years." Flo nodded gently. This was not going to be easy, either for Dot to tell, or herself to listen to. However, in her wisdom, she knew it was important for the girl to get all this off her chest.

"Come on, love, we'll go in the other room. It will be more comfortable in there. Bring your cocoa with you." They went through, and Dot sat down in the comfy, old chair by the window. Her father had sat in the same place when he had told Flo about Olivia, all those years ago. Flo sat down opposite Dot and smiled encouragingly.

So the girl continued her story. She first told Flo about her short spell of freedom. The strange way things had worked out. How kind everyone had been. Even Mrs Morris, her old head teacher, had given her a good reference, before feeling obliged to reveal her whereabouts, when questioned by the police.

"I wondered how you came to be back so soon."

"It was a shock, Gran, when Olivia turned up. She made an awful scene. Mrs Fergus is such a lady, I'm sure nothing like that had ever happened in her home before!"

Dot spent several hours that day telling Flo about life with Olivia. Her memory went back a long way. This was probably due to the cruel incidents that were impossible to forget. She could not tell the whole story at one time. There was too much. It was, however, a great relief to be able to talk about things at last.

When she left Flo's for the Railway house that evening, she felt as if she had shed a great burden. Her steps did not slow as she neared home. There was nothing to be afraid of anymore, just weeks and months to fill, until she reached her sixteenth birthday.

Edward, now nine, became a good companion. He was old enough to be aware of his mother's cruelty to Dot in the past, but too young to have done much about it. Joan at seven, and Meg at five, were unaware of the unhappy relationship between their mother and half-sister. Dot seemed quite grown up to them, but great fun to be with.

Saturday afternoons became special. Sometimes they went to visit Flo. Although she was Dot's Gran, they didn't know her. Flo welcomed them all with open arms. It was wonderful to have children to spoil again. In spite of money being short, she conjured up treats for tea. They loved the jellies made in rabbit moulds that wobbled on their plates. Delicious, evaporated milk was poured generously over each portion. Occasionally, when Flo had eggs to spare, there would be a plate of fairy cakes in the centre of the table.

On Sundays if the weather was fine, they all went to the park. The girls played on the swings. Edward usually played football with the other boys. Dot caught up on her reading. She had joined the local library and was continuing to work her way through everything she could lay her hands on by Jane Austin.

Olivia's nursing career was going well. She was more often "on duty," as she called it, than she was at home. It was usually just a case of someone sensible being present to administer medication or change dressings. On one occasion, shortly before Dot's birthday, and her planned departure, Olivia did bite off more than she could chew.

She had accepted a booking to deliver a baby. The mother and father were both blind and they were extremely poor. They scratched a living as best they could. Mr Bond doing odd jobs and his wife taking in laundry.

"We can't afford to pay you much, Sister Fisher," they said, when she answered their poorly written note, by visiting their home.

"You are not to worry," Olivia purred. "I can deliver your child. My rates are very reasonable. It is my vocation in life to help those in need. Do you have family to help you afterwards?"

"Oh, yes. That is not a problem. My sister will stay here for a few weeks."

"Fine. I will keep in touch. Here is my address, for when the time comes." Olivia left the shabby little house and walked home. Although she had given birth to three children of her own, she was no more competent than Dot to deliver a baby. This did not bother her conscience. She would cope.

The call eventually came. A small girl of about eight years knocked on the front door of the Railway house, late one afternoon.

"I've got a message from Mrs Bond. She says will Sister Fisher come as quick as she can."

Olivia, who had answered the door, felt a quiver of fear in her stomach, at the child's words. Usually so in control of herself, she realised she was out of her depth. She closed the door on the girl, simply nodding her acknowledgement. Then she went into the kitchen and made some tea. While it brewed, she wondered what to do.

Olivia was still sitting in the kitchen when Dot arrived home from work. Unusually for her, she confided in Dot.

"I can't go, Dot. I can't do this. You will have to go and tell the woman to get someone else. Tell her I'm ill, tell her anything, but go, go right away."

Dot was horrified.

"Olivia, I can't do that. The poor woman is relying on you. Whatever will she do?"

"She'll manage. Her sort always do. She is blind you know, and him. Shouldn't have kids, people like that. No sense of responsibility."

Dot thought, *And you have, I suppose.*

"Will you give me a letter to explain why you are not going?"

"I'm in no fit state to write letters. Tell her anything you like, just don't waste any more time. I don't want her husband coming round." Olivia's voice rose hysterically.

Dot ran all the way. If she was sorry for Mrs Bond before, she was doubly sorry when she got to the house. She could hear the screams from the front door as she pushed it open. Mr Bond, who had arrived home in the meantime, came down the stairs, stumbling in his haste.

"Is that you, Sister? Thank God, she is in a terrible state."

"I'm afraid it isn't Sister. I am her stepdaughter. She can't come. I am sorry."
Dot's words sounded lame, even to herself.

"Can't come. What do you mean? Of course she can come. It was all
arranged, months ago." His voice was shrill with fear. His sightless eyes seemed
to be staring into Dot's soul.

"There must be someone who can help," she replied desperately. "A
neighbour, surely there is someone."

The poor man was beyond thinking. His terror was as blind as his eyes were.
He clambered back up the stairs, clumsy in his haste to be with his wife. Dot
thought on her feet. She dashed out into the street and knocked at the next front
door. She shouted as she knocked, and an old lady answered almost
immediately. She grumbled at the disturbance. Dot hastily explained the
situation. For all her years, the woman understood the urgency of the matter and
took charge. She pushed Dot to one side, saying as she did, "Go and get her, at
number nine. Tell her what's happening, and to come right away. Hurry up, girl."
Dot did as she was bid, and "number nine" was soon on her way to help.

Dot stood in the road, uncertain what to do. She decided on reflection that
she had done what she could and went home.

All the family were back by now, even Archie. Olivia was washing up
unconcernedly, when Dot arrived back.

"There's some scouse in the pan. It'll need warming." Then as an after
thought, "What happened?" Dot told her. She was still upset by the whole affair.
She could hear the woman's cries in her head. She told Olivia what she had done,
and how the two neighbours had gone in to help. Then to her utter disbelief,
Olivia burst out laughing. She laughed until the tears ran down her face.

"I told you it would be all right. Those sort of people always land on their
feet. What a scream." She started to laugh again, holding her aching sides as she
did so. Dot was horrified at this grotesque outburst. She had no illusions about
Olivia, but this episode was the end. The woman had no scruples whatsoever.
Not a drop of human kindness ran in her veins.

"You disgust me, Olivia. I shall never forget this day. Heaven alone knows
what the outcome of all this will be." Olivia started to laugh again, uncontrollably.
Dot walked out of the kitchen. She could not bear to be in the same room as
her stepmother a moment longer.

They never knew if the baby was safely delivered, or not. Dot was too
ashamed, by association, to go near the Bonds, and Olivia too scared. She need
not have worried. The sad, little couple were in no position to seek justice, or take
revenge, on Olivia for her appalling behaviour.

She stopped advertising her services for a while. She kept a low profile. Maybe it would be better to concentrate on the elderly in the future. Possibly make a change of tack. She might become a lady's companion. There could be all sorts of opportunities in that line.

Dot did not stay around long enough to find out.

CHAPTER FOURTEEN

Leaving home the second time was quite different. Dot discussed her departure with her father and grandmother. Shortly before her birthday, she wrote to Mrs Roberts, asking if she could stay with her until she was settled in work. She planned to use the same agency again. "Could you make me an appointment with them, when I have a date?" All this would save time for her, and inconvenience for her host.

"I'd like to go into nursing," she confided to Flo, "but Dad is set against it. I can't start until I am eighteen anyway. Even then, I think I'll still need his permission, so I plan to go into service again. That will give me a roof over my head, and time to sort myself out."

Flo listened quietly to all these confidences. She thought how mature her granddaughter seemed, and felt that she need have no worries about her. When she went away, she would be able to look after herself.

The long awaited birthday arrived. Flo gave her a little tea party. Archie and the children were all there, but not Olivia. She had declined the invitation, much to Dot's relief. Archie and Flo had scraped up a small sum of money to give the girl a start. They gave her this, placed inside a new purse, along with a note wishing her good luck from all of them. Dot was touched by their kindness. She knew how hard it was to come by money to give away.

Edward, Meg, and Joan had bought her six handkerchiefs, and the girls had made her a card. Flo had given her a most precious gift. It was a photo of Emily, Dot's mother and Flo's daughter. It was mounted on thick cardboard, and wrapped in tissue paper. Dot had never seen it before, and her grandmother parting with it moved her to tears.

"I will treasure it, Gran." She kissed Flo gently on the cheek. "Thank you."

On the morning that she finally left, Archie accompanied her to the Pier Head. He waved goodbye from the landing stage as the ferry moved off. He shed a tear as Dot waved back. The breeze was already ruffling her hair. Her father's farewell words were fresh in her mind.

"Remember you are as good as the next one, Dot, but treat people with the respect they deserve. If you need me, I am here, not far away." Then he repeated what he had said once before: "This is the best thing you could possibly do, love. God bless."

Dot enjoyed the short crossing to Birkenhead. The September sun was warm on her back as she leaned on the ship's rail. The *Mersey* sparkled as the blunt bow pushed through the current.

Wouldn't it be marvellous to be going to America or somewhere? To sail on and on for weeks, she thought. *Maybe Birkenhead is far enough for today.* She looked at the Liverpool skyline, so recognisable to travellers. She felt that she could almost touch the Cathedral, it seemed so close in the clear autumnal air.

"Lovely day for a sail." A young man stopped beside her and propped himself up on the ship's rail, chin in hand. "I'm going to Cammell Laird to see if I can get an apprenticeship with them. They are the best ship builders in the world you know."

Dot grinned at him, thinking what a lovely smile he had.

"Snap! I am looking for work too, but not at Lairds. I am going into service until I am old enough to do nursing. I love it over this side of the water." The Wirral peninsula stretched away in front of them. They chatted easily together during the rest of the ferry crossing, and the time flew by. On arrival at Birkenhead, they wished each other good luck and went their separate ways.

Dot thought she would stop at the café, for old time's sake. She could tell the lady behind the counter about how she had got on last time. Of course, the woman was not there anymore, or maybe just not on duty. Dot was disappointed for a minute, but quickly accepted that everything was going to be different this time. Today was the beginning of a new life. She had to acquire a job with accommodation. There was no time to dawdle. She hastily drank the tea she had ordered, paid the bill, and left for Mrs Roberts' house.

This time she was expected. Mrs Roberts had a hot meal ready when she arrived. After initial hugs and greetings, they both sat down to eat. The steak and kidney pudding was delicious and Dot had two helpings. Cooking had not been Olivia's strong point. Mrs Roberts, on the other hand, prided herself on hers. After a good-sized portion of stewed apples and custard for dessert, Dot was replete.

They sat for a while, before putting the kettle on for a cup of tea.

"I have made an appointment for you at the job agency. It is for tomorrow morning at ten o'clock. So we can do what we please for the rest of the day, dear. If it takes a while to get you suited, don't worry. I shall enjoy having you here, and it is important that you go somewhere you are going to be happy."

The day passed pleasantly enough. They enjoyed each other's company. They went shopping in the afternoon, and in the evening they sat by the fire and chatted. They talked about all sorts of things, but mostly about Dot's life since returning home. Mrs Roberts was aghast as she heard of Olivia's escapade with the Bonds.

"Dear God, Dot, what an appalling thing to do. She will come to a sticky end, that one, mark my words."

Dot wondered about that, but kept her thoughts to herself. Olivia seemed to her to go through life unscathed, leaving a trail of unhappiness behind her.

In the event, Dot was fixed up with a job almost as quickly as the first time. Her stay with her old friend was subsequently quite brief. She had decided before leaving home this time that she didn't want nursery work. All her short life she had looked after her siblings. Her brief experience with the Fergus family had taught her that as a nanny's assistant, she would mix very little with the other staff. She decided to aim for a maid's position.

This time Dot went alone to the agency. The same lady was there when she went in, and she recognised Dot immediately.

"Hello, Dorothy. You are prompt. Take a seat and I will be right with you." Miss Armitage remembered this waif-like girl from the previous time she had used their services. There was something about her. She had a certain air of self-sufficiency, unusual in one so young.

"I am afraid that we have no vacancies for nursery maids at the moment. Would you consider anything else?"

"Actually, I would prefer not to work with children." Then she added, "That sounds awful, doesn't it?" Miss Armitage laughed, and Dot explained her reasons.

"I don't blame you. It is a bit limiting, the company I mean. Well, now, in that case, I think I have something that might suit you very well." Miss Armitage looked pleased. "The Hislops require a new tweeny. You could be just the one they are looking for."

Dot looked puzzled.

"A tweeny?"

"It's what they call a between maid. She waits on the cook and the butler, and the senior maids. She has household duties as well."

Dot had not stayed long enough at the Ferguses' to learn about the staff hierarchy. She had been cocooned away with Nanny, in the small world of the nursery.

"This is a very prestigious family, Dorothy. Mr Charles Hislop is a cotton millionaire. He is a most generous person, and a great benefactor to the local community. He is a self-made man, which is probably why he is so good to his staff. He knows how hard life can be for the working class. If you are successful in obtaining a post in his household, you will be very lucky indeed." The door to her future seemed to open for Dot as she listened to Miss Armitage. "Well, what do you think Dorothy," the woman continued, "shall I arrange an interview?" The girl did not need to think about it.

"Please, Miss Armitage, whatever time they say, I will be there."

So it came about, that two days later, Dot stood on the doorstep of the main entrance to Woodleigh, the beautiful home of the Hislop family. It stood surrounded by vast grounds in Oxton, an area favoured by the wealthy folk of Wirral. She reached forward and rang the bell. Her heart pounded within her chest, until she could hardly breathe. The excitement and anticipation of the moment were almost unbearable. She turned to look behind her at the long winding drive she had just walked up. The beautiful grounds stretched either side of it. Lawns, perfectly mown in stripes, were edged with autumnal flowers, gaudy dahlias, and bronze chrysanthemums.

Dot heard the clatter of shoes approaching within the house. The heavy door opened silently as she turned to face it. A young woman, wearing a crisp, blue cotton dress, with a white frilly apron and cap, stood on the threshold.

"Miss Fisher?" Dot nodded, and before she could reply, "Please come in. Mrs Hislop is waiting for you in the drawing room. She will see you right away."

Dot took a deep breath and stepped inside.

CHAPTER FIFTEEN

Enid Hislop heard the front door bell ring as she sat at her writing desk. She had been there for some time, trying to find the right words to send to her eldest son, Philip. He was taking medicine at Oxford, and finding it hard going. It was not that the work was difficult for him. He had a good brain, loved the subject, but found too many distractions at university.

Enid put down her pen as Hilda announced the arrival of the young applicant she was expecting.

"Do come in. How nice and prompt you are. Please sit down." Her voice was soft and welcoming, and Dot felt immediately at ease. The interview was fairly brief, following much the same line as the one with Mrs Fergus. This time she had references to offer. Mrs Morris, her head teacher, Greenaways Manager, and Jean Fergus had all provided excellent reports. It was obvious to Enid that the girl was of good character and a hard worker. All this was apparent from her references. In addition, she had an air of independence and a certain style about her, beyond her tender years and humble background. Enid felt that she could go far, given the chance.

"Do you think you would be happy working here, Dorothy? We have a big staff. A house of this size needs a lot of looking after. We do a great deal of entertaining, both social and business. It is hard work, but we pay a fair wage and you get your keep of course."

This elegant woman fascinated Dot. Her beautifully modulated voice had no trace of an accent. Tall and slim, she was dressed in the height of fashion. Her figure-hugging, linen dress was immaculately cut, the hemline falling between calf and ankle. Her hair was arranged in natural curls about her face. She smiled encouragingly at Dot as she finished speaking.

"I think I would love it here, Mrs Hislop. It is such a beautiful house." She looked around the room, her eyes wide in appreciation of the exquisite furnishings.

Enid rang a bell, and shortly, the maid who had answered the front door came in to the drawing room.

"This is Hilda, Dorothy," then turning to Hilda, "Would you take Dorothy to meet Cook please? She can introduce her to the rest of the staff, and perhaps give her a cup of tea. I will be along in about half an hour." Hilda bobbed a dutiful, little curtsy in Enid's direction.

"Yes, madam, right away." She grinned at Dot as they left the room together and went to find Cook. Enid Hislop returned to her desk, took up her pen again, and stared at the blank page.

Hilda chattered all the way to the kitchen.

"Are you the new tweeny then?"

"I hope so, I am not sure if it is settled."

"I have been here three years. Wouldn't dream of leaving. The Hislops are wonderful employers. We live off the fat of the land, and we go on holidays with them. Of course even then, we have to work, but we get lots of time off when we are away from Woodleigh." They reached the kitchen and the chirpy girl stuck her head of frizzy, blonde hair round the door.

"Cook, this is Dorothy, come for the tweeny's job. Madam says will you give her a cup of tea. She will be along in a bit." She pushed Dot into the kitchen and was gone. Cook looked up from the pastry she was deftly rolling.

"Come in then, girl. Don't stand there like one of Lewis's. Sit yourself down." Dot did as she was bid. She had the feeling that when Cook spoke, you jumped. Her instincts were correct. Mary Wilding was a force to be reckoned with, a cook in the best of traditions. Excellent in her craft, she ruled her domain with a rod of iron. Beneath her gruff exterior, however, she was a kind woman, if a little narrow minded. She took to the girl, but thought her far too thin.

"Need some meat on your bones, my girl, but we'll soon fix that if you come to work here." Dot looked at Cook's ample bosom, securely contained within her apron.

As long as I don't get like that, she thought.

Small, for the weight she carried, Mary Wilding's face was flushed by the heat coming from the great range. Her eyes were small and bright. She could look stern as well as kind, but was usually fair to the staff. However, like all cooks, she was at times likely to explode with rage, at someone's apparent inadequacy.

"What did you do before, Dorothy? Have you done any work below stairs?"

Dot was not quite sure. After all, the nursery at the Ferguses' had been upstairs. She did not want to appear foolish in front of this seemingly imperious woman.

"I was a nanny's assistant in my last post, Cook." This reply seemed not to require any geographic information.

"Oh, so you will be stepping down a peg or two coming here." Cook raised an enquiring eyebrow.

"Not in my opinion. There is not a lot of future in the nursery, unless you can afford to train properly. As a tweeny, I can get promotion, can't I?"

"Ambitious, are you? Well, that is not a bad thing I suppose. I think you'll do, my girl. I shall tell Madam when she arrives. You must have satisfied her, or you wouldn't have made it to my kitchen."

At this moment, another maid came through the door. Small and neat, she wore a smart uniform dress of pale, green cotton, with stiffly starched collar and cuffs. On her head she wore a crisp, white cap clipped to her brown hair.

"Elizabeth, come and meet Dorothy, soon to be our new tweeny." Turning to Dot, Cook added, "Elizabeth is the head maid here at Woodleigh. She is over all the parlour and kitchen maids. Therefore you will be answerable to her when working above stairs. Whilst you are on duty in servant's quarters, I am in charge."

Elizabeth came forward and shook her hand firmly.

"Hello, Dorothy, pleased to meet you. I hope you will be happy here."

Mrs Hislop joined the little group. She had not finished her letter. Indeed she had decided to leave it until tomorrow. Charlie would be home early today as they had an engagement that evening.

"What do you think, Cook? Will this young lady suit us?"

"I'm quite happy, Madam, if you are."

"Right, that is settled then. We could do with you starting right away, Dorothy. Is that possible?"

"I could start tomorrow, Madam." Dot was learning fast, and the title tripped off her tongue quite naturally.

"Good. Well, Cook, I will leave you get things moving. Elizabeth, will you arrange for the dressmaker to measure Dorothy for her uniform, and maybe you could find her something to wear until the dresses are ready? Perhaps there would be time to show her the bedroom that she will be sharing with you. By the way, Master James will be coming home at the weekend, after all. Will you see that his room is ready?" Elizabeth acknowledged the instructions with a slight bend of knees. Enid left the room, glad that the staff problem was resolved. She could now concentrate on sorting the boys out.

The two girls went up to the bedroom that they were to share from now on. Dot liked Elizabeth and hoped they might become friends. As they went upstairs to the staff wing, she realised that she had not thought of Olivia, the family, or the Railway house since leaving home four days before. She had a good feeling about the way things were working out.

Mrs Roberts will be thrilled when I tell her all about this, she thought.

"What a lovely room, Elizabeth." Dot gasped as they went into the bedroom. It was big, even for two. There was a separate dressing table, chest of drawers, and wardrobe for each occupant. Beside each of the twin beds was a soft woollen rug.

Elizabeth sat down on her bed, kicking off her shoes as she did so.

"Call me Lizzie, please, when we are not with the family anyway."

"I'm Dot." They giggled in the mutual satisfaction of being young and free, with all their lives in front of them.

CHAPTER SIXTEEN

Mrs Roberts was slightly disappointed when Dot got back that night. She was full of the job, the house, the girls, and the room she was to share with Lizzie. As she listened, she realised that she had been looking forward to having Dot around for a while. It was good to have someone to cook for, to talk to in the evening, especially a youngster who was so enthusiastic about everything.

"Mrs Roberts, they are all so nice. The girl I'll be sharing a room with is really friendly. She is four years older than me, she's the head maid, and she's going to teach me what to do above stairs. I have to help cook as well, you know, do the vegetables, wash pans and all that sort of thing." She stopped for breath, full of excitement and anticipation. "They don't have a butler. The mistress runs the house. She won't have a housekeeper either, says she prefers to keep the reins in her own hands. Lizzie says that Mr Hislop is a self-made man. He became a millionaire by sheer, hard work, with his wife helping him all the way. So, she runs the house herself. I suppose because she knows people so well. There are lots of staff to help of course, far more than at The Moorings. I met some of them before I left. Oh, I am going to be all right there, more than all right in fact."

"I am really pleased, Dot. You have waited a long time for this day. I have a good idea of what you have put up with over the years. That is behind you now and you must keep it that way. Don't let Olivia get involved in your new life. You know what she is. If she sniffs money she will want to try and wangle some for herself."

Dot thought of the Salvation Army collection boxes. Mrs Roberts was nobody's fool. She certainly had Olivia weighed up.

The next morning, Dot packed her small bag with a few personal belongings. On top she placed the photograph of her mother, still wrapped in tissue paper.

She planned to buy a frame for it when she could afford one. Enid Hislop had told Dot that a member of staff would collect her at eleven o'clock.

Mrs Roberts had found her an envelope and some paper to write a letter to Flo. Having told her of her new address, and about her position as a tweeny, she asked if Flo could let her father know her whereabouts.

Tell him I'm fine, Gran. He has not to worry. I dare not write home because Olivia will read the letter for certain, and I don't want her to know where I am. I will keep in touch, I promise. I'll come over to see you on my first day off.

She signed the letter, sending all her love, carefully folded the paper and slipped it into the envelope. Now she was ready to go to Woodleigh.

Just before eleven, there came the roar of a powerful engine outside the house. Mrs Roberts peered through the net curtain.

"Good heavens, what a noise. It is someone on a motorbike. He is coming here. I hope it isn't one of those awful telegrams." The motorcyclist knocked on the door. "Will you go, Dot? I am all of a bother." Dot opened the door. A man in his twenties stood there. He wore a leather helmet with the strap undone. A yellow woollen scarf was wound round his neck and tucked into his tweed jacket.

"Dorothy Fisher? I have come to take you to Woodleigh. I am Joe Martin, chauffeur to the Hislops." Dot looked at the motorbike in amazement. She had expected a ride in a car, which would have been a treat, but this was something else. Joe smiled at her surprise.

"It's my own bike. I thought you might enjoy the ride. Have you ridden pillion before?"

"No, but I have always wanted to. What a lark! Mrs Roberts, it's my lift. I am going on a motor bike." Dot laughed excitedly. Mrs Roberts merely looked doubtful. She watched as Dot climbed on the pillion seat, her bag tied on a pannier at the side.

"You be careful with that girl on the back, do you hear me?"

Joe smiled winningly.

"Of course. I am always careful. I could have come in the car, but it is such a beautiful day. I thought the bike would be more fun. Are you comfortable back there? Right then, we will be off."

"Bye, Mrs Roberts. Thanks for everything. I will see you soon."

Joe put the bike into gear and let out the clutch. Mrs Roberts waved as they moved off. Dot clung on tightly to Joe as they accelerated away. They weaved in and out of the narrow streets, soon reaching the open road. Dot's hair streamed out behind her as they sped along. Conversation was kept to a minimum. It was hard to hear anything as the wind tore away the words.

It was lunchtime when they arrived at Woodleigh. Lizzie was waiting in the kitchen with Cook.

"Hello again. Enjoy your ride? Joe loves his bike, no time for girls, have you, Joe?"

"No time for anything, working here. I will just have a sandwich please, Cook. I must wash the car before I go to collect Mr Hislop. They are going out to dinner tonight. I have got to pick him up early."

"That is a job for you, Dorothy. There is a piece of ham in the pantry, and a newly baked loaf. Cut Joe a sandwich, nice thick slices now, and plenty of butter. Make sure you wash your hands first. Use the butlers pantry." Dot had arrived.

"I will show you where things are, Dot." Lizzie stepped forward, taking her arm, and directed her to the pantry. "When you have done that, I will show you how to look after the staff's lunch. Cook prepares it, you serve it, and then you get your own. You will soon get into the swing of things."

Dot performed her first duties without any problems, and then had lunch herself. She would have called it dinner. She had never eaten so well in her life. There seemed to her to be enough food for an army. After ten minutes' rest, to let the food go down, as Cook put it, Dot and the scullery maid set to clearing the dishes from the table in the staff dining room. Cook sat in a comfortable chair in the kitchen and promptly fell asleep.

"We will wake her when we have washed up," said Vera, the scullery maid, running her hands over her tightly pulled-back hair, and catching the loose ends with hairgrips. She was one of those unfortunates who looked permanently harassed. Possibly she was. While they worked they chatted about life at Woodleigh, and Vera raved about her favourite film stars. Dishes finished, they put the enormous kettle on the range.

"Cook will want tea when we wake her." At this point Lizzie appeared.

"Come on, Dot, bring your bag and we will get you settled in. Madam will be home soon and she will want to see you. I hope the dresses that I have found for you will do until your own are ready."

They went up to their room. There on the bed lay the two dresses. Dot couldn't wait to try them on. They were loose, but passable by Lizzie's standards. Dot combed her hair and looked at herself in her dressing table mirror. She hardly knew the girl who looked back at her. She was so smart. She fixed the starched cap on top of her mop of dark hair. The shoes Mrs Fergus had given her still polished up well, although they were a little tight. She felt confident to meet her employer when she arrived home. The rest of the afternoon she followed Lizzie around. She watched closely everything that Liz did, determined to learn how to do her job well.

Their chauffeur drove Mrs Hislop home from the friends' house she had been visiting. As she went through the front door, she wondered how the new girl was settling in.

"I can imagine how she feels, poor young thing. Far from home, and no mother and father to return to tonight." She need not have been concerned. Upstairs, Dot removed an odd loose hair or two from her shoulders, and went down the servants' stairs. As she reached the bottom she practised the little curtsy that Lizzie had shown her.

Enid rang for tea, when she had discarded her coat and hat.

"I'll see Dorothy next, please, Elizabeth. How is she getting on?"

"Very well, Madam. No problems at all. I am sure she will fit in nicely." Enid relaxed with her tea. She touched neither the scones, nor the dainty cakes that Cook had prepared. She and Charlie were dining out, and she did not want to be full of afternoon tea, and not able to appreciate the meal. There was a knock at the drawing room door and Lizzie ushered in Dot.

"Welcome to Woodleigh, Dorothy. I hear you are settling in well. I will introduce you to my husband later this evening. My son James, and possibly my eldest boy Philip, will be home at the weekend. That will leave just Tim, my youngest, for you to meet. He is the same age as you, and still at boarding school."

Dot felt as if she was being slowly absorbed into the family. No wonder Hilda had said she wouldn't dream of leaving. Used to nothing but abuse from Olivia, it was a warm and wonderful feeling to be accepted, unconditionally, by this remarkable woman.

You will never regret taking me on, she said to herself, as Enid dismissed her, and she returned to the servants' quarters. There was a new spring in her step. She had, at last, moved on from the Railway house, and this time there would be no going back.

CHAPTER SEVENTEEN

Joe drove Charlie Hislop home from his office in good time for his dinner engagement. Enid was already dressed to go out and poured him a drink as he came into the drawing room.

"I hope it's not too strong, Enid. You know how generous Hesketh is with his measures, and we have a whole evening ahead of us." He smiled in the direction of his wife. A big, bear of a man, he had no particularly striking features. His hair was brown and well cut. His grey eyes were quite searching and missed very little. He adored Enid. She and the boys were his reason for living. Everything he had achieved was for them, and he had remained the same kindly man that he had been when he had started out. He was, however, nobody's fool, and was highly respected in the world of the cotton merchants.

"Had a busy day, dear?" Enid passed the crystal tumbler of gin and tonic to Charlie as she spoke. The ice clinked as he put the glass down on the table beside his armchair.

"So-so! The replacement clerk who started today seems promising enough. How about you, how is the new girl getting on?"

"Fine. She really is keen and quite mature for her years. I don't think she will be below stairs for long. She has too much about her."

"I will nip along and say hello when I've finished this." Charlie liked to know his household staff well. They all shared a home after all, and it was important to everyone that harmony reigned. He emptied the glass, kissed his wife on the cheek, and went to seek out the tweeny.

"This is Dorothy, sir." Cook beckoned Dot over. She came forward, wiping her hands on a towel as she did so.

"How do you do, sir?"

"I am well, thank you, Dorothy, and you, are you going to be happy here?"

"Couldn't be anything else in a place like this, sir. Everyone is very kind and making me feel at home."

"Good, that's what I like to hear. Well, I have to dash now. We will get to know each other as we go along. Just remember, I am responsible for you while you are working under my roof. You are very young and a long way from home and family. If you have any problems, my wife and I are here for you, and we are only too willing to help if needs be." He turned to his cook. "Looks like a busy weekend, Cook, with two of the boys coming home."

"Nothing pleases me more, sir. Those boys appreciate good food. It's a pleasure to cook for them. Not that you and the mistress don't—" Her voice faded and she looked quite flustered. Charlie laughed.

"I know just what you mean, Cook. I can expect lots of steamed puddings for a couple of days then can I?" With that he left the kitchen and made his way to his bathroom and started to run his bath. In the master bedroom, Enid had laid out his dinner jacket and black tie. He thought how he would much prefer to have a quiet evening at home, but he would probably feel differently after he had bathed and shaved.

That evening, after the staff had eaten, they retired to their sitting room. This was comfortably furnished, with three settees and several armchairs. One wall was lined with bookshelves. These were full of reading matter, ranging from detective stories to the classics. One shelf was devoted to reference books, dictionaries, and anthologies of poetry. Three occasional tables and a writing desk completed the furnishings. It was in here that the staff were allowed to entertain their friends on their day off, if they wished.

Dot and Vera joined the others, having first washed up the pans and dishes. Only when the kitchen was clean and tidy, and the supper trays laid, could they finish for the day.

That first evening, Dot sank into an empty settee, tired but happy. Lizzie came over and sat by her.

"Are you worn out?" she enquired kindly.

"No, just nicely so, I'll sleep without rocking, as my gran used to say."

Dot remembered the long walk, to and from Greenaways, six days a week. Her stepmother's frugal lunches, which had horrified the women she had worked alongside. Tired, then, meant exhausted, with more to do when she arrived home.

"Anyone fancy some music?" This from Hilda who was dance mad, and put on a record without waiting for a reply. The gramophone was carefully wound up, and a new needle fitted. The sound of Henry Hall's dance band playing the Charleston burst forth. Even as Hilda got Joe up to dance, the telephone began to ring. Lizzie dashed the length of the hall to answer it. She was back within minutes, looking anxious.

"Cook, it's Master Timothy's school. He has had an accident, and they are sending him home by car. Do you think that we should get in touch with Mr Charles, or not?"

"Not a lot of point," replied Cook. "It will take a couple of hours for him to get home, and the family will be back by then. Did they say what happened?"

"Only that it was a motor car accident. He has broken his arm and a couple of ribs. They will take a month or so to heal, won't they?"

"You are right about that, Elizabeth. Poor lad, he won't take kindly to sitting around for weeks. Proper live wire he is. He can go in James' room for tonight. It is all ready for the weekend. Tomorrow you can get Timothy's own bed aired."

"Looks as if we will have everyone home by the weekend," commented Lizzie. "That will be nice, having the place full of life." She turned to Dot. "It is great fun when the boys are home, always something happening."

Henry Hall finished playing his Charleston, and Hilda wound up the gramophone, and played the record again. Joe came over to Dot and asked her to dance. Hilda was not pleased.

Since collecting Dot earlier that day, Joe had found himself thinking of her quite a lot. It had been very pleasant having her arms around his waist as they had ridden his motorbike to Woodleigh. This rather surprised him. She was very young, and he was usually too pre-occupied with his bike to bother with girls. Hilda had been trying in vain for some time to get his attention, to no avail. He simply was not interested.

Dot laughed at his invitation.

"I can't do the Charleston, or anything else for that matter, Joe."

"Then you will have to learn, won't you?"

"Not tonight, she won't," intervened Cook. "Sorry, Dorothy, but we will have to get some supper ready for Timothy. Just something light, because it will be late when he gets home. Accident or no accident, I know Master Timothy, and he will be starving." She and Dot returned to the kitchen and prepared a chicken salad. "When he arrives we'll cut some thin bread and butter, and make him some tea. Mr and Mrs Hislop will be upset about all this. I wouldn't send one of mine to boarding school. They're supposed to look after them. This sort of thing shouldn't happen." She grumbled on about the school, until they were ready to go back to the sitting room.

Hilda had given up on the music by then and was curled up in a chair, looking sulky. Dot went over to the bookshelves and browsed among the volumes until she found something to read. She settled down with Charles Dickens, and was soon spellbound by the early pages of the story.

Enid and Charlie arrived home at ten o'clock. Joe, who had gone to collect them, had told them the news about Timothy. Enid was very anxious, but Charlie was less concerned.

"It can't be too serious, Enid, dear, or they wouldn't have sent him home tonight."

"I suppose you are right, but I won't rest until I see him."

"Can I pour you a brandy? It will calm your nerves and help you sleep later."

"Thank you, Charlie. It might help. I do hope he is home soon."

An hour later, the car arrived with Tim on board. Mr Black, the assistant head, had brought him home personally. The headmaster had wanted to make sure that the Hislops knew exactly how the accident had happened, and that it was no fault of the school's. Tim himself was remarkably cheerful.

"Just don't make me laugh, Pa. It hurts like hell."

"No need for that language, Timothy, especially in front of your mother."

"Sorry, Mum. It really does hurt though."

"I know, dear, broken ribs are awful. Have they strapped you up tight?"

"Tight! I can hardly breathe."

"You poor old thing. Are you hungry? I know Cook has some supper ready for you."

"I'm starving, Mum. Could I have it upstairs though? I am really tired." Enid looked at his pale face and thought how young and vulnerable he was.

"Yes, dear, you go up. You are in James' room for tonight. Pa will come and help you get undressed. It will be difficult to manage it yourself."

"I will be up in a minute, Tim. I just want a word with Mr Black."

Mr Black had waited quietly to say his piece, giving the three of them time to get over the upset.

"We are all very distressed that this should happen while Timothy was in our care. The truth is, his form were all walking back from the playing fields, with Mr Tilsley, the games-master. A car, driven by a lunatic, mounted the pavement and hit Timothy. The police have the driver in custody, and they will deal with the matter." It was never easy to be the bringer of bad news, and Charlie felt sorry for the man.

"Look, Mr Black, it could have been a lot worse. The boy will be fine in a few weeks. No one is blaming the school, although it is a pity that the rugby fields are so far from the main buildings."

The master looked relieved. He had spoken his piece. He refused Charlie's offer of hospitality, preferring to be on his way. It was a long drive back to Denbighshire. Charlie rang the bell for Lizzie as he thanked Mr Black for bringing Timothy home.

"The gentleman is leaving now, Elizabeth."

"Yes, sir." Lizzie saw the schoolmaster out. Then having given Timothy time to get ready for bed, she took up his tray. "You are a fine one, Master Timothy. Anything to get home from school!" Timothy grinned and tucked into his chicken. Charlie came up as promised.

"I'll stay with you until you have eaten your supper, Timmy." He rarely used his son's childhood name these days. He turned to Lizzie. "I will leave his tray on the landing, Elizabeth. It will do in the morning."

Enid appeared as Lizzie was going. She, too, felt happier about her son when she saw him emptying his plate.

When Lizzie returned to the sitting room, she found Dot all on her own. She still had her nose in her book.

"Come on, Dot, time for bed. You have had quite a day."

Dot closed the book, memorising the page number. She would find a bookmark tomorrow. Her first day at Woodleigh was over.

CHAPTER EIGHTEEN

James arrived home on Friday evening as planned. He drew up at the front door in a spanking new sports car. He jumped athletically over the side to be greeted by Joe.

"What a car, Master James! Isn't she a beauty?"

"She certainly is, Joe. It's a Standard, an Avon Special. Is there room for her in the garage? Actually, Pa does not know that I have bought her yet. I want to choose the right moment to tell him."

"Your father's Rolls is in there, of course, and Master Philip will be home tonight. If we tuck her in at the far end, she will be fine. It is not as if she was a big car."

"Excellent, Joe. Will you garage her then please?" With that, James leaned in and pulled his bag from behind the driver's seat. He bounded up the steps to the front door and burst into the house, shouting as he went, "Hello, Mum, I'm home."

He nearly bumped into Dot in his haste, and stopped to apologise. She accepted his apology gracefully, adding that his mother was in the drawing room. She then hurried off down the hall.

"Mum, it is good to see you, and marvellous to be home, it seems like forever."

"You have only been gone a fortnight, dear."

"I know, but work is different to school, and I am not used to city life." James was learning the cotton import business. Charlie hoped that his son would join him at Hislops eventually. It had seemed sensible that James should start off with another firm. He had joined Harry Meredith, an old friend of Charlie's, after finishing school. Meredith's was based in Manchester, so James had taken rooms there. It was a good arrangement, not too far to travel home, but far enough for him to make a new life and be independent.

"Mum, who is the new maid? I just met her in the hall. What an attractive girl."

"That would be Dorothy. Yes, she is attractive, James. She is also only just sixteen. I don't want you running after her and embarrassing her. There are plenty of girls in your own circle to chase. Your father is home. He made a point of being early, as you and Philip were coming for the weekend. I think that he is in the library at the moment."

"No I'm not." Charlie came into the room. "Whose car is that outside the front door?"

James was caught unprepared. He knew that Charlie was not going to be pleased.

"It's mine, Pa. I got it on Monday. I know that I should have spoken to you first. I got a loan from the bank. There was no problem getting the money."

"I don't suppose there was. They know whose son you are, that is not the point. You know that I was getting you a runabout, to enable you to get home easily. You are far too young and inexperienced to be driving a fast sports car like that. You also have to earn the right to own such things. We will discuss this later, however. We do not want to spoil the weekend for everyone."

"Timothy is home, James." Enid changed the subject. "Poor lamb was hit by a car on the way back from games. He has broken his arm and a couple of ribs."

"Probably some fool in a sports car," muttered Charlie. "I'm off to get ready for dinner before Philip arrives. I hope he is not going to upset me."

In the kitchen, Dot helped Cook with the preparations for dinner. After three days, she felt as if she had been at Woodleigh for months. She had made the acquaintance of the head gardener, Joseph, not to be confused with Joe, and his two assistants, Fred and Jack. She had also met Alice the dressmaker, and Gertie who came in to help Vera with the heavy cleaning. All of these lived out; therefore Dot would not see much of them. Joe lived in the mews flat over the big garage, which had once been the stables. He had all his meals with the rest of the staff, and tended to spend his evenings in the staff sitting room. Since Dot's arrival, he spent all his spare time in the kitchen. Cook was a bit concerned about this, but said nothing. Dot, herself, was blissfully unaware of his interest. There was so much that was new and fascinating to see and learn.

Just finding her way around the house took some doing. She had never had any sense of direction. The three floors, endless passages, and staircases kept her on her toes. She was enraptured with the furniture and fitted carpeting. At home they had linoleum and rag rugs, like everyone else. As for the paintings and ornaments, they took her breath away.

Philip arrived home in good time for dinner. It would seem that he had neither misfortune nor misbehaviour to report, and Charlie relaxed as they were called into dinner. Lizzie and Hilda served the meal of roast lamb. Enid chopped up Timothy's meat so that he could eat one handed. Charlie dispensed the wine. It was he who stocked the cellar, and he preferred to do all the handling himself. Good wine, after all, needs careful attention.

"Perhaps Dorothy could assist you with the coffee this evening, Elizabeth. It will help her get used to our routine."

"Yes, Madam, of course." Lizzie returned to the kitchen and broke the news to Dot.

"Heavens! Will I have to carry the tray? I'm sure to let everything slip off."

"No, you won't. Just follow me around, and watch what I do." Dot heaved a sigh of relief.

Having finished their meal, the family retired to the drawing room. This was their favourite place to relax. The big lounge was only used when they had company. Enid rang the bell for coffee, while Charlie poured himself a brandy.

"Anyone else want a drink, Enid, Philip?" Enid declined and Philip said that he might have a Scotch later.

Lizzie came in with the tray. She poured the coffee into the china cups, and checked who wanted cream. Dot stood at her side watching carefully. She helped Lizzie pass the cups to the waiting family. She gave Philip his black coffee, looking into his clear blue eyes as he thanked her. For some strange reason, her stomach fluttered disconcertingly, and she dropped her gaze.

"Philip." Enid glanced across at him. "You have not met Dorothy. She joined us a few days ago. You are settling in nicely, aren't you?" she said, turning to Dorothy. Dot felt herself blushing for some reason, and she could not wait to escape to the kitchen. Lizzie appeared not to have noticed anything, and Dot felt quite composed by the time she reached the end of the hall.

"All done in there?" asked Cook. Lizzie nodded. "Right, then we will get ours. It is pigeon pie tonight." She licked her lips in anticipation. Dot, however, was not so enthusiastic.

"Pigeon pie. That sounds awful." She remembered the scruffy birds pecking grit in the street outside the Railway house.

"You mind what you are saying, my girl. I am famous for my pigeon pie." Cook admonished her good-humouredly. They all ate their fill of the pie. To follow, Cook had made two syrup puddings. One was for the family, or more especially Timothy. The other was for the staff. So replete that they could hardly move, they settled down in their sitting room. Vera and Dot set to tackling the pots. The sound of the telephone ringing reached them in the scullery. They heard Hilda answering it.

"Good evening, the Hislop residence. Yes, that will be all right. I will get her for you." Hilda appeared in the doorway of the scullery. "It is for you, Dot. Your dad is on the phone."

Dot went pale. Telephones were new to her. She put them in the same class as telegrams, and they meant trouble. She hurried down the hall and with trembling hands, picked up the receiver and leaned forward to speak.

CHAPTER NINETEEN

"Hello! Dad? Can you hear me?" Dot's voice was raised, as if to send her words flying across the Mersey to her father.

"Dot, I am so glad that I got hold of you. I am phoning from the depot. I am just about to start a shift. Listen, Dot; somehow Olivia has found out where you are. After what happened last time, God alone knows what she will try. I thought that if you realised she knew your whereabouts, you would at least be prepared." Archie sounded agitated and upset. Dot digested the news with a certain amount of despair. Was there to be no end to Olivia's presence in her life?

"Oh, Dad, what am I to do? She made a terrible scene at the Fergus place. I would be so embarrassed if she started anything here. Can't you stop her coming?"

"You know Olivia, Dot. I can't physically detain her, not even if I was home all the time. Obviously I will talk to her and try and make her see reason."

"Why on earth did you marry her, Dad? I will never understand that." Archie did not answer her question. This was partly due to his discomfort at speaking on the telephone, and partly because he had no real reason to give her. How could he explain to anyone about Olivia?

"Just be ready for her, Dot. I have got to go now, or I will be late for my shift. Look after yourself love."

"Bye, Dad." The line went dead as she spoke. She stood there in the hall, shaking. Fear of Olivia flooded over her, threatening her newfound happiness.

"Whatever is the matter, Dorothy?" Philip Hislop was concerned to find the new maid in such a distressed state. Not waiting for an answer, he sat her down in one of the chairs that lined the long hall. "Sit there a minute. I will be back."

He hurried to the drawing room and asked his mother to come with him. Enid followed to where Dot sat dejectedly. Tears were falling down her cheeks.

"Leave this to me now, Philip. You get back to your father, dear. I won't be long." Enid put her arm around Dot's shoulders. "Come on, Dorothy, we will go into the library. No one will disturb us there, and you can tell me what this is all about." Not aware of the telephone call, Enid assumed that the girl was homesick, or had been upset by a member of the staff. Dot pulled a handkerchief out of her apron pocket and blew her nose.

"I am sorry about this, Mrs Hislop. I will be all right in a minute."

"You can tell me anything, you know that, Dorothy? I will be discreet if you are having trouble with anyone working here."

"No, it is nothing like that. It is my stepmother. Dad has just telephoned me. She knows I am here; she will come and spoil it all. I don't know what to do." Her voice rose with emotion, and Enid took control.

"Dorothy, Dorothy, calm down, my dear. Wipe your eyes, take a deep breath, and tell me all about it. Then we will see what we can do to help, all right?"

Dot looked uncertainly at this woman she hardly knew. She felt instinctively that Enid was someone to trust, and slowly she began to tell her story. She started with the fiasco between Mrs Fergus and Olivia, and that outcome. Then with gentle encouragement from Enid, she sketched in the story of her short life. She finished with her few days at Woodleigh, and told of her relief and happiness at being there.

"What do you think your stepmother will try to do, Dorothy? She cannot make you go home, now that you are sixteen."

"I really don't know, Madam." Dot was recovering her composure now. "That is what I am so worried about. She is capable of anything."

"Do you feel up to going back to the others now?" Dot nodded. "Good girl. You are not to worry about this woman anymore, do you hear? We will deal with her if she comes. I am glad you told me all this, Dorothy. It was very brave of you. It is not easy to open your heart to strangers, but you did the right thing." Enid accompanied Dot to the sitting room, where all the others were wondering what on earth was going on. "Dorothy has had some upsetting news. Hilda, would you get her a cup of tea?" Hilda nodded and scuttled off. "I will leave her in your care, Elizabeth, perhaps an early night?"

"I will see she is all right, Madam. Come and sit here by me, Dot."

Enid returned to the family. James had gone up with Timothy, who was feeling tired after dinner. The two brothers had lots to talk about, especially the new car. Downstairs, Enid told Charlie and Philip, as briefly as she could, the story that Dot had related to her.

"What a bitch of a woman!" Philip was incensed.

"Indeed," said Charlie. "What are we going to do about it?"

Enid, who had had more time to think, replied, "Tomorrow, I will phone this Jean Fergus, where Dorothy first worked. She has had a brush with the woman, and she may be able to help."

"Good idea," then Charlie added, "You don't think she was exaggerating the situation, do you?"

"I wish I did, Charlie. No, this woman is cruel, and it is time someone helped this poor girl out of her clutches once and for all."

Back in the sitting room, the others fussed around Dot kindly. Hilda brought her tea and gave her a hug. No one asked questions, for which Dot was grateful. She would tell them in her own good time. For tonight, however, she had talked enough and simply wanted to be quiet.

Sleep came slowly. Dot tossed and turned, the threat of Olivia ruining her new life invading her senses. Elizabeth, on the other side of the room, lay awake too.

The following morning, things were back to normal. Nothing untoward happened that day or the next, and Dot began to relax.

Enid was no nearer to discussing Philip's problems at Oxford with him. He managed to avoid being alone with her during the weekend, leaving early Sunday evening for the long drive back. James, however, had to face his father's disapproval. Charlie was disappointed in him, and left his son in no doubt about it. In spite of the upsets, it was a pleasant family weekend. It was not often that they were all together these days.

Philip, driving back to Oxford, found himself thinking of Dorothy. His face softened as he thought of her. He brushed his almost blonde hair back from his forehead, his blue eyes concentrating on the road ahead. He loved driving. No distance was too far for him. Most of all, he loved medicine, and his studies were going well. One or two undergraduates spoilt university for him. These came from the highest levels of society, and were inclined to despise those whose wealth came from sheer brains and hard work. The fact that Philip was proving to be a brilliant scholar, with a great career in front of him, did not make them like him any more. Philip had been to the same public school as James and Timothy. Few survived that sort of education without learning to take care of themselves. He was biding his time, confident that the right moment would come for him to deal with his tormentors. Meanwhile, he had to concentrate on his studies, and not let the mindless few get to him.

At the end of her first month at Woodleigh, Dot had her day off. Joe, who had an errand to do, gave her a lift on his motorbike. He dropped her off in

Birkenhead. She had a quick look at the shops, and then walked down to the ferry at Woodside. She was off to visit Flo as promised. The landing stage was a flurry of activity, and she enjoyed all the hustle. She suddenly remembered the young man, hoping to get a shipyard apprenticeship, and wondered how he had got on. There were a number of foreign sailors on the ferry this time. Dot assumed that they were from one of the many big ships in port. Some of them carried parcels and had obviously been spending their wages after weeks at sea. They jabbered away in their strange tongues, laughing and waving their arms about.

When the boat reached the Pier Head, Dot went ashore along with the hordes of other passengers. She set off to catch the next tram, stopping to buy a bunch of flowers for Flo.

At that same moment, Olivia paid her fare at Woodside. She had only to find the right bus to get her to Oxton, and she could put her plan into action.

No stuck-up little madam is going to get the better of me, she thought. A look of spiteful determination spread over her face. It quite destroyed her beauty, if she did but know. Her topaz eyes narrowed to slits, and furrows criss-crossed her brow.

An hour later, she arrived at Woodleigh. Wearing her nurse's uniform dress and coat, she strode up the long drive to the front door. She rang the bell, assuming a long-suffering smile, as she heard footsteps approaching. Hilda answered the door. Olivia announced herself as Dorothy's stepmother, and asked to see the lady of the house.

"Is Madam expecting you? She has not mentioned that you would be calling." By now, Hilda and the rest of the staff knew a good bit about Dot's story. The parlour maid stood her ground, determined to be as obstructive as she could. "I shall have to enquire whether or not it is convenient for Madam to see you. Will you wait there, please?" Hilda closed the door, leaving Olivia open mouthed on the steps.

She found Enid in the sewing room with the dressmaker. "I am sorry to disturb you, Madam, but Dorothy's stepmother is at the front door asking to see you. I did not ask her in. I did not really know what to do." Hilda floundered, knowing full well that it was the height of bad manners to leave a visitor on the doorstep. Enid digested the news for a moment. She then instructed Hilda to show Olivia into the hall.

"I will ring the bell when I am ready to see her. I may be a while so do not think I have forgotten." Then she smiled and added, "You did quite right not to ask her in, Hilda. Well done!"

Enid had telephoned Jean Fergus the day after Dot had told her story. She had confirmed everything the girl had said, and Enid was well prepared to deal with Olivia. She left her sitting in the hall for nearly an hour, giving her time to get a little agitated. Then she summoned Hilda and asked her to send Olivia into the drawing room. Enid sat with her back to the French windows. She looked up slowly as Olivia was ushered in and bade her sit down in a rather uncomfortable, straight-backed chair opposite her.

CHAPTER TWENTY

Dot alighted from the tram at the corner of Flo's road. Clutching the flowers in one hand and holding her thin coat down against the wind with the other, she ran the short distance to Flo's front door. As it opened, she shouted, "Surprise! It's Dottie, Gran." Flo was delighted.

"Come on in, love. Give your gran a hug." They went into the kitchen, Dot chattering away, as Flo put on the kettle.

"Your dad was here yesterday. He seemed a bit worried about Olivia knowing where you are working."

"She has not turned up yet, Gran. Maybe she won't now."

"Let us hope not," Flo said quietly, but not too confidently. She made the tea, and they went into the living room. A good fire was burning, and the warmth wrapped itself around Dot.

Meanwhile at Woodleigh, Olivia looked directly into Enid's face, waiting for her to speak first. Enid obliged.

"Well, Mrs Fisher, may I ask why are you visiting me?" Enid's tone was cold and formal.

Not discouraged, Olivia replied, "I've come about my stepdaughter. She ran away from home, you know, having stolen money from my purse. Not only that, she leaves us without the wages that she brought into the house. The money was little enough, but it helped me to keep food on the table. She is totally self-centred. She does not give a damn about anyone else, not even her young brother and sisters." Olivia stopped for breath. Enid seized the moment.

"I am not sending her home, Mrs Fisher. That is not what Dorothy wants, nor can you make her. You are aware of that?"

"I don't want her home, she is a thief. Do you know she stole from my Salvation Army collection boxes?"

"That is not quite the way I heard it." Enid was fuming. "Although I did hear something about the collection boxes. Maybe I ought to inform the Salvation Army. I am sure they would be most interested."

"There is no need for that." Olivia was taken aback at the way the conversation was going. She struggled to change her approach. Enid watched her discomfort with satisfaction and pressed home her attack.

"What exactly are you doing here, Mrs Fisher? I am very busy today and I have no time to listen to this nonsense about Dorothy. Please come to the point."

Olivia was nonplussed. This was not a woman to be fooled with. She decided to cut short her stay.

"I want you to send me the girl's wages each month. I know she gets her bed and board in a job like this. She has no need of money to waste on fripperies while her family starves." Enid was livid. She rounded on Olivia, her tone like ice.

"If what you say is true, I would have no need to send you Dorothy's wages. I am quite sure she would see to it herself. As it is, I know that your husband is working, as indeed, you are. You also have your little moneymaking schemes that are not strictly legal. We have already touched on that subject, have we not, Mrs Fisher? Now unless you wish me to take action on this matter, I suggest you leave my home immediately. You will also leave your stepdaughter strictly alone for the future. Should you appear so much as inside the gates of Woodleigh again, you will be ejected, and my husband will take legal action. I am quite sure that any investigation into your affairs would reveal a lot more than we have discussed today. Do I make myself clear?"

Olivia was reduced to silence. She shook with rage, astonished at this totally unexpected turn of events.

"I mean every word, Mrs Fisher, now please leave." Enid had rung the bell for Hilda, who appeared at precisely the right moment. "Mrs Fisher is leaving, Hilda. She will not be back."

Olivia pulled herself together and followed Hilda out of the room. She had never felt so angry or humiliated in all her life. It did not occur to her that what had happened was of her own making. She stalked off down the drive without a backward glance. She did wonder if Dot could see her from one of the windows.

Little bitch, she thought, *they are welcome to her. I hope I never see her again.* She reached the bus stop, the chill wind not making her temper any better. She turned her back to it, reflecting on her defeat.

In Garston, Dot and Flo enjoyed their afternoon together. Not much news for Flo to relate, but she listened to all her granddaughter had to say about Woodleigh. She liked the sound of the Hislops and their way of life. It seemed from what she said that Dot lived almost as well as her employers. From all accounts, the staff seemed to be a decent lot, and Flo felt happy and relieved about the girl's future.

Just keep Olivia out of her life, please. Flo offered up the silent prayer.

"Next time you have a day off, Dottie, don't come chasing all the way over here to see me. Now that I know you are all right, I will be quite happy seeing you just once in a while. You must spend your free day with new friends, doing new things."

"We will see, Gran, we will see!"

That evening, Dot arrived back at Woodleigh in time for dinner. As she was not on duty, she did not have to wash up the dishes. She sat with Lizzie in the sitting room, where the rest of the staff had congregated to listen to the gramophone. Hilda was bursting with news of Olivia's visit. Dot's heart sank when she started the tale, but by the time Hilda had finished, relief set in.

The following morning, Enid sent for Dot. She was taking coffee alone in the drawing room.

"Sit down please, Dorothy." Dot did as she was bid and listened quietly, while Enid told her exactly what happened yesterday. She smiled as Enid reported how the conversation had gone. "I hope most sincerely that you will not be bothered by the woman again, at least for as long as you work here. I am sure we both hope that will be for some considerable time to come."

"I don't know what to say, Madam. I am so sorry that Olivia came here bothering you. She was wrong to do that, but thank you for dealing with her the way you did."

"I think that it is best put behind us, don't you? We all have lots to look forward to. It is Christmas next month. We all have a wonderful time at Woodleigh. The boys will be home. Their friends come to stay. We have parties at New Year, oh, you will love it, Dorothy, you really will."

Dot felt a little surge of excitement as Enid talked. Then, the conversation over, she returned to her duties.

Mary Wilding, the cook, looked up from preparing lunch for both Enid and the staff. She gave Dot a warm smile.

"You all right, gal?" she enquired.

"Fine, thanks, Cook."

"Good. Right then, we had better get on. Make a start on those vegetables. When they are done, you can help Vera with the silver. We are having a big dinner party this weekend. Lots to do!" So Dot was swept up in the preparations, and her old life was put aside.

The weeks sped by, Christmas and New Year came and went, hard work for the staff, but exciting. Dot had never known such festivities. All the downstairs rooms were decorated. A giant fir tree stood in the entrance hall, covered in glass baubles that had been collected over the years, and dozens of candles that were lit each evening. The pictures were trimmed with holly, and a beautiful wreath hung on the front door. Visitors came to stay, which made extra work, but they were generous with their tips to the staff. The Hislops were also good to their employees. They all received a small personal gift and extra money in their pay packets at the end of the month.

Dot was unable to get home over Christmas, but early in the New Year she returned to the Railway house with presents for all, even Olivia who immediately complained to Archie, "She is obviously earning far too much." He ignored her. It was easier that way. He was amazed at Dot. She looked so well. The good food at Woodleigh had filled her out, and she looked like a young woman, not a half-starved child. She had matured, too, carrying herself well with an air of confidence. He was both proud and grateful.

The friendship between Dot and Lizzie grew. They were comfortable together, although quite different in personality. Lizzie was the quieter of the two, calm and sensible, inclined to be predictable. Dot was impulsive and ready for anything. Their days off did not often coincide, but when they did, the two would cycle to Lizzie's home. It was quite a ride to Moreton, but they were young and fit and thought nothing of it. The bikes were old, used by the Hislops in the past, but nowadays available for the staff to get around.

Shortly before Lizzie was twenty-one, she invited Dot to a party to celebrate her birthday.

"It is just family and a few old friends from school. Mum is determined to give me a do. I would rather not bother."

Enid gave the girls permission to stay over at Lizzie's after the party. It was too far for them to cycle at night. She would have arranged for Joe to collect them in the car, but she and Charlie needed him that night. The party went well. Dot met Lizzie's friends, including Bob, who had his eye on Lizzie, and had for a while.

"I will marry her one day," he confided in Dot's ear. He had drunk several pints of beer by this time, but he meant what he said. "I have known her for years, and I have never been interested in anyone else, believe me!"

"Oh, I do, Bob, I do."

The next morning as they cycled back to Woodleigh, Dot told Lizzie about her conversation with Bob. Lizzie blushed.

"I know he likes me, Dot, but I am not interested in walking out with him. Not yet anyway. I enjoy the job, and I am not ready to settle down. It is Abersoch in August. I would not get a month away like that, if I was married."

"Is Abersoch good, Liz?"

"Good! It is bloody marvellous, as Master Philip would say. We have our own bungalow, which is beautiful, right by the sea. It is in the grounds of the house. Mr Hislop takes us out on the yacht. We live like lords, Dot."

As August approached, the staff prepared to shut Woodleigh up for the month. Dustsheets were brought out, and the rooms closed one by one. Suitcases were packed. Tennis racquets and assorted sailing gear appeared in piles as the boys arrived home. James, the only one of the three working, was the last to get back. Charlie had used his influence to organise James' release from Meredith's for four weeks.

The day of departure finally arrived. The excitement was at fever pitch. The family and the housekeeping staff piled into the waiting cars. Joe drove the Rolls with Enid, Charlie, Timothy and Cook on board. Philip had Lizzie, Hilda, and Vera as passengers. Dot was driven by James in the Avon Special. The cars moved off together. The eagerly awaited holiday had begun.

CHAPTER TWENTY-ONE

The drive down to Abersoch, through North Wales, was an education for Dot. She, who had never been more than a few miles from Garston, found herself in countryside more beautiful than anywhere she could have ever imagined.

She felt like a captive bird escaped from a cage. The wind tore at her hair as the open-topped car sped along. James was quite talkative. He felt attracted to Dot, and in the way of most young men, he enjoyed driving his sporty car with a pretty girl at his side. Dot wished he would keep quiet so that she could soak up the scenery and enjoy the sense of freedom that she was experiencing.

After a couple of hours travelling, the cars turned down towards the sea. They came to a halt just above the shoreline, hazy mountains behind them, and below, the incoming tide.

"Come along then." Cook was out of the car with an agility that belied her size. "Let's get everything ready." Picnic baskets were produced from the cavernous boot of the Rolls, and travel rugs placed on the ground. Then Cook produced a picnic of thickly sliced ham and pork pies, jars of pickled onions, and English mustard. Loaves of crisp baked bread and pats of butter were laid alongside. There were strawberries, the very end of the crop, and jugs of thick cream. A great chunk of Lancashire cheese and a box of water biscuits were there for those who still had room to fill. Charlie produced two bottles of red wine, which he poured himself. All of the company received a small glass. This was the first time Dot had tasted wine of any sort.

"I'd rather not." Her words were ignored and a glass pushed into her hand. She was not impressed, and still preferred Cook's fresh lemonade or homemade ginger beer. The party tucked into the alfresco meal. Cook had excelled herself, everyone agreed. They did not linger. They had a fair way to go before they would reach their destination. The staff cleared away the picnic debris and loaded the baskets back in the boot. Then they set off once more.

It was early evening when they arrived at Abersoch. The sky was that turquoise blue, usually seen in June. The sun, starting its slow descent, cast a tangerine light on a few clouds out over the sea. Dot was spellbound.

"How beautiful," she said to herself. Philip, who was standing near her heard her comment and agreed.

"Indeed it is." Then he added, "I would like to live in Abersoch."

"Maybe you will one day."

"Dorothy," Cook called and brought Dot down to earth.

"Excuse me, Master Philip, I must go and help the others." She smiled as she left to join the staff. For some reason her heart was pounding in her chest. Philip, left alone by his car, felt more than ever that this girl was special.

"Come on, Phil old man, give us a hand. Mother is anxious to get everything unpacked before dinner." James was hauling cases up to the house. Joe had already taken some. Timothy had his arms full of tennis racquets.

"It's good to be back, isn't it, Phil? I hope this weather lasts while we're here."

So the holiday began. The house was not as grand as Woodleigh. It was smaller and more easily maintained. There was a caretaker who looked after it and organised the cleaning and airing of the place. When the family arrived, Cook and the rest of the Woodleigh staff took over.

Timothy need not have worried. The weather that August was perfect. There were a number of houseguests from time to time, mostly joining the Hislops for long weekends. The staff were kept very busy, working long hours, looking after the family and their guests. Enid, however, made sure that they each had time off to enjoy the weather, the beach, and Abersoch itself.

In the evenings, when the meal was over, they were allowed to go out to the yacht. Joe usually took them out to the *Valentina* in the launch. Forty feet long, with a fin keel, she needed plenty of water beneath her and was moored some distance away from the shore. In the spacious saloon, there was comfortable seating for all. They had their gramophone on board, and spent wonderful evenings imagining they were at sea, cruising to foreign parts.

On one occasion, Lizzie, Hilda, and Dot were all invited for a sail. The three brothers and two of their friends felt that a few girls around would add interest to the afternoon. Cook gave her consent on condition they were back to help with dinner. The boys assured her that they would see to that, and off they went.

It was idyllic. The sea was scarcely ruffled. With all the sail they could muster, they barely made three knots. Philip observed Dot discreetly. She was standing at the bow, leaning on the rail, looking down. The bow wave sparkled as the boat moved through the clear water. He went up forward to join her.

"How are you enjoying the sail?"

"It's wonderful, Philip," she said enthusiastically, turning round to face him. Her cheeks were rosy from the sun. Then her colour deepened as she realised that she had called him Philip, without the master. She started to apologise, but he put a finger to his lips.

"I don't mind," he said. "In fact I like it."

A wave of emotion swept over her. She had never felt anything like it in all her short life. Her knees felt weak, and she suddenly wanted this man to take her in his arms and hold her tight. Philip was looking down at her from his full six feet. It was all he could do to stop himself from kissing this young and lovely girl. He did resist, because she was young, far too young and inexperienced for him, at not quite seventeen. Philip, at twenty-three, felt it would be unfair to get involved. The moment passed, but something had happened between them. An awakening of feelings quite deep and disturbing had occurred.

"Ready about!" James shouted the warning of a forthcoming change of tack. It was time to return to their moorings and get the girls back for their evening duties. Philip and Dot joined the others in the cockpit, both of them quiet and thoughtful.

The breeze was lighter now. The *Valentina* barely moved through the water. James started up the engine, and the boat surged effortlessly ahead. The girls would be back in good time.

The following week, Lizzie had a surprise. Bob, her determined suitor, arrived, having cycled all the way from Moreton. With him was his friend John. They were both on holiday from work and thought the trip would be fun. It would cost very little and enable Bob to see Lizzie. Joe said they could share his room for a couple of nights if the Mistress agreed. Enid had no objections and the two dropped off their rucksacks and went to explore Abersoch. They had egg and chips in a little café, filling up with rounds of bread and butter. They were ravenous after their long days on the road.

"Would you like to go for a walk, Liz?" Bob asked that evening, when the staff finished work for the day.

"I should think you are too worn out for walking, after cycling all those miles."

"It beats sitting down at the moment, to be honest."

"Have you enough time to cycle back, Bob?"

"Oh no. The plan is to stay here until Saturday and put the bikes on the train as far as we can. Anyway, how about a walk?"

"I don't mind if that's what you want. I'll see if Dot wants to come." Lizzie was anxious not to be left alone with Bob. She felt that he was getting too serious about her.

"If she is coming, I might as well ask John." Bob was disappointed, but at least he would be with her. Maybe they could split up later.

So the four of them set off for the beach. It was a glorious evening, still warm with a gentle breeze from the south.

Dot liked John. He made her laugh and seemed very easy going. He was two years older than her, serving an apprenticeship with a master electrician. He lived in Moreton, near to Bob. They had been to school together, and although Bob was two years his senior, they had become firm friends.

They enjoyed their short stay. All too soon, they were cycling off to catch the train, to return home.

"Can I see you sometime, Dot, when you get back to Oxton?" John asked shyly, as they were leaving.

"Maybe," said Dot, her reply noncommittal. She did not want any complications in her life just now. Everything was so good at the moment. She was beginning to know who she was, slowly and surely. She wanted to simply enjoy her job and her friends at Woodleigh. She could see that he was hurt. It showed in his beautiful grey eyes.

"We'll see, John. It's a long time off yet." She laughed to lighten the moment. She and Lizzie waved them off from the gates. Philip, standing at his bedroom window, felt a pang of jealousy, far too strong to be justified. He sighed as he watched Dot walk up to the house with Lizzie, both of them laughing happily as they went.

"Dorothy, what am I going to do about you?" He whispered the words to his reflection in the window as she disappeared from view.

Chapter Twenty-two

Dot looked so well by the end of August that her own family would have found it hard to recognise her. No longer waif-like, her body had filled out to healthy proportions, and her face was lightly tanned. She wore her dark hair shoulder length now, and it shone with health.

After the sail on the *Valentina* with all the boys, there was little opportunity to do it again. The house was full of guests, friends of Enid and Charlie, and the three brothers. Then it was time to pack up and return home. It had been a wonderful month, the most memorable one of Dot's life.

On the journey back to Woodleigh, Hilda rode in James' car. Dot joined Lizzie and Vera in Philip's. She sat behind him, studying the back of his head. His neatly cut hair trying to curl at the nape of his neck made her want to reach forward and touch him. She thought about the day on the boat, and the moments together. Then, for some reason, her thoughts turned to John and what fun he had been.

* * *

"You look miles away, Mum. Have you been to sleep?" Dorothy had been so deep in her reverie that she had not heard Elizabeth cross the ward.

"No, dear, I was thinking about your father, and that first summer I went to Abersoch. You know it seems just like yesterday. Time is a funny thing, isn't it? What a pity they pulled Woodleigh down and built those awful flats."

Elizabeth agreed, thinking as she spoke that her mother looked much better these last few days.

"Any news about you coming home?"

"I see the consultant again next week, but the physiotherapist thinks it will be a while yet."

"Are you fed up, Mum?"

"Not a lot of point, is there? It will take as long as it takes. I do at least have my faculties, which is more than you can say for some of the poor souls in here. I spend a lot of time thinking about my life. It's funny, you know, it's as if most of it happened to somebody else. I should get you to write it all down for me one day. It would make a good book." Elizabeth laughed in dismissal of the idea.

"I don't think I'm quite up to that, Mum. Did Aunt Lizzie come last night?"

"Yes, dear, Bob brought her. They both looked very fit. They are well into their eighties, you know. Bob is still driving. How lucky they are to be together after all these years."

The visit flew by, as it always did. Elizabeth hated leaving her mother more and more as the weeks went by. Dorothy simply got on with it. She was determined to walk well enough to be allowed back home. She refused to be a burden to her family. She waved good-bye to her daughter and wondered if anyone would visit in the evening. She had enjoyed seeing Lizzie and Bob. If ever a marriage had been made in heaven, it was theirs.

* * *

After the trip to Abersoch, Bob had pursued Lizzie with fervour. He frequently cycled over to Woodleigh, spending time with Lizzie in the company of the staff in the sitting room. Sometimes John would turn up with him, and Dot and he would make up a foursome. They would go to the pictures or maybe for a walk together.

Christmas that year found Woodleigh full to capacity. The whole family was home, joined by several guests. Philip's friend was the sister of a fellow student at Oxford.

"Do you mind if Elspeth comes for the holiday, Mother?" Philip rather hoped that the answer would be no, when he phoned her at the beginning of December. Elspeth had angled for an invitation, having become rather smitten by Philip, when visiting her brother Ned at Oxford.

"He is so attractive, Ned. Does his family have money?" She was not the sort to waste her time on someone without.

"Rather," said Ned emphatically. "His father is a millionaire. Self-made man and all that. Old Philip is a decent type though, and he's doing rather well."

Elspeth almost purred with pleasure.

"Good husband material then, Ned?"

"I should say so, no good wasting your time on anything less!"

So Elspeth came to Woodleigh on Christmas Eve. Philip greeted her in the hall, not quite sure how all this had come about.

"Good to see you, Elspeth. You do look well."

So I should, thought Elspeth. She had spent a fortune on clothes for the visit and her dark auburn hair had been newly permed.

Dot had been promoted to the position of parlour maid. Enid considered her wasted as a tweeny and moved her upstairs when she could. Today, she answered the door to Elspeth. Philip came to greet her. Dot felt a wave of emotion as he kissed the girl's cheek. Excusing herself, she hurried back to the butler's pantry to help Lizzie with the afternoon tea trays.

"I hate her," Dot said vehemently.

"Who?"

"That friend of Philip's."

"You don't know her, Dot. She's never been here before."

"I don't have to know her. I hate her."

"What's brought this on?" Lizzie looked at Dot with some surprise. After all, Philip's friends were nothing to them.

"She is out to catch him, Lizzie. I know she is and she is not right for him."

"And who is? You, I suppose." She looked at Dot, expecting her to laugh at the idea, but was surprised at her reaction.

"I think that I have fallen for him, Lizzie. Seeing him with that girl made me feel so jealous and I have no right to be."

"Indeed you haven't. Dot, you are not eighteen yet. He is years older than you, going to be a doctor, and will probably marry a nob."

"I know, I know, but I can't help how I feel."

"Has he ever given you any encouragement, Dot? You know what I mean."

"No, Lizzie, nothing like that." She did not tell her friend about the magical moment on the *Valentina*. What was there to tell anyway? It was something indefinable, but unforgettable.

That second Christmas at Woodleigh was even more pleasant than the first. Working above stairs, she was able to enjoy the festivities. She took note of the fashions and behaviour of the guests. She was by now fully versed in the art of table arrangement. The variety of cutlery and glassware and their positions on the dining table posed no problems for her. She was completely comfortable in the company of the "nobs" as Lizzie called them. None of them daunted her, or made her feel inferior, except for Elspeth. Maybe Philip's friend had an instinct about Dot. She was forever demanding small services. Things that she would normally do herself she required Dot to do. She was difficult and condescending on occasions.

Philip overheard her one day being quite rude to Dot, and he stepped in angrily.

"Dorothy is not your personal slave, Elspeth. She is a highly regarded member of our staff, and not used to being spoken to like that." Elspeth turned an angry red. Dot fled. It might have been Enid speaking. Her boys had inherited her kindness and sense of fair play.

Mortified, Dot dashed up to her room. She washed her face and dabbed some powder on her nose. The incident revived memories of Olivia, and she pushed them away. Elspeth was not going to spoil Woodleigh for her. She would be gone soon.

On the way to continue her duties, she ran into Philip.

"Are you all right?" he asked kindly. He put his forefinger under her chin, lifting her face to look at him. "You mustn't let her upset you. She should know better than to behave like that."

"I'm all right, Master Philip. Please excuse me. Lizzie will be wondering where I have got to." Philip stepped aside, and Dot hurried off down the hall.

"Is there a problem, Philip?" Enid had seen him talking to Dot and gently lift her chin up. She felt somewhat disturbed. "You aren't interested in Dorothy, are you, dear, more than any other member of staff I mean?" Philip shifted from one foot to the other.

"She is a lovely girl, Mother, very intelligent, and amazingly good company."

Enid had not expected such a reply. She was suddenly concerned.

"You know, dear, she is very young and inexperienced. Anyway, she seems to be seeing that friend of Lizzie's young man. He is near her own age and from her own background." Enid was not a snob, nor had she any qualms about Philip on that score. However, as the wife of a self-made man, she knew that there could be problems if he got involved with Dorothy. He also had several years' hard work before him to qualify in medicine, and a serious relationship could become a complication.

"Philip, darling, are we going for a walk before it goes dark, or not?" Elspeth appeared, warmly dressed in an astrakhan coat and hat. She looked stunning.

"I'll be with you in a minute, Elspeth. I'll just get my coat." He kissed Enid on the cheek. "Don't worry, Mother. I won't do anything stupid. I'll see you at dinner." He collected his overcoat from the cloakroom. His mind was in turmoil. *Dorothy, why have you got under my skin like this? It's not the right time.*

He joined Elspeth. Through the pantry window, Dot saw them set off together, Elspeth taking his arm as they went. She felt a little empty inside.

CHAPTER TWENTY-THREE

Elspeth occupied most of Philip's time that Christmas and New Year. When he returned to Oxford she travelled with him, as her family lived not far from his college. The time spent together at Woodleigh had strengthened her determination to become his wife. He was eligible, handsome, and soon to become a doctor, what more could a girl want?

Dot tried to turn her thoughts away from Philip. There could be no future with him. Everyone told her so.

At Easter, Bob proposed to Lizzie, and she accepted.

"It will be a while before we get married, Dot. We'll have to save up for the wedding, and Bob wants us to get a place of our own. He says renting is a waste of money. I want you to be my bridesmaid of course. John is going to be best man."

Dot was thrilled at the prospect, even if it was in the future. She threw herself into helping Lizzie with wedding plans.

Alice, the Hislops' dressmaker, offered to create a wedding gown for Lizzie. Dot bought the material for her own dress, and Alice also made that. The wedding was to be a modest affair, the couple preferring to spend their slender savings on a deposit for a house.

Shortly before Dot's nineteenth birthday, the wedding took place. The Hislops lent the Rolls Royce to be used as the wedding car. It was a perfect, summer day. Lizzie, composed as always, looked beautiful in her classic, white dress. Her bouquet, made up of cream roses from Woodleigh, and her mother's own wedding veil, complemented the gown.

Dot, who was bursting with excitement and happiness for her friend, could hardly keep still during the ceremony.

John could not take his eyes off her. He listened to the words spoken by the vicar and found them moving.

"Marry me, Dottie Fisher," he whispered to her, as they stood together to be photographed outside the church. Dot smiled as usual at this request.

"I'm far too young, John. Everyone says so. Anyway, this is their day, let's not talk about us."

"I won't give up, Dot. I'll wear you down."

Joe drove the happy couple to their new home, where the wedding breakfast was laid out. Cook had contributed a magnificent cake as her gift, and it had pride of place on the table. The guests walked the short distance to the house, Dot feeling a little self-conscious in her bridesmaid's dress.

After the meal, John made an amusing speech as best man, and a toast was drunk to the bride and groom. The day went without a hitch.

The couple were going to the Lake District for a few days' honeymoon. Joe was to drive them to the station to start their journey. The whole party assembled to wave them off, and Lizzie tossed her bouquet over her shoulder as she left. She turned to see Dot holding it high above her head. John, ever the clown, was on his knees, his hands together as if in prayer. Everyone laughed at his antics, then turned their attention to the departing bride and groom.

"Have a wonderful time, don't do anything we wouldn't do." There was much laughing and joking, and they were gone.

The party was over. On his return from the station, Joe drove the staff back to Woodleigh. It was a squash, even in a Rolls Royce, but no one cared. They drove home in high spirits, revelling in the luxury of the car.

The Hislops were out for dinner, so they had no duties to attend to. They all assembled in the sitting room. No one wanted anything more to eat. The girls each had wedding cake to put under their pillows.

"You will all dream of the men you are going to marry," said Mary Wilding.

"Have you got a piece, Cook?" asked Hilda.

"I've got more sense," she replied gruffly, thinking of the lad who had not come back from the Somme in nineteen sixteen, but saying nothing.

That night, Dot dreamed of Philip.

After the wedding, things changed at Woodleigh. Lizzie gave up her job to become a housewife, and Hilda was promoted to head maid. She and Dot rubbed along. Hilda was, however, more than a little interested in John Gardner. He had obviously fallen for Dot in a big way, and this Hilda resented. The household ran smoothly still, but the happy days with Dot and Lizzie, working side by side, were over.

Visiting Lizzie on her day off, Dot found herself envying her friend the happiness that she and Bob shared.

"You are happy, aren't you, Lizzie?" It was not really a question, more of a statement. Watching Lizzie pouring tea into china cups, a wedding present from the Hislop boys, she listened to her chatter about running the house. Happiness shone out of her.

Sometimes, Dot and John would meet at the newlyweds'. One evening, walking her to the corner to catch her bus back to Oxton, John said, "That could be us, you know, Dot. We could have our own little house. I would decorate it just the way you wanted. We would have a lawn at the back and I could mow it on Sunday afternoons."

"You hate gardening, John!" she exclaimed in reply.

"I know, but I would do it for you."

"You are hopeless, John Gardner. What am I going to do with you?"

"Marry me, Dottie, that's what you can do."

At that point, the bus came and Dot jumped on.

"I'll see you soon," he called as it started off. Dot watched his tall straight figure become smaller as they moved away. She thought how handsome he was, with his black wavy hair and clear grey eyes. He made her laugh, with his quick wit and his funny impersonations of people. She could do a lot worse than to marry him.

That night, she dreamed of Philip again.

Serving tea the following afternoon, she heard news of him. He did not get home so often now. He was approaching his finals.

Enid was entertaining a friend. She and Gloria went back a long way. Their children had been born at the same time. Dot passed the cake stand round.

"Thank you, Dorothy." Gloria acknowledged her, smiling as she did so. She then turned to Enid, saying, "How about Philip? Has he long to go now at Oxford?"

"It's finals soon. Then he is doing a couple of years in hospital. After that, he will decide where he goes from there. I fancy he'll do surgery, you know, but it is a long haul and requires great dedication."

Dot hovered as long as she dared, fussing with the tea trays.

"Where will he do his hospital stint?"

"Oh, Oxford I think, Gloria. That's where Elspeth is after all."

"I see," said Gloria meaningfully.

"I don't know how serious he is about the girl." Enid looked at her friend ruefully. "You can't choose their wives for them, can you? We'd probably make a better job of it if we could. Elspeth is a fine girl, but a bit pushy for me. She comes from a good family, very wealthy and influential, but I'm not sure she is right for Philip."

Dot left them to it. The conversation had upset her.

Don't be stupid, she admonished herself. *Philip is nothing to you, never could be. He lives in a different world.*

"You've been a long time, miss," snapped Hilda.

"Sorry," muttered Dot, wishing Lizzie was back and they could talk together.

For the first time, John's proposals seemed a possibility. *Most girls would jump at the chance, especially Hilda.* Dot could not help smiling at the thought of Hilda's reaction if she accepted him. *That's no reason to get married, my girl,* she told herself, and she wished that she had a mother to confide in. Her father seemed remote now, after more than three years away from home. She met him occasionally when she visited Flo, but she had never been back to the Railway house.

Ah well, she sighed, *there is no rush to decide. If he really wants me he will wait a while.*

The following day, she had two pieces of news that were to help her make up her mind.

CHAPTER TWENTY-FOUR

Hilda picked up the morning post. Personal letters and bills for the family were placed on the silver tray in the entrance hall. These were usually read at the breakfast table. Any mail for the staff was placed on the huge dresser in the kitchen. Today, there was a letter for Cook, two for Joe, and one for Dot.

"Who's writing to her, I wonder?" Hilda was curious. Dot never received post. She scrutinized the envelope, trying to decipher the postmark, but was thwarted when Dot herself breezed into the kitchen.

"What a lovely morning, Hilda, I wish it was my day off."

"You've got a letter," came the reply.

"Thank you, Hilda." Dot put it straight into her apron pocket without looking at it. Hilda was consumed with curiosity. Dot, realising this, determined to leave the envelope unopened until later.

It was a beautiful day. Timothy, now nearly nineteen, was at home preparing for University. He was to study classics at Oxford, planning to teach when he got his degree. He came into the kitchen that morning looking for a snack.

"Dorothy, the very one! Is there anything to eat? I'm starving."

"Master Timothy, you know that's not up to me. You'll have to see Cook. She's out in the vegetable garden at the moment. Can you wait?"

"I might just go and weed her out." Laughing at his unintentional pun, Timothy turned to go. "I think you could drop the 'Master' now, Dorothy. It makes me feel about ten years old. I'm the same age as you after all."

With that he went out into the gardens to look for Mary. He found her instructing the head gardener as to her requirements for the week. Joseph would then pull the vegetables each morning, so that they were as fresh as possible.

"There you are, Cook." Mary turned round at the sound of Timothy's voice.

"Looks like it, Master Timothy. What can I do for you?"

"A tasty morsel, Cookie? A small meat pie, some cold sausage, anything to fill the gap until lunch."

"Mercy me, where do you put it all? It's only an hour since breakfast."

"I'm a growing lad, Cookie."

"Come on then, let's see what I can find."

They returned to the kitchen. Vera was busy making a drink of tea for the staff's elevenses. Mary made Timothy a cheese and pickle sandwich, and he sat at the well-scrubbed table to eat it. He loved the kitchen. Its warmth was as comforting now as it had been when as a child he had come to Cook for consolation. He was forever in trouble in those days, and she always helped him sort things out.

Cursed with a quick temper, he had worked out a way to relieve his feelings. There was a large, ancient umbrella hanging on the back of the kitchen door. When his anger overwhelmed him, Timothy would storm in, snatch the umbrella and march to the very bottom of the garden. There he would open and close the brolly as fast as he could, until his rage abated. He would then return it to the back of the door, thank Cook quietly and go on his way.

Today, however, he was at peace with the world as he sat demolishing the sandwich.

"When are you off to college then, Master Timothy?"

"Couple of weeks, Cook."

"Are you looking forward to it?"

"Yes and no. It's a bit daunting."

"You do surprise me, you being away at school all this time."

"I know, but this is different. Out in the big wide world and all that." He laughed self-consciously. "It's a pity Philip will be just about finished. He will still be in Oxford though. That will be good."

Dot and Hilda joined the others for their cup of tea.

"By the way, Cook," continued Timothy, "did you know Philip was engaged? He phoned us last night. He and Elspeth are tying the knot, I'm not sure when. Between you and me, I don't much care for her. She'll wear the trousers for certain."

"Master Timothy, that's no way to talk. Have some respect, please."

Timothy grinned, then having delivered his news, and filled the hollow in his stomach, he departed.

"Well, well," said Hilda, "fancy that, Master Philip and that stuck-up Elspeth, engaged. I hope they stay in Oxford. What say you, Dot?"

"I hope he will be very happy." Her voice was flat as she tried to hide her pain on hearing of his engagement. "Will you excuse me? I have come down without a hankie. I won't be a minute." She rushed up to her room, wanting to be alone while she digested the news. *He never was yours*, she thought, *but he might have been, under different circumstances.* She had not imagined those moments on the *Valentina*. They had both felt that deep attraction that knows no boundaries. Another time, another place, something might have developed, but it was not to be. He really was out of reach now; Elspeth would never let him go.

She pulled herself together. She combed her hair. Then she smoothed down the bedspread. The unopened envelope crackled in her pocket as she bent over the bed. It was from her father.

Dear Dot,

I am sorry to have to tell you that Flo has died quite suddenly. She did not appear to have been ill. Her heart simply gave out, and she died in her armchair at home. I can't think of a better way to go. I know you will be very upset, Dot. If you would like to come home for a while, Olivia says that will be all right. The children have taken it badly, especially Edward. You don't have to let us know, just come if you want to.

Your loving,
Dad

The paper slipped from her fingers, and she began to cry. She wept for her grandmother, and for the mother she had never known. She wept for Philip and the love that might have been.

Returning to the kitchen, she told Cook that she had to speak to the Mistress.

"What ever is the matter, duck? What's upset you?"

"It's Gran, Cook, she's died, suddenly. My gran has gone."

Enid heard the news in the drawing room. She knew what Flo had been to Dot and what a gap losing her would leave in her young life. Enid was sad for her. She had seen the girl blossom under her roof, and become a confident young woman. She had thrown off the desperate years of her childhood, and seized

101

her opportunities with both hands. There was no bitterness in her heart to eat away at her and spoil her life.

"What do you want to do, Dorothy? Do you want to go home for the funeral at least? If you don't want to stay, no one could blame you."

"I'd like to be there for the funeral, for Dad's sake as much as anything. Olivia won't go I'm sure. I don't want to stay any longer than necessary."

Enid took charge.

"Suppose Joe ran you to the ferry? That would make the journey a bit easier."

Dot felt relieved. She would only need to stay a couple of days.

"Thank you, Mrs Hislop, I'd appreciate that."

"Off you go then, and collect a few things. I'll see Cook and Hilda, and then I'll organise the car." Then on a different note, "Be glad for your grandmother, Dorothy. She was a fair age, and didn't suffer a cruel illness. Most of all, she saw you make a new life for yourself, and it is only just beginning, you know."

Dot gave her a watery smile and went to put her things together. Half an hour later, she was on her way. Joe, respecting her mood, kept quiet as the car purred along. Dot sat beside him in the front, almost lost in the roomy, leather seat.

Last time I was in the Rolls, it was Lizzie's wedding day, she thought. *How happy we all were that day.*

Joe dropped her at Woodside. It seemed so long since she had first arrived there from Garston. It was as if it had happened to somebody else. She hardly noticed the crossing, or the tram ride.

She stood in front of the Railway house, surprised that she felt nothing. She knocked on the front door, as a stranger would. Indeed, she felt she was just that, a stranger.

The door opened, and there stood Olivia.

"Oh, it's you. I didn't know you were coming today."

"If it's not convenient, I can find somewhere to stay."

"There's no need for that, you can share with the girls. You'd better come in."

Olivia had not seen Dot for three years. She felt slightly in awe of the composed young woman who stood before her, and for once her acid tongue was still. Dot stepped inside, amazed at how small the house seemed. Accustomed now to the spaciousness of Woodleigh, she felt suffocated in the atmosphere of coal fires and stale cooking smells. The place looked uncared-for. Evidently no one had taken over her chores when she had left.

"When will Dad be home?" She addressed Olivia coldly, conscious of the fact, but unable to muster any warmth. Dot observed her as she made a pot of tea. She was still quite beautiful in spite of the premature lines on her face.

At this point, Archie arrived back from work, delighted to find his daughter under his roof again.

"I'm so glad you could come, Dottie. Will you stay for the funeral tomorrow?"

"Yes, of course, Dad. That's why I've come." Relief spread over her. If the funeral was tomorrow, she need only stay overnight.

One by one, Edward and the girls arrived home. They each gave Dot a warm welcome. Edward at fifteen was mature for his age. Meg at twelve had grown to look like Olivia, but had not inherited much else from her mother. She was a bright girl and had won a scholarship to the Grammar School, where she was doing well. Joan, now thirteen, was quiet and gentle, taking after Archie.

The re-united family spent the evening together. There was a lot of catching up to do. Archie wondered how he had fathered such an elegant daughter. She made them all laugh with tales of her life at Woodleigh. An early night was deemed sensible, with the funeral tomorrow, but it was some time before Joan and Meg tired of talking to their big sister, as they snuggled beneath the feather eiderdown.

The following morning, the children left for school and Olivia caught the tram to her current job as a lady's companion.

Archie and Dot were about to leave for the church, when there was a knock at the front door. Archie answered it. Dot heard a voice say, "Is Dot here?"

It was John. He had heard the news of Flo's death. Knowing Dot's home background quite well, and what an ordeal the funeral would be, he had decided to come and offer his support.

Dot, hearing his voice, ran to him. He held her in his arms, and the tears flowed. She wept until she could weep no more, and he let her go.

"It's all right, Dot. I'll look after you. You are not on your own."

John, having arrived at the right moment, accompanied Dot and Archie to the funeral. Flo's neighbours had put on a meal for the mourners. It was a quiet affair, Flo having little or no family. The ham salad eaten, and the tea drunk, the three of them returned to the Railway house. Archie took a liking to John, and while he was out of the room he said to Dot, "Good lad that. Known him long?"

"A year or two. He's a friend of Bob's."

"Good of him to come to the funeral."

Olivia arrived home at this point. She saw John sitting at the kitchen table.

"Who's this then, Dorothy? A friend of yours?" She flashed her tawny eyes at John, eyeing him up and down, as she advanced to shake his hand. Archie turned away, unable to watch his wife in action. Dot was horrified as Olivia sidled up to John, blatantly making overtures to him.

"I hope I'm more than a friend, Mrs Fisher." John's tone was firm and dismissive. Olivia was surprised at his coolness, and not a little annoyed.

"Well, be warned, young man. This girl is not what she appears to be. I'd get to know her really well before you commit yourself. She's a selfish little madam."

"Enough!" Archie's angry voice silenced Olivia. She stared at him, open-mouthed. "Leave the girl alone. No wonder she never comes home. Haven't you done enough damage already?" Archie began to cough, his chest heaving with the effort.

"It's all right, Dad. I'm going now anyway. I'll keep in touch. I'm glad I came for the funeral. Gran would have wanted that." She collected her things from upstairs, kissed her father good-bye and left.

"What a woman." John shook his head in disbelief as they set off for the tram.

CHAPTER TWENTY-FIVE

"Do you think funerals are always like that?" Dot turned to John as she spoke. They were leaning on the rail, watching the water rush past the ferry.

"How do you mean?"

"Well, I thought they were gloomy affairs, but once everyone said how sorry they were, it was more like a party."

"I don't know. I don't remember my dad's. You're right though, they all got a bit noisy, telling jokes, and stories about the past."

"Well, I'm relieved it's over. I don't suppose I'll go back to Garston, now that Gran has gone. Dad will have to come to see me in future."

The short ferry crossing completed, John saw Dot to her bus stop. He left her, to make his own way home. He had lost a day at work to be with her, and he would have to make it up somehow. Jobs were not easy to come by. There was always someone waiting to jump into a vacancy. He was, however, glad that he had gone to be with her. He had certainly had a glimpse of Olivia's character. He wondered why Archie put up with her, but he was not the first to wonder that.

After the funeral, he and Dot spent more time together. They continued to bump into one another at Lizzie and Bob's. They went to the pictures on Dot's day off. She met his family, but was not impressed. He lived with his mother and sisters, all of whom thought Dot had too many airs and graces. She laughed when he unwisely told her this. She supposed that living at Woodleigh, even as a maid, must have changed her. When she had her own home, things would be done properly however modestly she lived.

"No girl would be right for you, John, in your family's eyes."

"Oh, they're not so bad. I suppose they are a bit possessive, me being the only man in the house."

Some months after Flo died, the bungalow opposite John's home became available to rent.

"Dot, it would be perfect for us. It's partly furnished, so we wouldn't have to buy much to start off. I would be on hand for Ma and the girls. Isn't it time you said yes, and we fixed a date?" On this occasion, there was no joking or fooling about. He had a feeling that this girl was going to slip from his grasp if he was not careful.

"All right."

"Pardon?"

"I said, all right. I'll marry you. I don't know if I love you, John. How do you know if you are in love?"

John did not reply. He was so overwhelmed that she had at last agreed he was speechless. Dot misread his silence. "Are you sure that it is what you want?" she added.

"Of course it is, you know it is! I'm mad about you, Dot."

Dot felt herself drifting into a situation, perhaps unwisely. John was a very persuasive suitor. There was no real reason to turn him down. She would have a home of her own, near to Lizzie and Bob. What more did she want? She pushed thoughts of Philip aside. His memory would fade as she got on with her life. She would be foolish to miss this opportunity to be happy with John.

The decision made and the bungalow available, there seemed no point in having a long engagement. They rented the property, and three months later they were married. It was a quiet affair. Lizzie and Bob stood for them, and the only guests were Archie, John's mother Gladys, and his sisters, Alice and Margery.

The Hislops were in Abersoch for their annual holiday. They had been generous in their choice of wedding gifts. Enid and Charlie gave them a china tea and dinner service, and the boys, household linen, from sheets to tea towels. Charlie also gave Dot a small sum of money.

"Open a post office account, Dorothy, just in your name. Then you will have an emergency fund. No one need know about it, but you." She did just that, keeping it to herself as advised.

The wedding took place early in the morning. Archie was hard pressed to get there in time. Dot wore a slim-fitting, pale blue, crepe-de-chine dress, which fell to her ankles. Her matching hat was broad brimmed, trimmed with tiny, white, silk flowers. She looked beautiful and poised as she stood beside John, handsome in his new grey suit.

The honeymoon was a disaster. A friend of John's had lent them a caravan at Rhyl. He failed to say that it was a gypsy caravan, and long past its useful life. Dot was horrified when she saw it. The journey on the bus and train had been arduous. The field in which the caravan stood was a muddy morass. As they arrived it began to rain. The interior was cold, damp, and uninviting.

"I want to go home, this is awful!" Dot turned to John in horror.

"We can't just go back, what will people say?"

"I don't care what they say, I want to go home."

"Look, we'll light the stove and make a cup of tea. Things won't seem so bad then. The sun will shine tomorrow and everything will look better."

The sun did not shine the next day, or the next. After five days of rain, they packed up and went home. They looked forward to their own bed, in their own place. The honeymoon had not been a success in any way, the weather dampening their ardour as well as everything else.

John put the key in the front door and carried Dot over the threshold. They felt better already. An envelope lay on the floor. John picked it up and opened it, as Dot went to put on the kettle. She sang a little song as she busied herself, happy to be home at last. She laid a tray with a white linen cloth, and the china cups and saucers. She put some biscuits on a plate. It was almost like being back at Woodleigh, but now, she was the mistress of the house.

John walked into the kitchenette, his face pale.

"I've lost my job, Dot, just like that. Why did they wait until now?" Dot was dismayed, mostly for him. He looked so defeated.

"Probably because you are out of your time, and on full pay. Don't worry, you'll get another job. You are a good electrician, and there's lots of building work going on around here."

"What a start to married life." He went upstairs and came down wearing his jacket.

"Where are you going?"

"To the pub. The lads will be there. They will know if there are any jobs going." Without so much as a peck on her cheek, he left. At twelve o'clock, Dot went to bed alone. She was fast asleep when John finally came home.

Nothing was said the following morning. Dot went out early to buy some groceries. When she got back, John had gone to tell his mother the news.

"Well, she'll have to go back to work, won't she?" Gladys was a hard little woman. Life had not been kind to her, leaving her a widow at an early age, with three children to bring up. She had sympathy to spare for no one, not even her son, and certainly not for her new daughter-in-law, stuck-up little madam.

Dot had already thought of returning to work. When John came home, she had bacon frying, the kettle on, and a letter half written to Mrs Hislop. She knew they would still be at Abersoch, but she felt as if she was doing something constructive. Her heart ached for John, he looked so anxious.

"Don't worry, we'll cope. I'll go back to Woodleigh until you are on your feet again. The rent is paid for a couple of weeks, and we have no debts. We'll be fine." Something held her back from telling him about the post office account, Charlie's words ringing in her ears.

That evening, John went off to the pub again. After a few days she realised that this was to be the way of things. He and his friends would meet for a game of snooker and a pint or two. Most of them were married, living on slender wages, but there was always money for a beer. Archie was not a drinking man, and this way of life was alien to Dot. She felt neglected and lonely, confiding only in Lizzie.

"Is Bob like this? John may be out of work, but I never see him. He is at his mother's most of the day, drinking tea. Then he is off to the pub as soon as he has eaten."

Lizzie was upset for her friend, and found it hard to say the right thing. She feared Dot had made a big mistake marrying John. They had certainly got off to a bad start.

"Maybe things will be different when he is working again."

At the end of August, Dot heard from Enid Hislop. She could start back at Woodleigh as soon as she wanted. They would be delighted to have her.

Working at Woodleigh now meant a half-hour cycle ride, each way. Dot did not mind. She was happy to be back where she belonged. The family and staff gave her a warm welcome, and she settled into the old routine.

John was still out of work when she discovered that she was pregnant.

"Lizzie, what am I going to do? A baby, I'll have to give up work, and quite soon. I can't cycle all that way every day, not for long anyway."

"You will manage, Dot. People always do. You are lucky. I wish it was me."

"I wish it was you, too, believe me."

John took the news calmly, almost disinterestedly. Having won his bride, he seemed a changed person to her. He loved her, of course, but did not see the need to change his lifestyle or give up his friends.

"I don't know what Ma will have to say," he said. "She'll think it is too soon."

"Too soon! I don't know how it ever happened, you are never here." Dot was angry for all sorts of reasons, mostly because he seemed not to care. Their lives were about to change forever, and he was quite unmoved.

It began to look as if she had made the biggest mistake of her life in marrying him. This time there was no escape. She must make the best of things, for the baby's sake, if no one else's. They must talk, make compromises, and make the marriage work.

Chapter Twenty-six

John did not want to talk. Whenever Dot tried to get him into a serious conversation, he would wriggle out of it. Eventually she gave up trying. She worked as long as she could before the birth of the baby, and simply did not have any more energy to argue her point.

"I'm sure," she told Lizzie, "that things will be different when the baby arrives."

Mary Wilding, the cook at Woodleigh, was most excited about the impending arrival. Denied a family of her own by the misfortune of war, she lived her life through the young people around her.

"Who is going to deliver the baby, Dorothy?" Mary was concerned for the motherless girl. She knew that Dot did not get on well with her in-laws.

"I have booked into a nursing home in Upton, Cook. Nothing would persuade me to have it at home." Memories of Olivia, deserting the blind woman in labour, all those years ago, had never left Dot. She had thought long and hard about her situation, and decided to use the money that Charlie Hislop had given her for an emergency fund.

"I didn't know you had money in the post office, Dot." John sounded quite put out. "That is an awful lot to throw away on a nursing home. Ma knows a good midwife, and she and the girls would look after you." John could not begin to fathom the girl he had married. She was not like his friends' wives. He loved her so much, but she tried his patience with her modern ideas and independent ways.

Dot shuddered at the thought of Gladys taking charge of things, and shook her head firmly.

"I have booked, John. Dr Griffiths will attend. It is all arranged." John said no more.

When the time came, there was no one to help her. She simply caught a bus, and went alone to the nursing home. John's meal was left for him, and a note placed on the table to say where she had gone.

The baby was safely delivered after a long and difficult labour, and Elizabeth was placed in her arms. When she looked down at the child, she felt a great wave of love and emotion flood over her. In her twenty-one years she had never felt anything like it. She looked at the crinkled face and the shock of black hair. She was perfect.

It is you and me, Elizabeth, from now on. She closed her eyes as she spoke and fell into a deep sleep, overcome by exhaustion. A nurse took the child from her and left her alone in the comfortable room. The late afternoon sun, shining warmly on her young face, revealed her vulnerability.

Lizzie was the first to visit. She arrived with an armful of spring flowers for Dot and a crocheted shawl for the baby. She leaned over Elizabeth, exclaiming, "Dot, she is beautiful. Look at her hair, just like John's, so thick and black. He must be thrilled with her."

"He hasn't been in yet." Dot's voice was expressionless. "I can't believe it, but it's true. His first child, and he isn't interested."

Lizzie didn't know what to say. There was a glass vase on the windowsill. She picked it up and filled it with water from the washbasin. She went over to Dot and hugged her, then silently returned to the flowers.

John did not visit the nursing home. Dot was heartbroken. She was also embarrassed. She could not imagine what the staff thought about her husband's absence. She hid her feelings as best she could. Mary Wilding came several times, as did others from Woodleigh. Nobody realised that John was not visiting. If they thought at all, they assumed that he was there in the evening after work. Enid Hislop arrived one day with flowers and fruit and good wishes from all the family. She offered Dot a lift home, when she was ready to be discharged.

"Get Matron to telephone me, Dorothy, and Joe will pick you up." Dot was grateful for this thoughtful gesture. The truth was she had no idea how she was going to manage before Enid made the offer.

On Lizzie's second visit, Dot asked her to be the baby's godmother. Lizzie was thrilled, even more so, to have the little girl named after her.

Two weeks later, Elizabeth and Dot were driven home by Joe. The Rolls Royce caused a stir in the Avenue, doing Dot no good in her mother-in-law's eyes.

"Coming home in a Rolls Royce! Who does she think she is, Queen of the May?" Gladys spluttered the words to her next-door neighbour. The woman felt rather sorry for Dot.

"She's a good girl, Gladys. She's made a comfortable home for your John. He looks well on her cooking." Gladys grunted and went indoors. It did not occur to her to go and welcome the girl home.

Dot let herself into the bungalow, hampered by the baby in her arms, and the bag slung on her shoulder. She had sent Joe away immediately on arrival, knowing what Gladys's reaction would be. She dropped the bag in the hall and took Elizabeth into the living room. She stopped dead in her tracks. Her first thought was that they had been burgled. Then she slowly realised that she was looking at the debris of the two weeks that John had lived alone. Newspapers were scattered on the settee and floor, and clothes were dropped just anywhere. She cleared the settee and placed the baby in a cradle of cushions. Then she went into the kitchen. Two weeks' dirty dishes lay on the draining board. The sink overflowed with pans and crockery. She sat down on the kitchen stool and wept.

All the pent-up emotions of childbirth, John's absence from the nursing home, and the insecurity of her marriage were swept away with her sobs.

Tears finished and exhausted by events, Dot pulled herself together. The baby must be fed and put down in her cot. This she did. Sensibly, she then made herself a snack of bread and cheese, followed by a cup of steaming tea. Refreshed by the food and rest, she set to and cleaned the place up. When John arrived home that evening, the bungalow was spotless, and his wife and daughter fast asleep in their bedroom.

He had the grace to feel ashamed, but said nothing to Dot when she woke up to feed the baby. He made no mention of his failure to go to the nursing home, or apologise for the disgusting state of the place.

"Do you want to see your daughter? You did know you had a daughter? I am assuming you phoned to find out?" He hardly recognised her voice. It was icy, and made him realise for the first time that his behaviour was unforgivable.

"I'm sorry," he mumbled, bending over the baby. Her eyes were closed. She was so tiny. He looked up at Dot, ashamed, and repeated, "I'm sorry." Dot did not reply.

The following morning he went off to work as usual. He had not been unemployed for long, and was working locally. Dot set to learning how to be a mother. It was different from helping with Olivia's children, or being a nursery maid. The responsibility of the tiny scrap of life depending totally on her was daunting. She worried about her feeding properly, or suffocating in the night. She was like all new mothers, but had no one to tell her so.

Gladys' neighbour proved to be a great help, when she finally risked the wrath of John's mother and called on Dot. After that, Dot went to her for advice from time to time. Gradually she gained confidence and the baby thrived. Her years at Woodleigh stood her health in good stead, and she quickly re-gained her strength.

That summer, Archie came to stay. He spent his seven days' annual holiday with them, delighting in his grandchild, and enjoying time spent with Dot. He did not see much of John as he was working, and was rarely home in the evening. Archie had never been interested in drinking. It saddened him to see Dot left night after night, but he said nothing.

He was not happy about John's family either. Gladys made no attempt to disguise her feelings about Dot when talking to Archie.

"She fusses over that child as if she was royalty. She is always putting clean clothes on her, making unnecessary washing. It's ridiculous." She would ramble on in a similar vein, each time she met Archie.

Those two have no chance of making a go of things if they stay here, he thought. *There must be something I can do to help.*

Towards the end of his stay, he and Dot took the baby out in her pram. It was a perfect summer day. Elizabeth wore a white sunbonnet and she strived, without success, to sit up. She fell back on her pillows, smiling at the fringe on her canopy, as it bounced around with the motion of the pram. Archie and Dot walked to the edge of the next village. They eventually arrived at a new housing estate. Dozens of small, modern houses were being built. John was working for the builder, wiring the properties. He spotted them at the top of the rough, new road, and hailed them.

"Do you want to have a look, you two?"

"Yes, please!" shouted Dot. They parked the pram and Archie lifted Elizabeth out. He carefully carried her up the road. John watched them approach, seeing for the first time, his young family, as others might see them. Dot, back straight, arms and legs brown from the sun, her dark hair tumbling onto her shoulders. Elizabeth, in her grandfather's arms smiling her ready smile, her arms held out towards him. Unexpectedly, he felt proud of his wife and daughter.

"Come on," he said gruffly to hide his feelings. "I'll show you over this one."

The house, though small, was as modern as it could be. The kitchenette had built-in cupboards, with an enamel worktop along one side. The opposite wall had a sink with a draining board, alongside which stood a wash boiler. There was room for a gas cooker beside that.

"Isn't it gorgeous?" enthused Dot, moving into the hall. "It's got everything you could want. Look, there is a larder through here, and two living rooms."

"There are three bedrooms upstairs, and a bathroom. Go up and have a look if you want."

Dot clattered up the wooden staircase, whooping with delight as she went. Archie looked around more carefully.

"Good workmanship here, John," he remarked.

"Oh yes indeed. The boss only employs the best tradesmen. They are well-built little houses."

Archie looked thoughtful.

"How would you feel about moving out here, John?"

"I couldn't raise the deposit on a place like this, Dad. We are only just keeping our heads above water." Archie refrained from saying that going out every night did not help. He looked directly at John, his blue eyes screwed up against the light that streamed through the big windows.

"I'll give the two of you the money, John, enough for a deposit. I want Dot to have a home of her own, a fresh start away from your mother and sisters. She has had enough unhappiness in her short life. I want you two to make a go of things. There is a lot that I have left unsaid, but I am sure you know what I mean."

This was possibly the longest sentence Archie had ever put together. He finally had the chance to make up a little for his shortcomings in the past. Would John take up his offer?

Dot came bounding down the stairs.

"Couldn't you just imagine it, decorated and furnished? A big fire in the grate and a cat curled up in front of it? I suppose we should be setting off for home, Dad. Elizabeth will be ready for her bottle before we get back if we don't make a move."

Archie carried Elizabeth back to her pram, Dot walking on ahead. John watched them go, thinking about Archie's words. He then hurried back to the job in hand. He had been missing long enough.

CHAPTER TWENTY-SEVEN

Dot looked around the bright little kitchen. She had put away the groceries in the white painted cupboards. The china tea and dinner service were safely stowed away. A new gas cooker was installed in the designated spot, and the shelf above was filled with gleaming pans.

John had told Dot about Archie's offer as soon as he arrived home, on the night of the visit to the new estate. She agreed it was too good an opportunity to miss, and wrote to her father at his work place the following day. Things were set in motion and the purchase of the house made quite quickly.

John had helped her move in, but had to get back to work as soon as possible. Dot did not mind. Elizabeth slept obligingly in her cot, which was installed in her own room. John had worked hard to decorate the bedrooms before they moved in. The other rooms would have to wait until they had the money, and time, to paint and paper.

Dot wandered slowly through the house. She still could not believe it was theirs. Predictably, Gladys had been annoyed about the move.

"This area not good enough for you then?"

"Don't be silly, Ma. Just be glad we are getting a home of our own, and it's not that far away, now is it?" John felt nothing but relief when it all went through. His mother's constant sniping was wearing and made Dot unhappy. Gladys felt guilty about her treatment of Dot, now that she had to face their going. She knew she would miss her sunny little granddaughter, but it was too late now for regrets.

The young family settled into their new home. They loved it. A retired couple moved in next door. They promptly adopted Elizabeth, becoming grandparents overnight. Lizzie and Bob visited regularly. Lizzie was pregnant herself now, and this seemed to bring them all even closer together.

They never knew how Olivia got to suspect that Archie had given them the money for the deposit on the house. Archie denied it, knowing that she would be furious if she knew for sure.

Olivia had stayed out of Dot's life since Enid's dramatic ejection of her from Woodleigh. John's obvious disgust at her attempt to gain his interest at Flo's funeral had discouraged her from attempting further mischief. Putting two and two together about the money had propelled her into action once again.

If they have taken money from Archie, I shall get it back, she promised herself. She had to get Dot on her own. She did not fancy tackling John. Olivia then began to work out the best way to deal with the situation. She thrived on scheming, and if Dot was involved so much the better.

In the event, things did not work out as planned. Mary Wilding had taken to visiting Dot on her day off from Woodleigh. She was besotted with Elizabeth, showering her with gifts whenever she came. She was only too happy to let Dot go into Birkenhead to shop, or just have a few hours on her own. It was on just such an occasion that Olivia turned up unannounced. It was a Saturday afternoon, and she reckoned John would be at the football match as usual. She was right, but surprised to find Mary there.

Mary had not met Olivia before this occasion. She was well aware of her treatment of Dorothy though, and instinctively recognised her when she answered the door. The slightly plump figure, the overly black hair, and the tawny eyes could only belong to Olivia.

"Is Dot home?" Olivia's tone was soft. Mary wondered what to do. Olivia solved her dilemma by pushing past her into the narrow hall, saying as she went, "Are you a neighbour?"

"No, I'm not." Mary's reply was curt. "Who might you be, may I ask?"

"Dorothy's stepmother." Olivia glared at Mary.

"You had better sit down in there." She nodded at the doorway into the sitting room.

"I don't know how long she will be." Mary tried to sound discouraging. Olivia went through, taking in the contents of the room as she did so. It was modestly furnished, but immaculate. The big modern windows sparkled in the afternoon sunshine. Olivia recognised some good pieces of china scattered around.

"They don't seem to be short of much."

Mary leaped to their defence.

"They were lucky enough to have been given some very nice wedding presents. Dorothy was popular at Woodleigh. Everything else, they have worked hard for." She knew enough about this woman to dislike her intensely, and the brief moments in her company confirmed her feelings.

"Exactly who are you?" Olivia asked bluntly.

"Mary Wilding. I am the cook at Woodleigh."

"Oh, one of that lot." Mary did not respond to the barb.

"I don't understand how these two managed to buy this house. They had no money, as far as I know. I think my dear husband must have helped them. It is the sort of thing he would do. Do you know how they raised the deposit? You are evidently very much in their pockets. I expect they confide in you." Olivia smiled encouragingly. The topaz eyes stared straight into Mary's. Alarm bells rang. Mary was nobody's fool.

She took a deep breath, and returning Olivia's direct look, replied, "I gave them the money." She added nothing more. She hated lying, but this was one of those occasions when she felt justified in doing so.

Olivia's jaw dropped open. She had not expected this. She had no way of knowing if Mary was telling the truth.

Just then the back door opened and in breezed Dot. She shouted to Mary, "I'm home, everything all right? Look what I picked in the field." She came into the sitting room carrying a bunch of wild marigolds. She looked the picture of health. Her cheeks glowed and her hair shone. She stopped in her tracks when she saw Olivia.

"I thought that I would surprise you, Dot. Archie was so full of the house and the baby, I thought I'd better come and see for myself."

Dot was at a loss for words.

Olivia continued, "I wish we had been so lucky as to have been given a deposit for a place of our own. It's always been my dearest wish to be a house owner, but we could never afford it."

Dot felt cornered. She knew her father wanted his gift kept secret. Elizabeth became restless upstairs and began to grumble in her baby way. Mary got up to attend to her. As she walked out of the room, she smiled at Dot, saying, "I have told your stepmother how you let me spoil you both and pay the deposit for you." Mary left the room to collect Elizabeth, shouting, "I'm coming, sweetheart!" as she went.

Dot swallowed hard. Olivia stared at her. She felt instinctively that she had been foiled somehow, but the cook was surely too stupid to outwit her.

"I'll put these in water before they wilt. Would you like a cup of tea before you go, Olivia?"

Olivia recognised the dismissal. She was furious at being thwarted in her quest for the truth. Archie and his brat of a daughter, not to mention the interfering cook, had outwitted her. Well, Archie would pay for it. She would have a place of her own if it was the last thing she did.

"Don't bother with tea for me. I am on my way. It is a terrible trek back to Garston."

"You must let me know next time, and I'll arrange to be home." Dot got in the dig with quiet satisfaction. She took Elizabeth from Mary's arms and accompanied Olivia to the gate. "Give my love to Dad and the others." Olivia slammed the gate in reply and stalked off down the road.

It was not until later that evening that Dot noticed the Dresden shepherdess had disappeared from the sitting room mantelpiece. She had just finished telling John about the visit, when she missed the ornament. She gave a wry laugh.

"Olivia always manages to benefit in some way from every situation. If she only knew, I would have given it to her. I didn't like the thing anyway! Let's hope that's the last we see of her for a long time." John agreed.

CHAPTER TWENTY-EIGHT

Peace did reign over the house for quite some time. John was kept busy, working long hours. He still visited his local regularly, but Dot felt that he probably earned his recreation. It would have been nice to share some leisure time together, but she realised that it was not likely. She gave up making suggestions about outings as a family, and she and Elizabeth became soul mates. The marriage became simply a way of life, undemanding and unexciting, but a bond nevertheless.

The event that shattered the peace shattered more than Dot and John's humdrum world. On September 3, 1939, Britain declared war on Germany. Dot, hearing the news on the radio, rushed out into the garden where Elizabeth was playing, and swept her young daughter up in her arms. It was as if she feared Hitler's planes would fly over immediately. An air-raid siren wailed its mournful sound. Neighbours came out of their houses, alarmed at the news. They sought each other out, finding comfort in togetherness.

The children were excited, not understanding what it all meant. War was for history books. For Elizabeth, it was just a word.

* * *

Lizzie waved at Dorothy as she arrived at the entrance to the ward. She was pleased to see her old friend up and about.

"You are doing well, Dot. Have you finished with the zimmer?"

"I hope so. I hate the thing. Sticks are bad enough!"

"Never mind, you are getting there. You have been so uncomplaining. I'd have moaned like heck if it had been me stuck here all these weeks."

"No you wouldn't. It is good to see you, Lizzie. Elizabeth isn't coming today. I told her to take a day off, go shopping or something. She comes every day you know."

"How do you fill the time? Are you reading?"

"I can't concentrate, it is too noisy. It is funny though, I spend a lot of time musing about the past. When you arrived, I was thinking about the outbreak of the war. Our war I mean. Do you remember the day we went to visit Woodleigh with the children, and got caught there in an air raid?"

"Oh yes," Lizzie gasped. "We sheltered under the billiard table and you got stung by a wasp. Your arm swelled up and you were quite poorly."

"Woodleigh was hit by an incendiary bomb the next night, lucky no one was hurt." The two old friends continued to reminisce about the war years until it was time for Lizzie to go.

Left alone, Dorothy's thoughts drifted. The third time Woodleigh was hit by incendiary bombs, Enid and Charlie moved out. They went to Abersoch, taking up permanent residence in their summer home. Their boys were all in the army. *That was just before John's call-up papers arrived.*

* * *

The brown envelope marked OHMS plopped onto the hall floor on a wet Monday morning. Elizabeth picked it up and took it to her mother.

"Letter for you, Mum." Dot took it from her, and looking at it, said, "No, darling, it's not for Mummy. It's Daddy's. He has been expecting it."

The war that had left them comparatively untouched up to now became stark reality. John was on his way, and she and Elizabeth would be left on their own.

John was philosophical about his call up. He had passed his medical with flying colours. His request for the navy had been refused because of his shortsightedness. Ironically, he was posted to the Royal Artillery as a gunner. Wearing glasses was apparently not a handicap when firing on bombers.

When the day for John to report arrived, he parted from Dot and Elizabeth with sadness and regrets for his selfish behaviour over the years of their marriage. Dot, now twenty-six, had survived her childhood years and become a well-balanced, caring woman. There was no bitterness in her to blight her life or pass on to the next generation.

She cried when John left, wondering when she would see him again. How she and Elizabeth would survive on the meagre Army pay, she had no idea.

Would they hold on to the house? A thousand uncertainties filled her mind. Then she took herself in hand. *You are only one of millions, my girl. We will all have to cope, and hang on until the war ends. Think of Elizabeth and her future.*

When the Government began to bring young mothers into the war effort, Dot's life took a turn in another direction. Mary Wilding had not gone to Abersoch with the Hislops, preferring to stay in the area she knew and loved. She found a live-in job, cooking for an elderly couple residing in Bidston. It was on the bus route to Dot's, which meant she could visit easily. In conversation one day she made a suggestion.

"If you want to get a job, Dorothy, I could help with Elizabeth."

Dot looked thoughtful.

"You know what I would love to do, Mary? Get into nursing. It is what I have always wanted, but Dad wouldn't hear of it. It would be a good way to help the war effort too."

"Well, then, see what you can find out. Elizabeth will be at school soon. My duties are very light, I'm sure we could make it work." They looked at each other excitedly. It would give them a new purpose in life. Mary missed the hustle of Woodleigh, and knew in her heart that those days would not come back. If they did she would be too old to cope.

Dot made enquiries and discovered that she could do a course at the local Cottage Hospital. This would get her started. If successful, she could then think about taking national qualifications at a later date.

Dot and Mary's plans came to fruition, and Elizabeth started school at the same time. Dot was pleased to be able to collect her daughter at the end of her first day. The child chattered all the way home.

"Mummy, our teacher is quite old, like a granny. She is nice. I like her. She didn't believe I could read. Nobody else can. I've got to help Mrs Stuart with the books." She continued non-stop, and on turning into the gateway to the house, she said in a final burst, "I'm starving, Mum!"

Dot thought about the meagre contents of the larder. Rationing was biting hard.

"There's a cottage pie in the oven. It won't be long."

"Yummy! I think I'll go and tell Ma and Pa about school. Is that all right?"

"Half an hour, no more, or the tea will be spoiled."

Elizabeth dashed to see their neighbours. The elderly couple enjoyed the company of the young child next door. Their own two daughters had no children. Indeed, one had not married, a teacher; it was she who taught Elizabeth to read at four, and introduced her to the pleasure of books.

Dot laid the table. She was due at the hospital that evening and expected Mary any minute. She heard the side gate open, but it was not Mary. In the doorway stood John. He looked so handsome in his uniform. His appearance was so sudden and unexpected, she felt quite shaken.

"Hello, love!" He kissed her gently. "God, I have missed you both. Where's Elizabeth?"

"She's next door. She won't be long. Today was her first day at school, and she's full of it." Then she looked at John and added, "I am on duty at the hospital this evening. I can't get out of it. I'd no idea you were coming home."

"I couldn't let you know, love. It is embarkation leave, seven days, then God alone knows."

Dot's stomach churned with fear. She knew it had to come, but not so soon. She had not got used to his being in the Army yet. Their lives were changing at such a pace.

"Well," she said brightly, "we must make the most of it. A whole week, that's wonderful." She hugged him tightly. "I'll go and put the kettle on. Sit down and make the most of being home." She bustled into the kitchen, thinking of the near-empty larder and wondering if the cottage pie would stretch. She reached in the bread bin and began to cut hunks of bread.

At this point Mary arrived, carrying a basket. She put it down on the side. "It is only an apple crumble and some plum jam. The old folks will never get through all the jars I bottled. They thought Elizabeth would like some. Oh, and there are a few scones as well."

"Mary, you are a life saver. John's in there. He's just arrived. I don't know if I am on my head or my heels."

Elizabeth greeted John with squeals of delight when she returned home. He listened amusedly while she told him of her day at school. He found it hard to believe how much she had grown in the months since he had seen her.

The four of them tucked in to the cottage pie, followed by apple crumble. It was a feast. They all delighted in each other's company. Then Dot had to leave for the hospital.

"I'll try and get some time off, but it won't be easy. I have only just started there." She tucked Elizabeth up in bed and kissed John goodnight.

"I'll see you in the morning."

"I'll probably go for a pint, as Mary is here. Do you mind?"

She shook her head. *What's new?* she thought as she hurried off for the bus.

John went upstairs to change into his civvies. He hung his uniform on hangers, and put it in his wardrobe. He took a photo out of his inside pocket and looked long and hard at it. A young, blonde girl smiled back at him.

Are you worth what I risk losing? he asked. He did not really need an answer.

CHAPTER TWENTY-NINE

They made the most of John's leave. Matron, sympathetic to Dot's situation, gave her the week off, on the understanding that the time would be made up over the next few months.

John got to know his daughter again, constantly amazed at her rapid development.

"She's a person in her own right now, isn't she?"

"She has been from the start if you ask me."

They enjoyed their new togetherness. However, the photograph in John's pocket was a threat to it. Reflecting on his foolish involvement, he decided he must write to Patsy and finish the affair before it went any further. Dot must never know about it. She would be hurt and no good would be done.

When the time came to say goodbye, they both wept.

"I'll write as soon as I can. Don't worry if you don't hear for a while. I have no idea what the post will be like once we are overseas." He did not mention the front line. There would be no mail from there.

A few weeks after John's departure, Meg, Dot's youngest sister, came to stay. Dot enjoyed her company. She was seventeen now and working as a secretary. She had wanted to continue her education and take her Higher School Certificate, but Olivia wanted her to bring home a wage.

Elizabeth adored Meg, who took her everywhere with her, and made her feel quite grown up. She would meet Elizabeth from school and take her to the park on the way back. On one such occasion, as they neared home, they had a frightening experience.

The sound of a low flying plane caused them to look up at the sky.

"Meg, look, the plane has got a big cross on it!" Meg seized her niece and flung her in the ditch at the side of the road. She then jumped in herself. The plane flew on, to the sound of ack-ack guns. These were strategically placed a mile down the road, to defend Birkenhead and Liverpool from air raids. The siren sounded, a little too late, as the girls climbed out of the ditch. They were both very shaken and Elizabeth was not quite sure what it was all about.

"It was a German plane, Elizabeth. They are coming over in the daylight to strafe the people leaving the cinemas after the matinees." Meg was terrified. She hoped she would never be closer than that to the enemy.

Dot was waiting anxiously when they reached home. She had seen the plane from the garden.

"How terrible, attacking innocent civilians. Are you both all right?" Dot thought Meg looked very pale.

"We are fine, but honestly, that plane was so low that I could have reached up and touched it."

"I wonder how long they will keep up this blitz. It is bad enough on Merseyside, but London is being razed to the ground. Thank God we only get stray bombs dropped here, although there are the Army and RAF camps just down the road. They must be targets."

While his little family coped with the war at home, John was becoming accustomed to active service in France. He lived with fear, as did all his companions. He had written to Patsy from his embarkation camp, finishing their fleeting affair. He made no excuses, simply said it was a mistake and it was over.

He was quickly promoted to corporal, having shown initiative and an ability to lead. This leadership was to be tested to the full when shortly after he got his stripes, France surrendered to Germany and the British were pushed back to Dunkirk.

John found his unit isolated from the main force. Along with his sergeant, a red-haired Scot, known simply as "Mac," he managed to get the men safely to the beach. Once there, all hell was let loose. John took some shrapnel in his leg and Mac managed to haul him to a medical unit.

"We can't do much for you here, mate, but we'll get you on a boat as soon as possible. It isn't serious, although I don't suppose you'd agree." The cockney orderly grinned at John. "At least you'll get away from this damned beach. I swear I'll never go to Southend again after this blooming war!"

Seven hours later John was afloat in an old tub of a boat. It was packed with men, squashed together, filling every available square inch of deck. The wounded were mixed up with the fit, the result of the scrambling chaos of the evacuation.

THE RAILWAYMAN'S DAUGHTER

"Now then, old man, what's to do with you?"

John looked up into the weary face of the doctor. He knew him immediately. "Its Philip Hislop, isn't it?"

Philip looked at John, slow to recognise the man who had married Dorothy. He was exhausted and unwell himself, with no time or opportunity to get himself checked out. Then light dawned.

"John Gardner, well I'll be damned." He set to and made John's wounds as clean and comfortable as he could.

"You will need surgery when you get back to Blighty, John. You are not to worry though; it isn't serious, old man. You will get a bit of leave out of this, that's one consolation. How are Dorothy and your daughter?"

"Fine, when I last heard, thank you. How about your family?"

"They are safe and well, down in Abersoch with my parents. Elspeth is expecting again. The way things are, I may well be home when the baby arrives."

"Good luck, Philip, or should I call you, sir?" John indicated the officer's pips on Philip's uniform. The young doctor laughed, briefly released from the nightmare of recent days, by this contact with home.

"See you in civvy street, John. You can buy me a scotch." He hurried off to continue the endless task of patching up men to get them home.

They did not meet up again. The boat was so crowded that it was barely possible to move. John went straight into military hospital on reaching England. He had the shrapnel removed, and went home on leave when the wound was sufficiently healed.

Philip was found to be suffering from tuberculosis. He was admitted to a sanatorium for an indefinite stay. His war was over.

John was home for four weeks. It was the longest time they had ever spent together. They made the most of every minute. John tired easily at first, but slowly regained his strength.

He told Dot of his meeting with Philip.

"I couldn't believe my eyes, Dot. It was so strange to meet someone I knew so far from home in the middle of a war. He asked after you and Elizabeth."

Dot had to turn away. She could not let John see her face. She felt as if all her feelings were written there, for him to read.

Philip, she thought. *It seems a lifetime since I last saw you.*

"What a coincidence, John. How was he?"

"He didn't look well actually, but he must have been worn out. So few doctors, and so many wounded, most of them worse than me."

All too soon, it was time for him to return to his unit.

"I'll write as often as I can, love. Take care of yourselves for me." He held her tight, fighting back the tears. "Don't go falling for any of the patients now!" he said and then left abruptly. Dot heard his heavy boots on the path. The sound faded away, and she was alone.

Some weeks later, she realised that she was pregnant again. Her emotions were mixed. She did not want Elizabeth to be an only child, but she would be eight when the baby was born. There was no sign of the war ending. It was going to be difficult.

John was delighted.

I hope I am still in England when the baby is born. I want to make up for last time, he wrote. *Take special care now, Dottie, remember, I love you.*

She held the letter close to her, then read the words again. He really had changed. They would have a good life together after the war.

Elizabeth was unperturbed by the news of the baby. Her world was full of school, her mother, Mary, and Ma and Pa next door. She could not imagine a baby in the house, but was content to wait and see.

The following May, John Gardner junior was born. Mother and child were well, and John got compassionate leave. They were all deliriously happy. Elizabeth was devoted to her brother from the start. She was surprised to feel somewhat pleased that the baby had turned out to be a boy. She had not consciously minded one way or the other.

John's leave was soon over.

"Are you going to manage all right, Dot?"

"Of course I am. You know me. I'll be fine. Mary will stay for a while when you have gone."

John returned to camp. The war dragged on, a misery of separations, shortages and worry.

Later that summer, on a beautiful August afternoon, Dot was gardening. Pa had given her lots of geranium plants that spring, and now they were a blaze of reds and pinks. She weeded the border and stood back to admire her handiwork. John was lying in his pram gurgling happily. He looked so appealing that she picked him up and kissed him. Mary had taken Elizabeth out for an hour, so Dot and the baby had each other to themselves.

"I am lucky," Dot told him. He squealed in agreement. "Come on, John. Let's put the kettle on and have a cup of tea. I have finished out here." As she went in, there was a knock at the front door. Still holding the baby, Dot opened it to find a strange woman standing there.

CHAPTER THIRTY

Patsy Parker drew herself up to her full five feet two inches, tossed her long blonde curls away from her face, in preparation for her inquiries. She was taken aback at seeing Dot and the baby.

"Have I got the right address? I am looking for John Gardner's house. I was told this could be it."

"Yes," said Dot. "I am his wife, can I help you?" As she spoke, an instinctive feeling of dread swept over her. She hugged the baby tightly as if to protect him from harm. She looked expectantly at Patsy, who was obviously struggling for words. Eventually she spoke.

"I haven't heard from him for nearly a year. It has taken until now for me to find out where he lives. He could be dead for all I know."

"He's not dead, I can assure you," Dot said acidly, adding, "This is the proof of that." She looked down at baby John, tears blurring her vision. The appearance of this woman and the words she uttered could mean only one thing. John had been unfaithful. The realisation was like a knife in a surgeon's hand, cleanly removing her vital organs. She felt empty.

"You had better come in." She turned away from the door and the girl followed her into the sitting room.

"I didn't know that he was married. I knew he was about to go overseas, but nothing more. He said he would write when he could, but if he did, I never got it." Patsy's stumbling words ground to a halt. She looked helplessly at Dot. "How long have you been married?"

"Seven years," Dot replied automatically. She was having difficulty in getting to grips with the situation. Then with a supreme effort she said, "Just tell me what

127

you are doing here. My daughter will be home soon and I don't want you here when she arrives."

"I came to find out about John!" The girl's voice rose shrilly. "I love him. I didn't know he was married, I have already told you." She quietened down after her outburst. "What a mess."

"It isn't really." Dot's voice was dull, her face expressionless. "You thought John was yours, but he's not. He is my husband, and my children's father. He was wounded at Dunkirk and came home to me to recuperate. If he still wanted you, he would have written then. Please go now. I don't want you here in my home."

"I'm sorry." Patsy could not help admiring Dot's dignity, wondering how she herself would have coped if the position had been reversed. She looked longingly at the baby and went to stroke his cheek with her forefinger. "He's like John," she said softly.

Something snapped within Dot at that moment. She turned the baby away from Patsy's reach.

"Just go."

Patsy left, tears pouring down her face, as she ran down the road. Dot stood as if unable to move, shocked by the interlude. Her whole world had fallen down. The marriage that had taken such hard work to get off the ground was now a meaningless word.

John, John, how could you do this to me? I deserved better than that, and what about the children? How could you? Surprisingly, tears did not come; Mary would be home with Elizabeth any minute. No one must know about this until she knew what it all meant. Whatever the future held, something died in Dot that day.

She put the kettle on for tea, and then went out into the garden. She laid John in his pram and stood gently pushing him back and forth. His eyes closed reluctantly as he gave in to sleep. The air was scented from the roses in the garden next door. Pa's geraniums were blinding in the late afternoon sun. Their vivid colours were almost fluorescent. An odd petal or two fell to the ground, signalling the end of their blooming.

How transient their beauty is, she thought, *just like happiness.*

The side gate squeaked and Mary arrived with Elizabeth.

"We're home."

"Hello, Mum." They spoke in unison and Dot was brought back to her everyday world.

"Hello, have you had a good time? I missed you, I should have come with you both."

It was not until later in the evening, when Mary had gone home and the children were in bed, that Dot realised she did not even know the girl's name. She had no idea how far she had come, probably from a good way north, if her accent was anything to go by. Dot made some cocoa and took it up to bed. She was on duty at the hospital in the morning and would need to be down early to get the children organised for Mary.

What would I do without Mary? she thought. The old cook was like a mother to her, and Elizabeth and Johnny loved her.

Dot tried to read, but the same line came to her attention over and over again. She gave up, turned out the light, and opened the blackout curtains. A bomber's moon hung in the sky. *Don't let them come tonight*, she prayed.

Nor did they, what is more, John slept through. Dot did not sleep until it was almost time to get up. The loud tick of the alarm clock kept her company all night, and all too soon its harsh bell rang out its message.

The night of trying to sort out her thoughts had brought little order to her troubled mind. She bathed in the few inches of water allowed by the War Ministry and prepared the children's breakfast. Mary arrived promptly and Dot left immediately for the hospital.

Walking through the side entrance, the familiar smell, common to all hospitals, pervaded her nostrils. She was in her chosen world. Marriage, children and mistresses had no role here. Leaving her cloak and bag in the staff room, she went to report to Sister Cole.

* * *

Mr Robinson stood over Dorothy's bed. He respected this woman who had nursed geriatrics herself until she was seventy, far older than many of her patients.

"Dorothy, you are doing well. They tell me you passed the stairs test this morning. Well done."

"If you only knew," Dot muttered under her breath. It had been a struggle. She smiled benignly at the consultant. "When can I go home?"

"Soon," replied the doctor, equally benignly. This independent woman was not fooling him. He knew she was still in pain, in spite of her determination to be on her way. Her antipathy towards her walking aids, even her two sticks, was amusing, but touching at the same time.

Mr Robinson moved on to the next bed. His entourage of eager, young students, puppy-like in their desire to please, closely followed him.

Dorothy picked up her magazine and started to read how to make a picnic fit for a prince, in twenty minutes, with what was in the fridge.

What do these editors think we are, brainless? She was exasperated with the magazine and everything else at that moment.

"Dorothy, I have a telephone call for you. It's your son, phoning from Scotland." The voluntary worker called to her as she pushed the telephone trolley towards the bed. "Here you are, dear," she said, dropping the phone on the bed clumsily. Dorothy picked it up.

"Hello, dear, it is good to hear from you," Dorothy said. She was surprised to hear from Johnny. He had given up his job as a programme presenter with a local radio station to return to the cinema business, his first love. He was now in his forties, and not long married. Dorothy loved his wife like a daughter.

"I thought you were away on business."

"I got back early. Elizabeth has been keeping in touch with Paula." Johnny sounded worried. He had never been good at disguising his feelings. He had been shattered to hear the news of his mother.

"Oh, it was a silly accident, dear, just one of those things. I should have been home weeks ago, but there have been complications. They tell me it won't be long now."

"I wish I had known sooner, Mother. I would have come home."

"You couldn't have done anything, dear, if you had. Elizabeth's been wonderful. She has looked after the flat and my financial affairs. She has visited every day. It must be a bore for her, but you'd never know."

"We all owe her a lot, Mother, not just you. Anyway, I must wind up, I'm calling from the cinema."

"You take care, dear."

* * *

CHAPTER THIRTY-ONE

Dot and Lizzie sat towards the back of the stalls. *The Pathe News* was all about the D-Day landings in Normandy. Four years after Dunkirk, the boys were back in France.

"I suppose Bob and John will get sent overseas soon." Lizzie sounded matter of fact. This news of the invasion had been expected for so long that it was a relief to hear it.

"Probably," replied Dot. John had avoided being posted to North Africa and spent the last two years on the south coast. His regiment and several others were guarding the vulnerable ports down there. He had taken well to Army life, and by this time, had been promoted to the rank of sergeant.

The News came to an end, and the trailers for next week's films started. Dot and Lizzie's eyes were glued to the screen. This was their once-in-a-while night out. The lights went down properly and the big picture started.

"I love Greer Garson," whispered Dot as *Mrs Miniver* began.

"Shush," said someone behind them. Dot and Lizzie giggled, and then fell silent.

Dot did not challenge John about Patsy until his next leave came round. She could not bear to open the subject in a letter. No one knew what the next day would bring in these uncertain times. Whatever the outcome of it all, she wanted it to be clean, honest, and final.

The conversation, when it finally took place, was worse than Dot had imagined it would be.

"I don't even know her name, John. She simply came into my life and destroyed everything we had built up over the last seven years."

John had listened to her description of Patsy's visit without interruption. His face became drawn and pale. He lit a cigarette and drew deeply on it. When Dot finished, he asked quietly, "How long have you known?"

"Months, does it matter?"

"How could you keep it to yourself all that time? Did you tell Mary or Lizzie?"

"What has that got to do with anything? Don't you want anyone to know about the girl you were keeping somewhere while I was expecting Johnny, and struggling to keep a home together for Elizabeth and myself? A home for you to come back to." Her voice rose emotionally.

"Dot, calm down please, you will do yourself a mischief. Remember the kids upstairs." He swallowed hard. "Listen, love, it was nothing, a fling, a bit of fun. I was a damn fool. I never meant to hurt you. I was lonely and fed up. Scotland was a long way from home. Patsy was available, and fun to be with. I am not making excuses, I'm just telling it the way it was. I am sorry." His voice broke as he continued.

"It was a very brief affair, just before I went overseas. When I came home on leave and we had those few wonderful days together, I realised what a fool I was, taking a chance like that. I wrote to Patsy when I got to embarkation camp, finishing the thing once and for all. I suppose I was unkind really, but I wanted there to be no doubt about my decision. She could never have got my letter." His voice faltered and he said no more.

Dot felt exhausted. She went silently into the kitchen and put on the kettle. Without thinking, she put two spoons of tea into the pot. The meagre tea ration would not stretch to such extravagance.

"Damn, what a waste." She brewed the tea and took it in to John.

"What to do you want to do, Dot?"

"Nothing." John looked at her in disbelief.

"Nothing! You mean that?" His hopes lifted.

"When you told me that you had written to her, finishing it all, well, that made a difference. I have had a long time to think about all this. I don't want to throw the marriage away if there is a chance of saving it."

"You mean we will carry on then, the way we are?"

"Yes." Her brief reply disguised the sadness that she felt. Deep down inside she knew that it would never be the same again. Maybe she had never loved him enough, but she had given all she could.

The war continued. It seemed to all that it would never end. John was posted to France, and later to Belgium. He was never at the front line again. Bob escaped overseas posting altogether for some reason.

When Germany surrendered in 1945, Dot and her neighbours threw a street party for all the children. Everyone rallied around, each making jellies, or cakes and sandwiches. They used whatever they could lay their hands on to give the children a treat.

Japan surrendered in August of the same year, after the atom bombing of Hiroshima and Nagasaki. The celebrations were more muted on that occasion. The effects of the bombs were so horrific that people could hardly comprehend the aftermath. However, the forgotten Army out in the Far East could start to come home, to say nothing of the prisoners of war who had survived the camps.

Except for the lifting of the threat of the enemy, life carried on much the same for a long time. Rationing continued. Men came home looking for jobs that just were not there anymore.

Shortly before John was demobbed, Mary had word from Enid Hislop. The Ministry of Defence had taken over Woodleigh early on in the War, and was now handing it back to its owners.

It is only partly habitable, Enid wrote. *The MOD didn't repair the bomb damage, and left the rest in a not very desirable state. We would dearly like you to spend your remaining working life with us, Mary. Your duties would not be a burden. Our entertaining days are over and unlikely to return. We are just glad that we all survived the war. Our aim is to tidy and repair Woodleigh, when we can get a permit to do the work, and live there quietly.*

"What are you going to do, Mary?" Dot looked enquiringly at her old friend.

"I'll go, Dot. You don't really need me now that John is coming home. The Hislops have always been good to me. They need me now, and they will see me all right when I give up work. I'm sure of that."

"I am glad, Mary. It is where you belong. I will come and see you. I'll bring the children."

"I'll come and see you too, often. What else would I do on my day off?" They laughed and smiled at each other, aware that times were changing, as were their lives.

Matron had put Dot forward for training to gain her qualifications.

"You are a born nurse, Dorothy, but you won't get anywhere without your exams." Dot was flattered, but terrified at the prospect. Her poor schooling had left great gaps in her education. Matron soon squashed her protests.

"Good Heavens, woman! You can read and write, just put your mind to it. You will never regret it."

By the time John was demobbed, Dot had a place at the teaching hospital, a few miles away, and was ready to begin her career.

The war had brought great changes to her life. She now must learn to live with John full time. Life had moved on a lot since his call-up. Her training had to be fitted in with looking after the children and running the home.

"You can do it, Dorothy," assured Mary.

"I hope you are right."

Mary's words rang in her ears the morning she started at the hospital. She had never felt so nervous in her life. For some reason she thought of Olivia, and her posing as a nurse. She rarely thought of the woman nowadays, although Archie came regularly for short stays.

Her new life began.

John started back with his old firm, and the family began to learn how to live together once again.

CHAPTER THIRTY-TWO

Twelve-year-old Elizabeth hopped from one foot to another impatiently. The bus was late. Her school bag bulged with homework and pulled heavily on her shoulder. Her mother would be late for work if she did not get home soon to take care of Johnny.

Elizabeth was worried about her mother. Dorothy was not happy. She worked hard at the hospital, and at home. John had gradually slipped back into his old ways after his demob. He took little interest in his home and family, preferring the company of his friends down at the local, and his pint of bitter.

"John, if you put some of your beer money to one side, we could take the children away on holiday. We could even consider getting a secondhand car. We would be able to drive into Wales for the day, now and again."

"I'm not interested in driving, Dot. I had enough of that in the Army. I don't want to go away either, I am quite happy at home."

"I was thinking of the children, John, not you."

John's expression turned from indifference to anger.

"All you ever think about is the kids. I'm sick of it. If you want to go on holiday, you take them, but count me out." He stalked out of the kitchen, down the garden and into his tool shed, banging the door behind him. Dot sighed and set to making the tea.

Elizabeth, who had heard all this, felt disturbed, as if somehow her safe little world was threatened by this minor tiff.

She and Dot had inevitably grown very close through the war years. The two of them had shared hardships and difficulties. Elizabeth, like many others of her age, had grown old beyond her years as a result of the war. She saw what was happening to her parents' marriage and feared the outcome. Divorce was not unusual nowadays. Her mother was used to independence and did not take kindly to the subsidiary roll of housewife and mother. Her father was indifferent and aloof from the family.

The red double-decker bus rounded the corner, Elizabeth heaved a sigh of relief, and put her worries to one side. She would just make it. Dot was ready at the door as she arrived.

"Sorry, Mum," the breathless girl gasped, "but the bus was late."

"Don't worry, love, I'll make it. There is a letter from Mary on the sideboard. Read it, she wants us to go for tea at Woodleigh on Saturday. See you in the morning."

Young John was in the garden, playing soldiers with two of his friends. Elizabeth washed her hands and took her tea out of the oven. Corned beef pie; her mouth watered. Her mother's delicious pastry, stuffed with corned beef, potatoes, and fresh peas from Pa's garden next door, she would enjoy this, and then do her homework. It would be time to get Johnny to bed then, before her father came home. His pie would be dried up, but he chose to visit his local on the way home instead of enjoying his meal while it was fresh.

She would save the letter from Mary until last. A visit to Woodleigh for tea meant that the Hislops were away, and she could explore the house.

Saturday dawned, a glorious, sunny day. It was a day just begging to be enjoyed. It had all the right ingredients. Dot had two clear days off work. As it was weekend, the children were home from school, and she planned to make the most of her time with them.

They caught the two o'clock bus to Oxton. This gave them the whole afternoon at Woodleigh. Mary was delighted to see them, although Dot thought she looked a bit on the thin side these days. She seemed well enough though, and in good spirits. They had a cup of tea on arrival, and then Johnny went off to play in the gardens. The rhododendron bushes made wonderful cover for escaping prisoners of war. The grown ups would not see him until hunger drove him in for food.

"Can I explore the house, Aunty Mary?" asked Elizabeth, anticipating the attic rooms and their treasures.

"No, dear, I am afraid not. Master Timothy is home for the weekend. It would not do for him to find you roaming round."

Elizabeth was bitterly disappointed. The house was full of such interesting things. She particularly loved the glass case in the library, with the carved ostrich eggs, ivory fans, and jade Buddha carvings. She followed Johnny out into the garden. She would seek out the lesser treasures of the summerhouse. There was a fund of paperback books and pre-war magazines to browse through on its dusty shelves. She smiled in anticipation of their pages.

Elizabeth's disappointment, however, was Dot's pleasure.

"Timothy, home? I haven't seen any of the boys for years."

"I told him you were coming. I'm sure he will drop in if he is back in time. He has just started a new school, deputy head. He is doing very well. It is not easy to get teaching posts in public schools, you know."

Shortly after this conversation, Timothy appeared.

"Any tea, Cookie?"

Dot was taken back to her early days at Woodleigh at the sound of these words. Memories came flooding back. Timothy, spotting her sitting by the window, greeted her enthusiastically.

"Dorothy, how good to see you! You look just the same. How long is it since we met?"

He stopped for breath and Dot replied, "It is years, Timothy. The beginning of the war probably. I haven't seen any of you since then, not your brothers anyway."

At this point Elizabeth appeared.

"John is all right, Mum. He's playing games in the garden. I am going to sit in the summer house." She stopped suddenly as she saw Timothy. "Oh, hello, I'm Elizabeth." She smiled, and her whole face lit up. She was inclined to be a serious child, not given to smiling.

"Your daughter, Dorothy, she has to be, she is so like you."

"Not really, she is more like John."

"Ah, in looks maybe, but it could be you standing there when you first joined us."

"I hope not, I was a scrawny little thing."

"You know what I mean, Dorothy. Do you fancy a walk round the gardens for old time's sake, maybe catch up on some news?"

Dot looked at Mary.

"You go on, duck. The fresh air will do you good. You spend too much time shut up in that hospital with all those germs." The older woman looked at Dorothy kindly, concerned that the girl was doing too much. Dot picked up her cardigan from the back of her chair.

"If you don't mind then."

Dot and Timothy went out of the kitchen door, and Elizabeth followed, intent on her afternoon of reading. The main garden was mostly lawn now, for ease of maintenance. Johnny could be heard in the shrubbery.

"Come on, chaps, one at a time, as fast as you can. Keep your heads down."

"I suppose that is what the war is to John's age group. Another game, like cowboys and Indians."

"I hope it stays that way, Timothy. I hope we never see another."

They walked slowly across the lawns, shuffling their feet in the leaves that were lying in wind-blown piles. They reminded her of her first visit to Woodleigh.

"I love this house. I am so glad your family came back after the war. Although it must seem a bit empty to your parents nowadays."

"Maybe, but we all come back from time to time. Of course we don't keep a staff like we used to do. Those days are over. A good thing too, I suppose." Timothy looked thoughtful. "The world is a very different place for us all."

They walked along, comfortable in each other's company. It was as if the intervening years had never happened, but they were no longer son of the house and servant. Times had changed, and so had they.

"How are James and Philip? Are they well?"

"They are fine. You know Philip was invalided out of the Medical Corps with tuberculosis? Well, it took a couple of years, but he is fully recovered now, working in London. Elspeth left him. She couldn't cope with the illness. She took the children and went out to Rhodesia after the war. Her brother Ned is out there. I expect she will remarry when the divorce is sorted out. I can't see her living on her own." He sighed. "I never liked Elspeth, I am sure Philip is better off without her, but it was hard for him, losing the children like that. James hasn't married, although he has had a few close shaves." Timothy laughed. "I expect he will settle down one of these days. He is more engrossed in the business than anything else. It is taking a lot of effort to get it moving again after the war."

They reached the edge of the grounds and turned back towards the house. Dot's head was buzzing with all she had just heard. Mention of Philip had disturbed her. She was distressed about his illness, and shocked to hear about Elspeth's behaviour.

They sat down under the old cedar tree. Its branches were almost touching the ground. Timothy asked about Dot's life.

"Oh, I am fine. I am nursing, training properly. It is a bit hard to study at my age, but I am coping." They chattered on for some time, and then returned to Mary's domain. The tea was ready. Timothy chose to join them in the kitchen.

"It is good to see you again, Dorothy. Taking tea with you and Cookie makes me feel about fifteen again."

Elizabeth arrived, closely followed by Johnny. The afternoon had proved a success after all. Young John's cheeks were red with excitement and fresh air.

"Wish we had a garden like this, Mum. Can I go out there again after tea?"

"It will be time to catch the bus then, Johnny. Maybe Aunty Mary will ask us again sometime." She smiled at Mary, who clucked her agreement.

"Come when I am here again." Timothy was surprised to hear himself say, and he was even more surprised to realise that he meant it.

"We'll see." Dot's words were non-committal.

Shortly after tea, the visitors left for home. Dot's thoughts were full of memories of her days at Woodleigh. The children chattered to one another, seated side by side on the top deck of the bus. Dot looked at her reflection in the window. She suddenly felt that there was more to life than this. The constant struggle to make ends meet and the endless studying for her qualification were beginning to wear her down. John's lack of co-operation in her quest to give the children a better quality of life did not help. His disinterest weighed her down.

Elspeth made a new life for herself. Why shouldn't I? The thought hit her like a physical blow. She shocked herself. *Could I leave John, take the children, and start again?* She stifled the thought, almost before it was born. *Maybe in years to come, when the children are older.* Her thoughts faded as the children stood up.

"Come on, Mum, we'll be past the stop." They charged ahead, jumping down the stairs, shouting as they went, "Come on, you will be left behind."

Dot followed as fast as she could, her mind now full of more immediate things, such as John's tea, and Johnny's bedtime. They stepped off the bus and rounded the corner into their road. A cool wind blew into their faces as they set off. The children dashed on ahead, plucking leaves from the privet hedges as they went. Dot walked briskly, her head down against the strong breeze. She became conscious of the fact that her throat felt sore.

I'm glad I am off duty tomorrow, she thought.

CHAPTER THIRTY-THREE

"She needs a doctor, John." Ma was adamant as she addressed him.

"It's Sunday, Ma, I can't call a doctor out for a sore throat." John resented his neighbour's interference, and this was reflected in the tone of his voice.

"It's more than a sore throat, man. You can see for yourself how ill she is."

Elizabeth hovered in the doorway. It was she who had called on Ma for help, at her mother's request. Dorothy knew she was in trouble.

"I'll get the doctor tomorrow." With these words, John retreated to his shed, leaving the anxious old lady and child alone.

"I'm worried, Ma. Mum looks awful." Elizabeth's distress propelled Ma into action.

"You go and sit with Dorothy. I'll be back as soon as I can. Don't worry, dear, I think I can help your mother." She hurried off, and Elizabeth went upstairs. Dot lay bathed in perspiration, her face scarlet from the high temperature she was running.

"Ma won't be long, Mum. She thinks that she can help you."

"Has your dad phoned for the doctor?" Her voice was scarcely audible, her throat almost closed. She felt as if she was choking to death.

"Just try to lie still a while, Mum. You know Ma is good with herbal remedies."

Dot did not attempt to reply, thinking to herself that it would take more than a few herbs to fix this.

After about twenty minutes, Ma returned. John was presumably still in his shed. She let herself in and climbed the stairs to Dorothy's room.

"It's only me," she called as she walked in. She held a muslin bundle in her hand. "It is a linseed poultice for your throat. We will soon have you to rights."

Ma came from Coventry, and her gentle Black Country burr was as soothing as her poultice proved to be. She placed it firmly round Dot's throat. Then she hurried off to prepare another to apply when the first one cooled. So she spent the morning continually applying new poultices. At one o'clock that afternoon, Dot felt a sharp pain, and then relief, as the abscesses burst, first one, then the other.

When the doctor saw her the following day, he diagnosed quinsy, in the form of two enormous abscesses on her tonsils.

"It is highly likely that your neighbour saved your life yesterday, Mrs Gardner. It is as severe a case as I have seen." He took a bottle of medicine from his bag and handed it to Elizabeth.

"See that your mother has this four times a day. Don't worry," he said, looking at the girl's anxious face. "She is over the worst, but you should have called me sooner," he reprimanded. Elizabeth felt indignant at this remark, but said nothing. How could she, without being disloyal to her father?

Dorothy was over the worst, although it took her a couple of weeks to recover fully. She did a lot of thinking as she lay in her sick bed, too weak to get up. She thanked God for her daughter, who kept the house running smoothly. Elizabeth saw to Johnny and put food on the table for those who wanted it. John was hardly home. He could not cope with Dot being ill and simply walked away from his responsibilities.

Dot slowly recovered and became aware of what was happening. Her resolve hardened. She would leave John when the children were old enough. This goal would help her through the years ahead. She was good at waiting.

On Johnny's seventh birthday, Mary died. It was quite sudden, and she did not suffer. She had stayed on at Woodleigh, long after she finished work. Charles Hislop had given her a bed sitting room of her own, enabling her to remain with the family until the end.

Dot was saddened at the death of her old friend. Mary had replaced her unknown mother and her departed grandmother. She would be greatly missed.

The Hislops informed her of the funeral arrangements and invited her to Woodleigh afterwards. Lizzie, and other old members of staff, had been contacted. Mary, having no known relations, would hopefully be sent off on her final journey by many of her old friends.

John declined to go, so Dot went with Lizzie and Bob. It was a brief service, followed by burial at the nearby cemetery. There were several dozen mourners in the flower-filled church. The family led the congregation down the aisle after the service. Dorothy moved to follow on behind the family. She came face to face with Philip Hislop. Her heart stopped and she felt quite faint for a moment. His face lit up on seeing her.

"Dorothy, after all these years." Philip said no more; he was so overwhelmed at seeing her that he felt like a gauche schoolboy, inarticulate and stumbling.

Dot said nothing. She simply nodded politely and proceeded down the aisle, followed by Lizzie and Bob.

The family, including James and Timothy, returned to Woodleigh by car. The rest walked the short distance to the house that had once been both their home and workplace.

Dorothy used the time to compose herself.

CHAPTER THIRTY-FOUR

The get-together at Woodleigh lasted less than two hours. It was a strange gathering. The Hislops had been the best of employers, but times had changed. Apart from Dorothy and Mary, none of the old staff had returned to the house since the family had moved to Abersoch during the war. The men had all been called up while the women had married and started families, or gone to do war work in factories. It never entered their heads to go back into service when the war ended. Meeting the Hislops now was surprisingly uncomfortable. They felt they should touch their forelocks or bob a little curtsy. They felt awkward in the company of their old employers.

"Lizzie, Dorothy how good to see you, and Bob, how are you?" Charlie Hislop broke the ice with his old joviality.

"Fine," they answered in unison, and conversation began to hum around them.

Enid started to hand around the plates of sandwiches and vol-au-vents. Her old staff jumped up to help, as they would at one of their own gatherings. Bob and Joe, the ex-chauffeur, helped Charlie with the sherry.

"There's beer through there if you chaps would prefer." Charlie nodded in the direction of the kitchen as he spoke.

"I don't mind if I do, sir," replied Joe, using a catch phrase of the day. They all laughed.

Dorothy, glass in one hand, china plate in the other, wandered around talking to old workmates and catching up on their news. Some of them she had not met for years and would probably never see again. The Hislops moved amongst their old staff, genuinely interested to hear how life was treating them. Only one had not survived the war. Fred, one of the young gardeners, had been killed during the D-Day landings. The others had either been lucky or avoided being sent abroad. The drawing room began to buzz with conversation as people became more at ease. Dot remembered her grandmother's funeral, and how it had seemed to turn into a party after a short while. John had said that seemed to be the way of things after funerals. She remembered their trip back over the Mersey, thinking what a lot had happened since then.

Suddenly she was in front of Philip Hislop.

"Dorothy, how good to see you. I'm only sorry it is such a sad occasion. I know how close you and Mary were, especially after you left Woodleigh."

A tear trickled down Dot's cheek. She swallowed a lump in her throat before answering.

"She was like a mother to me, Philip," She called him by his first name without embarrassment, or even thinking about it. "Where are you working now?"

"Still in London, but I'm thinking of moving back here. I'm not really a city type. I miss the sea and the fresh air."

At this point Enid Hislop joined them.

"Hello, you two. Quite a good turn out, isn't? I'm so pleased. We were all very fond of her. These last few years she really was part of the family."

Dot thought Enid did not look well. She had no idea how old the Hislops were. Enid moved on, the perfect hostess as always. Philip made no effort to circulate having reached Dorothy.

"Tell me about yourself. How is life treating you, are you happy?"

Dorothy, taken aback by the directness of his questions, looked him straight in the eye, replying, "Fine, thanks. I am kept busy working, studying, and running the house. Elizabeth helps, she always has, bless her. Johnny is a handful, typical boy, always up to mischief. He is a worry though. He had pneumonia a year or two ago and suffers from bronchitis as a result."

"I'm sorry to hear that." He paused and then said, "You haven't mentioned John, how is he?"

Dot's gaze fell away momentarily, and then looking round the room she answered, "He's well, quite well, thank you. Oh! There's Alice. I'll say hello to her then I must be off."

"Can I offer you a lift home, Dorothy?"

"That's kind of you, Philip, but I came with Lizzie and Bob."

"That's no problem. I can take the three of you. I'll go and have a word with them."

Dorothy watched him walk across the room. A faint feeling of uncertainty came and went as quickly as it had come.

"Dorothy, how are you?" She turned to find Timothy Hislop standing by her, hand held out in greeting.

"Timothy!" She was genuinely pleased to see him. He still had that boyish grin. His smile radiated warmth. She remembered their last meeting at Woodleigh, when she had visited Mary with the children.

"Shame about dear old Cookie. The parents will miss her. So will I, she was so kind to me when I was a kid."

"Her kitchen was your refuge many a time, I remember that well." Dorothy smiled as she pictured the hot kitchen, Mary slaving away preparing the next meal.

At this moment Lizzie came over to tell Dot that she and Bob were ready to go.

"Philip's gone ahead to the car. It's very kind of him to run us home, isn't it?" Dot nodded in agreement and went to thank the Hislops and say her good-byes. As she left the house she thought sadly that she was unlikely to visit Woodleigh again, or see many of the old staff. It was a page closed on a chapter of her life.

Bob climbed into the front seat alongside Philip. Dot and Lizzie sat in the back. As the car moved off, Dot realised that she had not spoken to James Hislop at the gathering. She had not seen him since her wedding.

Too late now, she thought and she settled back into the luxurious leather covered seat.

"This beats the bus, Dot." Lizzie grinned as she spoke. "Reminds me of the trips to Abersoch. Remember the picnics?" They all sighed in agreement.

"Those were good days," Philip said.

Bob gave him a sideways look. He had joined his trade union since the war and was making his way up the ranks. He did not think too highly of the "them and us" system of the pre-war days.

Dot soaked up the scene as the car rolled down the long, curving drive. The perfume of the freshly mown lawns pervaded the open windows of the vehicle. *Woodleigh*, she thought emotionally, *you taught me so much, repaired so much damage. Made me what I am today. I won't forget. I'll do something with my life and pass it on to the children.*

"If you drop Dot off first, then us, I think that will be easiest for you, Dr Hislop." Bob was enjoying the ride and wanted to stretch it out as long as he could.

"Right you are, Bob, you direct me, will you?"

On arriving at her address, Philip opened Dot's door and helped her out. She left the soft cushioned seat reluctantly.

"Bye, you two, see you soon. Thank you, Philip, for the lift."

"It was my pleasure, Dorothy. I do hope we meet again sometime." Philip shook her hand firmly and returned to the car.

"Bye-bye." She turned into her pathway looking for her key, when the front door flew open. John stood there shaking with anger.

"What was all that about? Where have you been?"

Dorothy walked passed him into the hall as the car drew away.

"Did she mean so little to you? I've been to Mary's funeral. Remember, you were too busy to come?"

John had the grace to look a little shame faced.

"Of course, it just slipped my mind. I've got a lot on my plate at the moment. Where are the kids anyway?"

"Ma's picking Johnny up from school. Elizabeth will be home soon. I'd better get the meal going." As she prepared the vegetables Dorothy thought about John's reaction to her arriving home by car. It wasn't like him. He seemed to not notice her comings and goings at all. They never went out together, nor did he bother with the children. She sighed as she lifted the pans down off the shelf. *There has to be more to life than this*, she thought.

The next week it was Lizzie's turn to visit Dot. It was a glorious day and they took their lunch outside to eat it.

"Philip Hislop talked about you all the way home after the funeral last week." Dot looked at Lizzie in amazement.

"What do you mean, Lizzie?"

"What I said. Where were you working, were you happy, was John good to you? All that sort of thing." Dot looked blank.

"Why would he ask all that?"

"I think he's got a soft spot for you, always has. I remember how he used to look at you when we were at Woodleigh. It made me think though, you don't look well, Dot, are you all right?"

Dot looked at her old friend. Should she tell her how miserable she was? Maybe one day, but not at the moment, she could not do anything about it just yet anyway. The children were too young.

"I'm okay, Lizzie, just a bit run down. I'll be better when I have finished my exams. I'm not going in for further qualifications. It's too much. I haven't enough time for the kids. Especially Elizabeth, she's growing up fast."

"That's a shame, Dot, when you've come so far."

"I know, but it has taken me so long to get here. I'll never be finished." Seeing that Dot had made up her mind, Lizzie said no more. Dot rarely complained about John's behaviour, so Lizzie and the world in general thought they were the ideal couple. It never occurred to her that Dot might be deeply unhappy.

The day after the funeral, Dot received a letter from Meg, her youngest sister. She recognised the beautiful handwriting immediately. Her family rarely wrote. Dot tore the envelope open carelessly.

Dear Dot,

Can I come and stay next weekend? I haven't seen you for ages, and I want to talk to you about something. Dad is not too good in spite of giving up work. The rest of us are well. We haven't heard from Edward for ages, what's new? Joan is still having a rough time with Jimmy. I'll get the eleven o'clock train from Liverpool. Hope you don't mind.

Love Meg XX

Dot did not mind at all. After the funeral Meg would be like a breath of fresh air. She had often visited during her school holidays, but now she was working and had the occasional boy friend, she didn't come so often.

The next day Dot sorted out the sleeping arrangements. Meg would go in with Elizabeth. The two got on well. Elizabeth had been pleased to hear of the coming visit. The following Saturday, Dot and the children met Meg's train.

"There she is," shouted Johnny excitedly, "right at the far end!" Meg saw them, waved, and hurried along the platform towards them.

"Mind the doors, please." The guard's warning came as the automatic doors closed on the electric train. Meg's ticket was collected, and they all walked, chattering up the path at the side of the station.

"It looks just the same, Dot. Are the swans still on the pond?"

"Yes, they had cygnets this year. They haven't flown off yet, but they are quite big now."

When they arrived home, Johnny went out to play.

"Would you go to Ma's for me, Elizabeth? She has some eggs ready. I'll need them for lunch. You can stay a while, there's no rush." Dot had a feeling Meg was bursting to tell her something. How right she was.

147

"Dot, I need your advice." The words came tumbling out. "You remember Steve, the young joiner where I work?" Meg had a secretarial job with a big building firm.

"Yes, of course I do, he's been here. Nice lad."

"That's just it, he is a lad. He's been asking me to marry him for months, but I think we are too young."

"I was only twenty, Meg," said Dot.

"I know, but I want to make something of myself, Dot. I wanted stay on at school but Mum wouldn't hear of it." Dot looked at her thoughtfully. Poor kid, she wouldn't have much of a chance against Olivia.

"Anyway everything's changed now, I'm pregnant."

The words seemed to hang in the air between them. Meg looked stricken as she waited for Dot to speak.

"I'm sorry, Meg, what a mess. What are you going to do?"

"I don't know. It's my own fault. Steve's a lovely man, but I am not ready for this. I'll be like all the other girls at home, pushing a pram, rushing back to get tea ready." She began to cry.

"Oh, Dot, what am I going to do?"

Dot put her arms round her and hugged her tightly.

"My poor little Meg. I think you really have no option. Steve is a good man. He may be young, but he loves you. He'll take care of you."

"I know that, Dot, but we'll be stuck there in Garston with both our families. At least you got away from all that. You have seen a bit of life and you don't live in town."

At this point John arrived home from work. He liked Meg. She was a lively girl, bright and intelligent, and although she looked so like Olivia, she reminded him of Dot in her ways.

"We'll talk later, Meg. Have a chat with John while I rustle up something to eat." Dot was worried about her sister. Although she was nearly twenty-three, she was young in her ways, and ambitious, certainly not ready to settle down. Dot sighed as Elizabeth came back with the eggs.

"Just in time, I'm ready for those." Elizabeth looked at her mother.

"Are you all right, Mum?"

"Yes, dear, why do you ask?"

"I don't know. You look bothered."

"I'm fine, go and talk to Meg and your dad. You can call Johnny in to wash his hands soon."

They all enjoyed their omelettes and salad, especially Meg. She loved the way Dot set the table. The cloth was always fresh, and the cutlery sparkled. She thought about home and Olivia's slapdash ways. When she had a place of her own it would be just like Dot's.

After lunch Johnny went out to play. Elizabeth and Meg went to the Saturday matinee at the local cinema. Meg was more like a sister than an aunt, and they got on well.

Dot cleared away the lunch things and put her feet up on the settee in the sitting room. She was on duty that evening, the last of a run of nights. She would have two whole days at home then. She drifted off to sleep.

It was John, listening to the cricket on the wireless, who heard the knock at the front door. Muttering to himself, he struggled out of his old armchair and went to see who it was, yawning as he opened it with a curt, "Yes?"

"Hello, John." There stood Steve, his bicycle leaning against the hall windowsill. John stared at him in amazement.

"Have you cycled all the way from Garston?"

"Of course. I came through the tunnel. I could murder a drink."

"Steve!" Dot, hearing the noise, had come to investigate. "What a surprise. Have you come chasing after Meg?"

Steve blushed, answering, "Yes, in a way, but I'd like a talk with you, Dot, if you wouldn't mind."

"Of course not, come on in. Meg and Elizabeth will be back soon." Dot felt sorry for the lad. He looked so hot after his ride. He stepped inside the narrow hall, wiping his brow with a white handkerchief.

"Go in the sitting room. I'll bring you a cold drink."

John had already gone back to his cricket. Dot took a stone jar of dandelion and burdock out of the cool pantry. She filled a tall glass and took it through to Steve.

Chapter Thirty-five

Steve lay sprawled on the settee. He accepted the drink gratefully and gathered his thoughts together as he sipped it.

"Meg has told me your news." Dot was seeking to make things easier for him. He looked so young for his twenty-three years, and rather vulnerable.

The ice broken for him, Steve looked gratefully at Dot and replied, "I do love her, Dot. There has never been anyone else. I'll be a good husband. My sister has offered us two rooms in her house for the time being. It would be a start and Meg would get away from Olivia." He looked sideways at Dot as he spoke.

She nodded understandingly, saying, "So you've seen through my stepmother already, Steve?"

His face reddened.

"Has she made a pass at you?"

"And how! I didn't know where to put myself." He squirmed on the settee. "I didn't tell Meg."

"You should, Steve. She did the same to John before we were married. She even tried a couple of times afterwards."

Steve looked astonished.

"No, you are not the only one by a long chalk, but that's another story. You don't need to know. Just make sure Meg hears about it before Olivia tells things her way. She is a dangerous woman. Getting back to Meg. Do you want to marry her?"

"More than anything, long before this happened. I'd rather things were different, you know, a place of our own and a few bob in the bank."

"Well, I'll talk to her while she is here. I think you are perfect for one another, but I won't push her, Steve. It's her decision."

At this moment Elizabeth and Meg arrived home. They saw the bicycle outside.

"That's Steve's bike!" exclaimed Meg. "What's he doing here?" They dashed in to the house excitedly, shouting as they went. John snorted to himself and turned the sound up on the radio.

"Can't a man have any peace, even in his own house?" he muttered. Nobody heard him in all the excitement. Dot closed the sitting room door on Meg and Steve, pushing Elizabeth ahead of her into the kitchen.

"We'll leave them in peace for a while. They don't get much time together at home. Let's make some sandwiches for tea. I'll open that tin of salmon I've been saving. It's a good job I baked yesterday."

In the front room the young couple talked about their situation, quietly and sensibly. In the peace of Dot's comfortable room it seemed easier to talk, and things didn't seem so bad. Steve told Meg of his sister's offer of accommodation, which cheered her up no end. By the time they had eaten Dot's tea, and Steve prepared to cycle home, they had made up their minds to marry as soon as possible.

Meg's visit came to an end. She left with her half-sister's good wishes ringing in her ears.

Their wedding was a quiet affair in the register office. Their witnesses were a couple of their closest friends. They lunched in a hotel nearby and went off to the Lake District for a weekend of hill walking. Nothing too strenuous was attempted because of Meg's condition. They came back glowing from the fresh air to find some unexpected and wonderful news waiting for them.

Steve's firm had won a big building contract on Anglesey, where a chemical firm was setting up a new plant. It was likely to take two years to complete, and Steve was given the opportunity to go. Married men would be provided with rented houses, all recently built and ready for occupation.

"I can't tell you how happy I am, Dot," said Meg in her short phone call. "Everything is working out so well. It's as if it was all meant to be."

Dot was thrilled and relieved for her much-loved sister. She would be away from Olivia and her interfering ways, living in the country as she had dreamed of doing. How strange life was, everything could change in a minute by the opening of an envelope.

Life continued uneventfully at the little house. Elizabeth was in her second term at grammar school and Johnny was now at primary. Managing her job was more difficult now for Dot. Johnny had to be met from school. Elizabeth had to get home in time for Dot to leave for the hospital. It seemed to Dot that the family was growing apart. They were never together for meals. Even on a Sunday when they were all home, John disappeared to the pub before noon, and arrived home at varying times. His Sunday dinner would be dried up in the oven. Elizabeth went to Sunday school each week, thus avoiding Dot's growing anger at John's behaviour.

Dot came to a momentous decision. She would leave the hospital. She had her basic nursing qualification, which was enough to get her another job if she wanted.

"How would you feel about me giving up the hospital?" she asked her husband.

"Makes no difference to me, Dot." John was working for himself and doing quite well. "A spell at home would do you good."

Her heart lifted at the thought. There would be time for the children, and to enjoy the house and garden. She remembered the excitement of getting the house, with Archie's help, and the thrill of the move. The relief of leaving John's interfering mother and sisters behind had been another bonus.

It was good to be home. The house shone with freshly washed curtains and paint work. The garden was ablaze with colour that summer, packed with annuals as well as the lupins, marigolds and poppies, and others that bloomed regardless of lack of attention. Dot pruned the climbing roses and the profusion of raspberry bushes that had taken over yards of the back garden. She was content for probably the first time of her married life. The children thrived, apart from Johnnie's occasional chest problem in the winter. Elizabeth enjoyed school. She made no great effort, knowing she would have to finish at sixteen. There simply was not the money for further education even if her mother went back to work. Nothing was ever said about the matter. It was simply understood by both parents and child.

John's business thrived, and he took an old friend into partnership with him. It worked well for a couple of years, until he and his partner fell out about something. They were both too pig-headed to back down, and the partnership floundered. They both had debts to clear as a result, which was difficult for both of them.

"You don't deserve this." Dot tried to comfort John. Whatever he lacked in strength of character, he was loyal and honest and would never let anyone down.

"It's my fault as much as Bert's." He worked every hour he could to pay off his share of the debts. Dot took a part-time post at a local nursing home to help keep the household ticking over. Between them they rode the storm and sorted the business out. Sadly it did not draw them closer together.

At sixteen Elizabeth did her "O" Levels and took a Civil Service entrance exam outside of school. This was at the suggestion of Ma and Pa's son-in-law. Their daughter and her husband had moved in to care for them during their slow decline into old age. Phyllis and Henry decided to stay on in the house when the old folk died. They knew Dot and the family well, and grew fond of Elizabeth and Johnny. Having no children of their own they took an interest in them both.

Debts cleared, John slowly slipped back into his old ways. Dot carried on at the nursing home. She liked the work, and there seemed no reason not to.

* * *

"Hello, Mum how's things?"

"Not too bad, dear." Dot smiled at her daughter. "They tell me it won't be long before I'm free. They are taking me home to see if they think I can manage. However, I have to go up and down their stairs well enough for them to fix a date."

"You have been so patient all these weeks. We should have moved you into a ground floor flat or a bungalow years ago."

"Well, it's my own fault, I wouldn't listen to you. I couldn't see this coming. You could, obviously. What beautiful flowers!" Dot said, changing the subject. Elizabeth never knew what she did with the cards from the Council. They came each year asking if she wanted to remain on the waiting list. Dot felt guilty as she remembered her replies.

Yes, please, but there is no urgency.

"They're from Aunty Lizzie and Bob. They sent their love and say they will see you soon," answered Elizabeth, blissfully unaware of her mother's thoughts.

"How's Tom, still working too hard?"

"He's fine, Mum, and yes, he is working too hard."

Dot never ceased to be grateful for Elizabeth meeting Tom. She knew no other couple quite like them. She had no doubts about them from the moment she met Tom. They had been too young to marry of course, but had proved the doom merchants wrong.

Looking at her daughter now all these years on, Dot thought about the chain of events that had brought them together.

* * *

The letter arrived with Elizabeth's Civil Service exam results in early July. She had passed with honours and would be notified of a suitable post, probably sometime in August. Her O levels were not so remarkable, probably due to lack of incentive, but sufficient to meet the Civil Service requirements, along with her excellent results in their exam.

Dot enjoyed that summer. The children were well and happy, and Elizabeth had a job to look forward to.

"Shouldn't you have heard something from the Civil Service by now, Elizabeth?" Dot asked, one day at the end of August.

"I would have thought so." Elizabeth had begun to get worried herself.

"Perhaps you should phone to find out what's happening."

Elizabeth rang the next day, and was told that they would look into the matter and get back to her. The following day the phone rang.

"Miss Gardner?"

"Yes," she replied, breathless from her dash in from the garden.

"It's the Civil Service, Wentworth House here, Margery Gawne speaking. We seem to have a problem I'm afraid. All records of your results have been mislaid. You are not on the list for a vacancy." There was a pause then, "We are very sorry."

"What happens now?" Elizabeth was angry and upset.

"Can you send us the letter and results we sent you in July? Address them for my attention. It might be advisable to send them by registered mail. We can then put you at the top of our October intake."

There was a short silence and Elizabeth replied, "That will have to do, I suppose, thank you." She was shaking as she ran outside to tell her mother.

"Never mind, dear, sometimes these things happen for a reason. Shall we collect Johnny from next door and go for an ice cream?" Dot was desperate to cheer her daughter up, and take her mind off things. Jobs were scarce in these post-war years. The July school leavers had taken up all the local positions. If the Civil Service post fell through it could be a long wait for Elizabeth.

The following week, Dot was telling the tale to the manager of the local pharmacy. She knew Mr Roberts well, being a regular customer with prescriptions for Johnny.

"It just so happens that we are interviewing for staff on Wednesday, Mrs Gardner. I'm sure I could get your daughter included in the group. She will need at least five O Levels, including Maths and English to qualify."

"That's no problem," said Dot eagerly.

"Right, will you ask her to call in tomorrow, and I'll be in touch with the area manager in the mean time."

Dot fairly danced home, anxious to tell Elizabeth the news. So it was that after a successful interview, Miss Gardner, dressed in a white coat, began her working life as an assistant on the drug counter. She loved it from the word go, making friends with the other girls, and beginning a social life. When she finally heard from the Civil Service in late October, she politely refused their offer, explaining that she had accepted another more suitable post.

Dot's daughter had grown up and begun to manage her own life. Her mother was both proud and not a little sad at the same time.

CHAPTER THIRTY-SIX

The following year Elizabeth brought Tom home to meet her mother. The one or two boys Elizabeth had previously brought home had not impressed Dot. This one, however, was different. Neither mother nor daughter ever forgot that day. John was out, and Johnny decided to retire beneath the gate-legged table in the dining room. He refused to come out, replying with a grunt when introduced to Tom. Elizabeth was embarrassed, while Tom laughed and said, "Best place for him!" This broke the ice, and later when Johnny was invited to see Tom's motorbike out in the road, he shot out from under the table.

"I'll put the kettle on while you are out there, tea or coffee, Tom?" Dot could not contain her laughter. She warmed to the lad by the minute.

"Coffee, please, Mrs Gardner, two sugars." He and Johnny went to look at the big Ariel motorbike.

"Can I have a ride, Tom?"

"We'll see what your mum says after. We'd better go in for that drink or it will be cold."

Elizabeth moved onto another plane after meeting Tom. Dot was highly amused. She certainly had never felt like that about John. Memories of the *Valentina* down at Abersoch came back, and the fleeting moments with Philip. Her heart lurched at what might have been if they had been young today, when the class system was losing its grip. She sighed and chided herself for dreaming rubbish.

"Don't you think that you are seeing too much of that lad?" John asked of his daughter some time later. What had started as a once- or twice-a-week meeting had rapidly become an everyday occurrence.

"No, Dad, I don't. I'm only happy when I'm with him. We like the same things. We like being together. There's no harm in that." Elizabeth was suddenly scared of what her father might say about her going out so much. John had to stay in for Johnny while Dot was working in the evening. He said no more, however, they had television now, and the pub seemed to have lost some of its attractions.

Meg had invited Elizabeth to stay for a holiday that summer. She wanted her to see her new home in Anglesey and meet her baby cousin Stephen. Dot had been delighted. None of them had ever had a holiday, apart from her disastrous honeymoon. Elizabeth had also been excited. Meg had said she could bring a girl friend and it had all been arranged. This of course was before she had met Tom, and now she didn't want to go.

"You have to go, Elizabeth." Dot was firm. "You can't let Meg down by not going. Tom will still be here when you get back."

June arrived and Elizabeth and her old school friend Angela went off to Anglesey on the bus. It was a beautiful journey partly hugging the North Wales coast, and across the bridge over the Menai Straits onto the Island. The landscape slowly changed from lush green fields and trees to the stark Northern coastline, battered by the prevailing winds.

The girls had a wonderful time. The sun shone all that June, perfect holiday weather. They walked miles, and took the bus to beaches galore. They swam in the cold clear water, the days flying by. Returning to Meg's on the next to last day of the holiday, Elizabeth spied a motorbike outside the little white house. It was Tom's.

"It's Tom, Angela, he's come to see me." She raced along the dusty road, Angela trailing along behind her, and flew into the house. Tom heard her coming and went into the hall to meet her.

"Tom, what a surprise. I can't believe it." He kissed her and held her tightly for a moment, then Angela arrived and they all went into the living room.

After tea Meg suggested that she and Steve could go to the pictures with Angela, if Elizabeth and Tom wouldn't mind looking after the baby. Elizabeth blessed Meg for her discretion. Angela then said, "I'm not keen really."

"Oh you'll enjoy it, Angela," said Meg, nodding meaningfully towards the young couple.

"Okay," replied Angela, the light slowly dawning.

Elizabeth settled baby Stephen down when he was ready for bed, and she and Tom curled up together on the settee.

"I've missed you so much," said Elizabeth softly. "I didn't want to come."

"I know, but you couldn't have let Angela down."

"I have enjoyed it. Meg has made us both so welcome, and I love the island."

"You know I was born here?" asked Tom.

"No! You never mentioned it."

"Yes, I was born a few miles away, and lived there until I was seventeen. Dad was moved to Cheshire with his job. Which brings me to why I came to see you." Tom looked anxious. "You see, he has been posted to Hertfordshire. They move in November."

"That's only five months away, Tom. What will happen, will you go with them?" Elizabeth jumped up from the settee, her heart pounding; the thought of losing Tom was too awful to consider.

"That's partly why I've come." He stopped talking for a while, and quietly stood up beside her. He then took her hand in his, looking down at her the way he had done when they had first been introduced. He had been hers from that very moment, now he looked so serious. At last he spoke. "Will you marry me, Elizabeth?" She stared at him, silent and trembling. "Say something please." He could stand her silence no longer.

"Tom, of course I will." They clung together holding on to the magic of the moment for as long as they could. Then they sat down again, still holding each other tightly.

"I'll have to speak to your dad. How do you think he'll feel? You are very young, but we will have to wait a few years anyway. I haven't done my National Service yet. I wanted to finish my apprenticeship first."

"I don't think Dad will mind. Mum certainly won't, you can't do anything wrong in her eyes." They heard the sound of the others coming back. "Better not say anything just yet, not until we have seen my family."

Meg suggested that Tom slept on the settee for the night.

"It's too late for you to drive that far." Tom accepted gratefully.

They all shared breakfast on the Sunday morning. Elizabeth, bursting with their news, just about managed to contain her excitement. Tom left soon afterwards, and the girls packed their bags, ready to catch the mid-day bus home.

"Thanks for a wonderful time, Meg," the two visitors said in unison.

"Our pleasure," replied Meg. "Many a good holiday I have had with Dot over the years. You must persuade her to come next. It would do her so much good. Johnny is old enough now to be left with you and John."

"I'll see what I can do, I promise." Elizabeth kissed Meg and Steve on their cheeks. She hugged little Stephen and they were on their way.

The bus was prompt and the girls enjoyed their run home. It was a beautiful day. Where the road hugged the coast, the sea was flat calm. Elizabeth could see her reflection in the bus window. She wondered if she looked different. She certainly felt it, and somehow so did the world. The grazing sheep looked woollier, and the sea gulls whiter.

Angela chattered away. She was unaware of the change in Elizabeth's life. She certainly didn't see any difference.

The girls parted at Birkenhead and took their separate ways home. Elizabeth continued by train.

Dot was at the station to meet her.

"Mum, what a lovely surprise." Elizabeth had not realised how much she had missed her mother.

"Hello, love, it's good to see you. It seems an age since you went." They hugged and set off down the hill, past the pond with the swans and the coots, towards home.

"I've some news, Mum."

"So have I."

"You first."

"No you, Elizabeth, you look very excited."

"Tom's asked me to marry him." She looked anxiously at Dot for her reaction. Her mother was taken aback. *They are so young*, she thought.

"We don't plan to marry right away. It's a long story, I'll tell you later. Let's hear your news first."

Dot took a deep breath and spoke quietly.

"I'm expecting a baby, Elizabeth."

Her daughter looked at her in amazement. She was eighteen, and getting married. Johnny was nearly twelve. Then she saw her mother's stricken face.

"I've been dreading telling you."

"Why, Mum?"

"I didn't know how you would take it."

"How do you feel about it?"

"I was shattered at first. It wasn't planned, I'll be thirty-nine, for heavens sake. I will have Johnny off my hands soon. I was beginning to think about the future." Her voice trailed off. There was so much she couldn't burden her daughter with, not now anyway.

"Mum, you'll get used to the idea. I'll help with the baby." Her mother began to weep uncontrollably. "Mum, don't cry. Come on; let's get you home. Is Dad in?" Dot shook her head.

"Of course not, where would you expect him to be?" Her angry retort stopped the flow of tears, and the two of them stepped up their pace, both anxious for the privacy of home.

Johnny was next door helping Henry with something in his workshop. The two women made tea and sat quietly drinking it.

"Tell me about Tom. What's the rush to get engaged?"

"His dad's been promoted down South. They move in November. Tom has his National Service to do. We don't know where he'll end up with the Army. I think we are just frightened of this slipping through our fingers. I'd like to marry as soon as possible, then at least we could spend his leaves together. I would get a marriage allowance. If I could stay on at home, I would save it to set us up in a flat when he finished with the Army."

Dot looked at her daughter. Two weeks ago she had seemed not much more than a child. She had grown up overnight. It was hard to believe she was the same person. Tom had to face John yet, and Dot had no idea how he would react. Nothing much had been said about the other forthcoming event. Elizabeth wasn't sure what to say about her mother's news.

"When is the baby due, Mum?"

"The end of January I think. The doctor's not quite sure yet. It's a bit early to tell." She looked anxiously at Elizabeth. "You don't mind about it, do you?"

"Why would I mind? As long as you're happy, Mum, that's what matters. Dad as well, of course, is he pleased?"

"Oh, he's thrilled to bits. I'm amazed really. Of course he'll have me at home all the time." Dot thought bitterly to herself, *That will please him. He'll have his freedom again. At least Elizabeth wasn't upset or embarrassed.*

In actual fact Elizabeth was so wrapped up in Tom and their future together, that her mother's news hardly touched her. Dot soon began to realise this, but understood her daughter's self-absorption. She was barely eighteen with her whole life in front of her. She glowed with happiness, and sang around the house as she did things.

Dot was burdened with guilt. She did not want this baby, by the time he was grown up, it would be too late for her to make the break from John. She felt trapped, could tell no one, and had simply to get on with what life had thrown at her.

Tom called round to see John on the Monday evening. Knowing what he had come for, John made it easy and opened the conversation.

"Are you going to be in a position to support a wife, Tom?"

"Yes, Mr Gardner. I finish my apprenticeship in November and I hope to get further qualifications in the Army, providing I can get in the Engineers."

"Engineering, eh? What sort?"

"Electrical, that's what I've served my time in."

"You'll be handy to have in the family." John laughed. "You'll do. Just make sure you take care of her now or I'll be after you." They shook hands and went into the other room to join Dot and Elizabeth.

The golden summer flew past. The young couple spent every free moment together. They were continually surprised at the things they had in common. They enjoyed the same films, music, and books. They shared ambitions to travel to the same destinations. Her friends became his, and his became hers.

One by one the boys were called up for their National Service. Dot worried about how Elizabeth would cope with their separation. November found Tom getting ready to go. The Army, renowned for its contrariness, assigned him to the Royal Signals. Dreams of furthering his qualifications in engineering were snuffed out. He joined his regiment, angry at the waste of time as well as being torn apart from Elizabeth. They, however, agreed that it made sense to marry as soon as possible and save what they could to set up home when Tom finished his stint. Mr and Mrs Kay, Tom's parents, moved to their new home in Hertfordshire shortly after Tom's departure, having met Elizabeth's family beforehand.

Tom was to let Elizabeth know the date of his first leave. They planned to make arrangements then. This left Elizabeth to break the news to her parents and organise a quiet wedding. It was this thought alone that made their parting bearable for Elizabeth.

Tom learned that his basic training would finish in January.

Let's hope I can get home then, wrote Tom. *I'll have to be there to organise the banns, and there will be other things I'll need to sign I'm sure. The rest I'll have to leave to you, darling.*

Tom did manage to get a forty-eight-hour pass, but when they began to arrange things, the unexpected happened. Dot watched her daughter's world fall down around her. Surprisingly, it was John who suddenly stepped in and put a stop to everything.

CHAPTER THIRTY-SEVEN

John stared at his daughter, anger rising in him as looked at her.

"You are going to visit who?"

"The priest at Tom's church to arrange the banns. I don't have to convert. It just means we won't have the full Mass. We're not bothered, we just want to get married."

"You may not be bothered, but I am. I will not give you permission to marry in that church. I had no idea Tom was a Catholic."

"He's not really, he doesn't go to mass anymore. He's not been since he was sixteen. There is too much he doesn't agree with. This is to please his parents really."

"What about your parents, Elizabeth?"

"You don't go to church, Dad." Elizabeth was shocked and defiant. "Why are you being like this?" She looked pleadingly at her mother, who shook her head and touched her closed lips, signalling Elizabeth to say no more. John stomped out of the room.

"I'm going out, don't bother with dinner. I'll see you later."

When he was gone, Dot made a pot of tea.

"There is a lot you don't know, Elizabeth. Your dad's sister Alice married a Catholic boy. There was a lot of trouble with the priest who did not approve of the mixed marriage. It really upset Dad and turned him against all things Catholic. If I had known about Tom's family I could have warned you."

"It wouldn't have made any difference, Mum. I'm marrying Tom. We'll find a way." She burst into tears and ran upstairs. Dot let her go. It broke her heart to see what was happening.

Later that evening Dot heard Elizabeth on the phone to Tom. She closed the door, not wanting to hear the conversation. Eventually the call ended and Elizabeth came in.

"Mum, we have decided to marry in the register office. Tom thinks it will be more acceptable to his parents than another church. Apparently his eldest brother was in the same position and he had a civil wedding. What do you think, will Dad accept that?" Elizabeth was desperate, at eighteen she had to have her father's consent to marry.

"I honestly don't know. He'll be home soon, leave it to me. I'll talk to him."

John was genuinely worried about his daughter. The Parish priest had nearly split up Alice and her husband. Finally John arrived home. Dot settled him down with some supper and told him what Elizabeth had suggested.

"That's fine by me, at least she won't want an expensive dress and a lot of fuss."

"I think she has had fuss enough, John. She is very distressed, and this should be the happiest time of her life."

"Why can't they marry in our church?"

"Tom's parents wouldn't be happy about that."

"Would they be happy about a register office wedding?"

"I can't see it, John, but this is the kids' idea of a compromise."

"Oh, for heaven's sake. Why don't they run off to Gretna Green?"

"They might just do that yet, and who could blame them?"

By the time Tom's short leave was over, the basic arrangements for a register office wedding were made. Mr and Mrs Kay, Tom's parents, accepted the decision, but could not attend the ceremony. The wedding day being on a Monday made it impossible for John to attend. He had far too much work on. Elizabeth rose above it all. She simply wanted to marry Tom before his posting, which might be abroad. They could then spend every moment of his time off together. They wondered if their parents knew what love was.

The expected baby also threatened the wedding arrangements. Due at the beginning of February, it seemed loath to put in an appearance. Dot was beside herself, having visions of giving birth at her daughter's wedding.

Richard Gardner finally arrived towards the end of February. He weighed nearly nine pounds and Dot had a difficult time. He was a beautiful baby and due to his late arrival, he hardly looked newborn. From the moment he was born, they all loved him, and Dot was overcome by her feelings for this beautiful child.

Although his late arrival had its funny side, it was hard on Dot. In her fortieth year she had little enough time to recover from Richard's birth to then cope with the wedding. All agreed that it was just as well it was to be a quiet affair.

The day arrived, it had snowed all the week before, but although cold, it was pleasant enough. Elizabeth was dressed in a dark, cherry red suit and a white fur hat. Tom wore a grey suit, miraculously tailored in two weeks. The ceremony was short, but the registrar was kind. They went home to Dot's for a buffet lunch, and then off to catch the train to Wales for their all-too-short honeymoon.

Dot felt sad as they left. They had not had much of a start to married life. She prayed that Tom would not be posted too far away and be unable to get home on leave.

The honeymoon over, Elizabeth returned home alone, while Tom went back to Catterick to await his posting. Richard grew like a weed, loveable but demanding. Dot could not remember the other two needing so much attention. She asked herself what else could she expect at her age?

John adored his new son. Dot was amazed at his patience. Richard didn't sleep at night. The whole household was desperate for rest. It got easier, however, as the weeks went by and everyone was happier. The baby had Elizabeth's room, while she made a bed-sit in the sitting room. Tom's parents had bought them a good bed settee for a wedding present. This way they were comfortable and private on the rare occasions Tom was home.

At the end of April he got his posting. He had applied for Germany, hoping that in its contrary way, the Army would station him in the UK. He phoned Elizabeth. "It's Egypt, eighteen months, no home leave."

"Tom, no!"

Dot heard her cry from the dining room.

"I can't bear it. Eighteen months, I won't see or speak to you for eighteen months."

"I go in June. I'll have two weeks' embarkation leave, and then down to Devon until we sail."

Dot had closed the door. She didn't want to eavesdrop. She had heard enough. *How would Elizabeth get through this?*

Tom hired a car for part of his leave. Dot waved them good-bye on their way to the Lake District, happy for the moment at least. The rest of the time they toured around on the motorbike, which Tom had arranged to sell at the end of his leave.

The day he left for camp, Elizabeth walked to the local train station with Tom. They walked up the hill, past the pond. The swans were sailing around, close together, leaving small waves behind them. Only death would part them. Elizabeth thought that she would choke on the lump in her throat. At the top of the hill she buried her face in his unfamiliar khaki and wept. Tom lifted her chin in his shaking hands and kissed her goodbye.

164

"I'll phone you as soon as I can." He could barely bring himself to look at her tear-stained face. "Look at the moon each night, Elizabeth. I'll be able to see it too wherever I am. It will link us together." They heard the warning horn of the electric train as it approached. Tom picked up his kit bag and slung it over his shoulder. "Bye." He turned and ran the last few yards to the station, while Elizabeth slowly walked home alone.

Dot was busy while Elizabeth was away. She collected all Tom's clothes and possessions and stowed them away in the wardrobe in the baby's room. She tidied up, placed some early roses in a vase on a small table by the settee, and closed the door.

On arriving home Elizabeth went straight to her room and cried for the rest of the day. Dot was distraught. She took tea in from time to time and tried to persuade the girl to eat.

"I am so worried," she told John when he arrived home from work.

He shrugged. "She'll be all right. It's early days, you'll see." He hugged her and went off to find Richard.

"Maybe you're right," Dot said next morning. "She seemed better today. She went off to work as usual." Dot watched her daughter closely over the following months. Richard was a diversion for all of them. They watched him learn to sit up, start to crawl and say the odd word. He was a beautiful boy and the apple of his father's eye. Dot could hardly believe it. He had displayed little interest in the other two. She assumed it was his long absences in the war. Each time he came home they had changed, and of course now he was much older.

Mrs Kay visited Dot several times before she joined her husband in his new job. She was the kindest woman imaginable and they got on well.

"Please call me Emily. We are family now after all," this on her first visit after the wedding. Although she had not attended the ceremony, she had been at the house helping get things ready for the buffet. Charles, her husband, had already taken up his post as stationmaster on the main Crewe to Euston line.

"I'd be pleased to," replied Dot. "I'm usually Dot or Dorothy."

"I'll make it Dorothy if I may. It's a lovely name. I would like to take this opportunity of saying how fond we are of Elizabeth. I always wanted a daughter, and what did I get? Three boys!" She laughed. "I now have two daughters-in-law, and I love them both."

The matter of the wedding was never mentioned again. Their only regret now was Emily's imminent departure down South, just when they were getting to know one another.

Dot enjoyed being home all day with Richard. She and Elizabeth spent a lot of time together as her daughter had no inclination to go out. Dot was concerned that Elizabeth spent so much of her free time at home. She knew the girl was saving hard for Tom's return, but felt it would do her good to go out occasionally.

Dot was able to see more of her old friends now she was not working. Sometimes on Elizabeth's day off, the two of them would walk the seven miles to Lizzie's house, pushing Richard's heavy pram. The two friends would talk of the old days at Woodleigh, and catch up on the news gleaned by one or other of them, about the staff and the family. Lizzie had four children, with quite long gaps between them. For this reason she had never returned to work. She and Bob had struggled financially for years after the war, but now things were getting easier.

"I heard that Philip Hislop was working over this way again. I don't know which hospital. James and Timothy are both married, I believe, but I don't think Philip ever married again," said Lizzie as she and Dot shared a cup of tea one afternoon with Elizabeth.

"What a waste, Lizzie, and how sad that she took the children abroad. Rhodesia, wasn't it, to her brother's?"

"I think so." Lizzie looked at Elizabeth, who seemed far away. "Tell me, Elizabeth, how are you managing without Tom? I expect the time is dragging." The girl's eyes filled with tears and she struggled to regain to her composure.

"I keep busy, just five months to go."

"She's saved hard to set them up in a flat," said Dorothy.

The weeks began to pass more quickly. August came and went, and on into September and eventually November. There was a lull in the letters as Tom's unit sailed home.

One Saturday afternoon, Elizabeth's manager unlocked the front door of the shop and pulled up the faded green blind. Elizabeth was unlocking her till, when she felt eyes staring at her. She looked across at the girls on toiletries. They turned their heads to the door. She followed their gazes and there stood Tom. He was in full uniform, bronzed from his time in the sun, and smiling that broad smile she remembered so well. She left the counter and ran to the door. She buried her face in that long-remembered scratchy khaki, laughing and crying at the same time. She heard a voice behind her. It was the manager.

"Get your things, my dear, and go home. You have waited long enough for this."

"Thank you, thank you so much. I'll see you on Monday!" They left the pharmacy, arm in arm, walking the length of the village. They were both unaware of anyone else as they caught the bus home.

"I'm only here until tomorrow evening." Elizabeth's stomach did a somersault at the words. "I have to report to Chester for my demob. It's only because I live so near that I was allowed home."

"It doesn't matter, Tom. Soon we'll be together forever, and nothing will matter then." The short journey completed, the two jumped off the bus and hurried the last bit home.

"Don't ever leave me again, Tom, will you?" Elizabeth looked at him, her blue eyes brimming with tears of unbelievable joy.

"No," he replied and he meant it.

CHAPTER THIRTY-EIGHT

The money Elizabeth had saved during Tom's time in the Army had fully furnished and carpeted the first-floor flat they had been lucky enough to rent. Saving to put a deposit on a house was difficult, because property prices were rising so quickly. Eventually they managed, and bought a house close to Dot and John.

It worked well, Dot helping Elizabeth with evening meals through the week, and in turn they baby sat for Richard when necessary. Elizabeth was now working as a dental nurse. She loved it, but the hours were long. However, she was off on Saturday, and so was Tom. A lot of their free time was spent improving the house. It was the twin of Dot and John's, but needed modernising. Property was hard to come by at the time and they had been lucky to get it.

Johnny became a regular visitor.

"It must be great having your own place, Elizabeth." Johnny now in his late teens envied his sister.

"You'll be next, Johnny," Elizabeth teased.

"I'm not getting married for years," came the typical male reply.

Tom's parents moved up north again. Charles retired early at sixty, with a comfortable pension and a golden handshake. They had settled in a bungalow in North Wales. They were near the sea and very happy. Tom had another motorbike by then, so he and Elizabeth could visit them often.

One August when they were visiting Emily and Charles for a short holiday, Elizabeth phoned her parents to wish them a happy anniversary. It was a Sunday afternoon. Dot had cooked a lovely dinner, roast beef with all the trimmings, John's favourite, with apple pie to follow. He had forgotten to buy Dot a card, and felt bad about it. He had gone off for a quick pint, promising to be home for dinner in good time. At two o'clock she fed the boys and Johnny went out for the afternoon. At five o'clock she switched off the oven and took out the plates, so much for the celebration. It was about then that Elizabeth phoned. Dot burst into tears at the sound of Elizabeth's voice.

"I can't take much more off this," she sobbed after explaining what had happened. "He'll never change, my life is just work and worry. I get no support from him." She stopped abruptly, feeling that she had said too much to her daughter. She did not want to spoil their holiday. She took control of herself.

"Never mind me, are you having a good time? Are Emily and Charles well?"

"Yes, Mum, we are all fine. The weather is glorious, and we are getting quite brown. We've done some touring on the bike. Mostly we have taken picnics up the hill with Emily and the dog." The warning bleep went on the public phone as the money ran out. "See you next Sunday, Mum. Love you—" The line went dead.

The phone call home left Elizabeth feeling disturbed and unhappy.

Dot's phone rang again almost immediately. It was Lizzie.

"Happy anniversary to you both."

"That's a joke, Lizzie. Oh, I'm sorry, dear, I didn't mean to snap. It has not been a good day. John's not here, he's at the pub. I cooked a lovely roast dinner to celebrate the day. He knew I was doing it but he has not bothered to turn up. I know I sound pathetic but it is not just that. This marriage is on the rocks, Lizzie. I don't know how much longer I can keep up the pretence. I really don't care anymore."

Lizzie was stunned. She had known for years that all was not well between Dot and John, but this was something more serious than she had suspected.

"Would you like me to come round, Dot?" She felt that Dot needed someone there, and Elizabeth was away.

"No thank you, Lizzie. I'll be fine. This is nothing new. Actually, I can hear someone now, I think it's Johnnie. Yes it is, I'll speak to you soon. Thanks for calling."

"Is Dad home?" Johnnie looked wary as he approached his mother.

"No, I haven't seen him since this morning."

"Well, Mum, as he is out, I'll take the opportunity to tell you that I am looking for a job away from home. It is time I moved out anyway, but I can't live with Dad anymore. He is rude to my friends if he takes their phone calls. I try to please him like Elizabeth did before she was married, but it is a waste of time. I think he is jealous of me."

Dot looked at him hard. She was shocked at his words but not surprised.

"I think you are right about the jealousy, Johnny. He was away when you were born. You were a sickly baby and needed a lot of my time and attention. We are lucky you came through it all, believe me. I'm not making excuses for your father. I quite agree with you, and if you can get away then I wish you all the luck in the world. I will miss you of course more than you might imagine, but I want you to be happy." Mother and son hugged each other, quickly separating as they heard John coming in through the back door.

"I'm home, Dot, sorry I'm late. I met up with a bloke I haven't seen for years. We got talking, you know how it is." He looked in the oven and made no comment about the empty shelves he saw. Dot went upstairs without a word, as did Johnny, leaving John to make himself a cheese sandwich.

Things continued in much the same fashion in the family home until Johnnie landed his job in Scotland. He went quietly without fuss as was his way, and he was missed by all but John who had never taken much interest in his elder son.

When spring arrived again, Tom, who had bought and renovated an old car that winter, had a bright idea.

"Elizabeth, how about a holiday abroad this summer? In the car I mean, down to Spain. We could take our mothers. They both need a holiday, what do you think?" Elizabeth was wide eyed at the prospect.

"It sounds fabulous, Tom, but what a long way to drive."

"We would do it in easy stages, no rush, just enjoy France on the way." Their excitement grew as they made enquiries about Channel crossings, hotel costs, insurance, and other such necessities. When they had explored the idea thoroughly they approached Dot and Emily.

"How wonderful." Emily was ecstatic, but Dot seemed strangely indifferent to the idea. She thanked them kindly but no, she would not be joining them this time. Elizabeth and Tom were surprised and disappointed at Dot's decision. She offered no reasons for her refusal and they did not press her. There was something about her that made them feel the matter was not up for discussion.

* * *

Dorothy sat by the open door at the side of her bed. The scorching weather continued, and her hospital stay dragged on interminably. The other patients continually moaned about the draught, while she yearned to get out in the sun. It was probably the heat that aroused memories of the children's invitation to go to Spain with them in 1964. How could she have told them her reasons for not going? It was all so long ago, and yet it seemed like yesterday. Johnnie's leaving had saddened her, although she had known it must come.

She had decided to go back to work. With only Richard and John at home, the time seemed right. She had taken a post in a nursing home, a bus ride away, with hours that fitted in with Richard.

That, she thought, *was how it all began.*

"Hello, Mum." Elizabeth's cheerful voice interrupted Dorothy's thoughts. "Guess what? I have permission to take you round the grounds in a wheelchair." Her mother pulled a face.

"A wheelchair!"

"Yes, dear, a wheelchair. I know you use one all the time when I'm not here."

Dot grumbled then agreed. Elizabeth disappeared momentarily, returning with a wheelchair. Dot sat herself in it without any difficulty and off they went through the open doorway.

"The air, Elizabeth, it's wonderful. Oh, I've got to get home. I can't stand that ward much longer. All those old women moaning all day, demanding attention." She stopped talking and soaked up the scene. The hospital grounds were well kept, and the flowerbeds were full of dahlias and chrysanthemums. The grass was newly cut and the air carried that incomparable scent. A gardener touched his cap as they passed.

When did I last see that? thought Dot.

"This makes me think of Woodleigh, newly mown lawns and the autumn flowers. Can you remember it, Elizabeth?"

"I can, Mum, I loved those visits to Aunty Mary."

"I owe a lot to Woodleigh. It's strange how it has kept touching my life. I was remembering earlier today, how you asked me to join you on your trip to Spain. You weren't to know how my life was changing at that time. I wasn't sure myself what was happening."

"It must have been hard for you, Mum, trying to tell us when the time came."

"I don't know which was the hardest, telling you, or actually making the move."

Elizabeth noticed her mother was becoming emotional, and changed the subject.

They walked right round the grounds, stopping now and then for Dorothy to look at something of interest. After an hour of meandering Elizabeth said, "I think we had better make our way back. It's close to teatime. Hasn't it been lovely out here?"

"Oh yes, I have enjoyed it. I'm sorry I was difficult."

"Mum, think no more about it. We'll do it again if you are not sent home soon." Dot looked rueful, but said no more. Once inside Elizabeth made her comfortable. They could hear the tea trolley rumbling down the passage.

"Just in time, I'll see you tomorrow, Mum. Keep your pecker up. It won't be long before you come home with me." She kissed her mother's soft cheek. "Bye, Mum, I love you."

Dorothy watched her depart for as long as she could, and turned her attention to her tea.

* * *

Shortly after Elizabeth and Tom's return from Spain in September, Dot dropped her bombshell. Elizabeth had called round to see her mother one Saturday afternoon. Tom was working overtime, it was a lovely day, and Elizabeth guessed her mother would be sitting in the garden catching the sun. She was right.

"Hello," she called as she walked into the back garden. "Isn't it gorgeous, Mum?"

Dorothy was sitting in a deck chair. Her dark hair made her tanned skin look even browner.

"Gosh, you look well." Dorothy did, and for good reason.

"I'm glad you have come. I hoped you would. I need to talk to you seriously, Elizabeth."

She sat down beside her mother, suddenly sick with apprehension.

"What is it, is somebody ill?"

"No, nothing like that." There was a long pause. "I'm leaving your father. I am going next week. I'm taking Richard with me of course." She stopped and looked at her daughter. *Is this when I lose her forever?* she thought. *Please, God, let her understand.*

CHAPTER THIRTY-NINE

Dot could never have imagined the consequences of Philip's first lift. Cold, wet and tired, waiting for a bus home after her shift at the nursing home, she would have accepted a lift from Old Nick himself that night.

"I thought it was you, Dorothy." Philip Hislop looked both pleased and concerned as he leaned across the passenger seat to speak to her.

"Philip, good heavens! This is a surprise."

"Jump in, I'll run you home, what a night."

"You are kind, I must admit I am frozen." She climbed in, sinking into the luxurious, leather-covered seat with a sigh. "This is Heaven."

"Not quite, but I know what you mean." Philip's heart was pounding. He could not believe that she was here beside him after all these years. "How are you, and your family?" he added quickly.

"I'm fine, we all are. Elizabeth is married, Johnnie is working away from home, and Richard is ten in February."

"How about John?"

"He's the same as ever. How about you?"

"I'm still on my own. You knew Elspeth and I separated years ago?"

"I had heard. She is in Rhodesia I believe."

"She was, but she came home before Independence. The children are grown up, both with careers in banking. Neither was interested in medicine. That's why I didn't go into general practice. It's hard work, and with no one to pass it on to it didn't seem worth it."

"You remember where we live?"

"Yes, I ran you home after Mary's funeral. You are at the end of the road, aren't you?"

"Yes, we are nearly there." The time had gone too quickly. Dot wanted it to go on forever.

"I'll look out for you in future, Dorothy. No sense in you getting soaked if I'm around." The hospital and nursing home were on the same route.

"That's very kind of you," replied Dot. She did not tell him that she had recently been accepted as a nurse in the same hospital as him. It was better hours and pay. The car drew up at her gate and she thanked him. "It's been lovely seeing you again." She closed the door firmly and ran up the path shaking the rain from her hair as she went.

"You'll never guess who gave me a lift home, John," she said as she went into the sitting room. There was no reply. John sat, chin on his chest, fast asleep in front of the television.

"What did you say?" he mumbled as he roused himself, then not waiting for a reply, "I'd love a cuppa if you are making one." Dot, exhausted from her long shift, sighed and went to put on the kettle. Her thoughts were a long way from John and his thirst, and suddenly she felt light-hearted and began to hum a tune to herself.

It was a few weeks before she saw Philip again. Long enough for her to stop looking out for him as she waited for the bus. It was raining as before, but he was already at the bus stop when she arrived.

"Hello, this is a nice surprise." She tried to sound casual as she asked him, "Have you waited specially?" She kicked herself mentally for sounding so inane. Why else would he have been there?

He sounded like a schoolboy as he answered, "I didn't want you to get wet." Dot, who was used to fending for herself, and had to bring coal in for the fire herself when she had flu last winter, burst out laughing at this. He looked hurt, his kind blue eyes showing his embarrassment at her laughter.

She climbed into the car, saying, "Oh, I'm sorry Philip, it is really very sweet of you to be so thoughtful. I'm not used to it, forgive me?"

He looked relieved.

"I thought I'd overstepped the mark."

"By being kind and considerate?" Dot looked at his gentle face. "You are a dear man, and you'll never know how long I have dreamed of a moment like this. Of course I knew it would never happen, so this has to be a dream."

"It's not though. I have thought of little else since I last saw you."

"I'm not free, Philip, you know that."

"You could be, Dorothy."

She was suddenly scared. This was going too fast.

"Come on, let's get you home," he said suddenly. She climbed in and took the opportunity to tell him of her change of job.

"It starts next week, so I won't be at this stop after that." He nodded.

Dot could not read his mind, but she knew how she felt. She had loved him since those first moments alone on the *Valentina* when she had been free. If only he had spoken out then. It would have been difficult. The eldest son of a rich and influential man and a servant falling in love, but love was strong. Elspeth already had her claws in, and Dot knew that Philip was weak. It went with his gentleness, which was one of the things she loved about him. So the moment had slipped away.

This was a second chance, but one fraught with difficulties. It could hardly be called an affair, not in the accepted sense. They began to meet for lunch, usually going somewhere on the Welsh border, far enough from home to avoid anyone they knew. Their occasional meetings were spent catching up on each other's stories. Philip's life had been empty of love since Elspeth's departure with his children all those years ago. He had concentrated on his career, rising steadily through positions, eventually returning home to his present consultancy.

Dorothy, as he always thought of her, had lived a life worthy of a film script. How had she remained so sweet natured and caring with all she had lived through? Olivia's brutality should have turned her into a bitter, harsh mother. John's indifference was beyond Philip's understanding, yet he had met the man and liked him. It was all an enigma.

The exchanging of their life stories brought them closer together, and their mutual love, stifled by time and events, began to grow.

The day inevitably came when they exchanged their first meaningful kiss. It was not the polite social kiss of acquaintances, but one that lifted their feet from the ground and made the sky whirl round above them.

"Dorothy," Philip murmured, "this is not going to go away, you realise that?"

"I know," her voice was a whisper, "I don't want it to." He took her in his arms and kissed her again. The world was spinning round, now there was no going back. They both knew their lives would never be the same again.

They continued to meet as often as possible, their growing love binding them ever closer. They began to speak of a future together, neither of them wishing to live a life of deceit.

Then, unbelievably after twenty years, Elspeth returned home. Philip had held on to his old house through all his career changes, hoping that one day it would be a home again, and then, suddenly, she was there. Philip was stunned. He was home early, his final operation of the day being cancelled at the last moment.

"What the hell are you doing here?"

"I heard a little rumour, darling, that you had someone new in your life. You don't think I am going to let another woman get her hands on all this?" She waved her arms around the beautiful room. "You must have plenty of money stashed away after all these years as well." She smiled acidly. "I've come to clean you out, Philip. I'm so glad you never bothered to divorce me."

Philip was furious.

"I have paid you maintenance, and for the children's education in spite of your despicable behaviour. I owe you nothing. I'll divorce you now, by God I will."

"It won't be that easy, Philip darling. You have left it a bit late, especially as I now want a reconciliation." She smiled thinly.

He looked at her, speechless, stunned by her blatant behaviour. Then anger took over.

"You stupid, unbelievable woman. Do you think I want you back? You couldn't get away fast enough when I was ill and needed you. You dragged the children off to another continent without my permission. I have missed them growing up, and God knows what lies you have fed them." He stopped, shaking with the rage that had been bottled up for years. Then, "I don't want to look at you, never mind live with you. You are wasting your time. You might as well go back where you came from. Clear out."

Elspeth's sophisticated coolness fell apart. She had never seen him like this.

"Who is this bit of skirt you have found for yourself? I can't believe you have waited so long. Is she someone I know?"

"Oh! Your spies are not that efficient then, Elspeth!" She flushed, suddenly out of her depth with this man she once had wrapped around her little finger. "You might as well know, it will be common knowledge shortly. It's Dorothy, Dorothy Gardner, she worked for my parents before the war."

Elspeth looked blank for a moment then she screeched, "Dorothy, that maid! Good God, Philip, have you gone out of your mind?" She fumbled in her bag for her cigarettes and lighter. She lit up, her hands fumbling uncertainly. She was lost for words.

Philip kept control of himself with difficulty.

"When you have an address let me know and I will send it to my solicitor. I will get things moving as soon as possible." Philip could not look at her as he spoke.

"What do you mean?"

"Divorce, of course, that's what you want, isn't it? However, don't think you are having it all your own way. You walked out on me, remember. Now go, get out, I don't want to see you again." She picked up her bag and coat, her face contorted with fury.

"We'll see, Philip darling," she sneered. "I have friends at court, if you'll pardon the pun. I think I came back just in time to spoil your fun." She stalked out, her stiletto heels biting into the block floor in the hall. She slammed the front door, rattling the stained glass window, and she was gone.

Philip was shattered. He poured himself a large gin and tonic and picked up the telephone, hoping he was not too late.

"Jenkins, Jenkins and Smythe Solicitors." The voice was business-like.

"Hello, can I speak to Andrew Jenkins please? It's Philip Hislop, I'm a personal friend, and it is rather urgent."

"Hello, old man, what's all this?" Andrew was put on immediately.

"Andrew, I think I am in trouble. Could you meet me at the club tonight, about seven-thirty?" Andrew consulted his diary. Philip was not only a good friend, but also his consultant.

"That's fine, Philip, I'll see you then."

Philip sighed with relief. He felt better now that he had made a move to get the ball rolling.

When Dot heard all this the next day she was stunned. Suddenly, their slowly developing relationship, cautiously moving along at their own chosen speed, was a matter of public knowledge. Whoever had informed Elspeth had doubtless told others. Although their social circles were worlds apart, in a small village gossip soon spread.

"I will have to tell John. He mustn't hear a whisper of this from someone else. It would be dreadful for him. It is going to hit him hard anyway." Dot's voice broke.

"Don't cry, Dorothy, this had to come one day. I'll find a flat for you and Richard. That will make things easier. You couldn't cope seeing John every day. It would be impossible for you both, and bad for the boy." They held each other closely, their kisses more comforting than passionate. "It will be all right, darling, at least we will be able to see one another now without driving down side streets and hiding in Wales for our lunches." Dot smiled a watery smile and kissed him.

True to his word, with the help of a friend in the property business, Philip found a flat for Dorothy. It was to be vacant in two weeks, and she could move in as soon as she liked after that. Dorothy's relief was immense.

She had now to break the news to John. There could be no good time, so Dot chose to tell him after the evening meal, and before he went out for a drink. Richard was out with friends so they had the house to themselves.

"John, I have something to say to you. This is probably the most difficult thing I have ever had to do." John raised his head questioningly. Dot continued.

"I am leaving you. I am leaving soon. I'm going to be with Philip Hislop, eventually." John's face drained of colour. "We have been seeing one another for some time and feel we have a future together. You must realise that our marriage is dead. I have tried to talk to you so many times." She sighed as his look turned to one of resignation. "I will be taking Richard with me of course. There is no way you can care for him on your own. You will be able to see him as much and as often as you want."

John said nothing. He went off to the pub banging the door behind him, leaving Dot shaking and drained of emotion. She could hardly believe his behaviour afterwards. He simply put his head in the sand after he finally took the news on board. She found him rooms with an old friend of his, sorted out his belongings and all his business invoices and accounts in the jumble of his desk. She boxed stuff and labelled it clearly, wondering how on earth he would manage without her to cope with his business affairs. During all this John simply spent his days in the pub and the bookies. He was broken hearted, but simply went along with Dot's arrangements like a child being sent to boarding school. He told no one what was happening until Dot told Elizabeth.

CHAPTER FORTY

Elizabeth stared at her mother. The shock was like a physical blow. She tried to speak, but no words came. Dot had anticipated this moment for so long, and it was worse than she had ever imagined. Eventually Elizabeth found her voice.

"Does Dad know?"

"Of course." Dot's reply seemed curt. She didn't want it to, but her tongue seemed tied.

"I'd better go, I'll speak to you later." Elizabeth struggled out of her deck chair. She was awkward in her haste. She had to get away and think. She wanted Tom; he would know what to do. Her stricken mother watched her go, wondering if she would ever see her again. She began to weep knowing that her newly found happiness was going to cause grief for all her family.

Tom's car was in the drive. Elizabeth let the tears go as she went in the back way. Tom was putting on the kettle.

"Hello, have you been to your mum's?"

"Yes, Tom, and you'll never believe what she told me." She poured out the story incoherently, words punctuated by sobs. There wasn't much to tell really.

Tom listened quietly and then asked, "Where is she going? Has she met someone?"

"I don't know. I didn't stay to find out. I just ran home."

"What on earth do you think she is feeling right now? You running off like that, she must be in a dreadful state."

"I don't know, Tom, I just wanted to be with you. I want everything to be all right like before."

"Was it all right before? Was your mother happy? As far as I know she has had a wretched life for pretty well most of it."

179

Elizabeth looked at him. She had stopped crying. Tom hadn't reacted the way she thought he would. He was more concerned about her mother than her.

"Tom, it's awful. Johnnie has already gone. Dad will be alone; the whole family will be split up. I can't bear it." She stopped, suddenly aware of how selfish she sounded. "What a mess," she said and flopped down in her leather swivel chair.

Tom disappeared into the kitchen, returning with a mug of coffee.

"Get that down you, Elizabeth, it will help. Let's talk about this sensibly." He looked at her tear-stained face, wiping her cheeks with his thumbs, and kissing her forehead gently. "We don't know half the story, do we? You know your mother has been unhappy for as long as you can remember. You have even considered talking to your dad about the situation, haven't you?" She nodded. "It is her life, darling, she isn't stupid, she will have thought long and hard before coming to a decision as drastic as this. I hope that she has met someone who will make her happy."

"It will mean a divorce, Tom, I thought you didn't believe in that. You told me so when we first met."

"Yes, I know, I think it was a leftover from my Catholic upbringing. I certainly wouldn't deny your mother a chance of happiness. I think you should go round and talk to her, find out a bit more about what is happening before you condemn her."

Elizabeth wiped her face with the back of her hand. Tom shook his head. "You can do better than that." She smiled faintly, hugged him and ran upstairs. She washed her face and brushed her long hair and pulled it into a ponytail. Downstairs she asked Tom, "Will you come with me?" He held her close, his heart aching for her. He knew she loved her mother, but her world was falling down around her and she was very confused.

"Of course I'll come, be brave, think about your mum. She has never had what we have, Elizabeth, try and remember that." Tom locked the front door, took Elizabeth's hand in his, and they walked round the corner to the house where she had grown up. Dot had gone inside. She heard the door open and rushed out of the dining room.

"I didn't think I would see you again, Elizabeth. I thought I'd lost you for good when you ran off like that."

Elizabeth flung her arms around her. "I'm sorry, Mum. I didn't give you a chance. It was a shock, but I've no excuse for leaving like that. Tom calmed me down and made me come back to hear you out properly."

Dorothy never forgot Tom's intervention. Things might have turned out very differently if he had not been so level headed.

"Do you want to tell us about it, Mum?" he asked, ushering them both into the sitting room, once their old bed-sit. They all sat down and Dot began to speak.

"I am leaving to be with Philip Hislop."

Elizabeth gasped. "Do you mean Philip Hislop from Woodleigh?"

"The very same. We met again after many years, apart from a brief moment at Mary's funeral. I was waiting for a bus after work. It was raining and I didn't have an umbrella or anything to put on my head. I was soaked. Philip passed by in his car and spotted me. I don't know how he even recognised me under the conditions. He turned round as soon as possible and drove back for me. I was so grateful; I'd have taken a lift from anyone that night. I was cold and miserable. He brought me to my door, said 'good-night' and that was that. I thought a lot about him afterwards. We had feelings for one another when I was at Woodleigh, but nothing was ever said. We had no future together anyway. He was the son of the house and I was a much younger, upstairs maid." Dot stopped talking.

"Would you like a cup of tea, Mum?" Elizabeth asked quietly.

"I would please."

Tom jumped up. "I'll get it. You carry on, Mum, I'll hear you through there." Until this evening he had never called her Mum. It comforted Dot, and she blessed the day her daughter had brought this fine young man into their lives. He was wise beyond his years.

"I didn't see Philip again for some time. Then one very wet evening, he was waiting for me at the bus stop. Then it became a regular thing. If the end of his session at the hospital coincided with mine, he looked out for me. During these lifts we talked a lot and caught up on each other's lives. The magic was still there, incredible though it was after all these years." Tom brought in the tea. Dot sipped hers, piping hot. It burned her mouth as she drank it.

"Mum, where do you go from here? What about Dad? Where are you both going to live?" A thousand questions tumbled around Elizabeth's brain. They came out in no particular order of importance. "What about Richard? He and Dad adore one another."

Dot looked at her, sad beyond belief at the anguish she was causing. She had to be strong. She had found love for the first time in her life, Elizabeth and Tom's sort of love. How she had mocked them at the beginning of their relationship. She felt ashamed now, but at almost fifty she suddenly knew what love was all about. She also knew that it was worth the fight. Had her marriage to John proved to be a comfortable one, compatible and sharing, she would never have considered leaving him. It was sterile, in spite of the children. They simply existed side by side, ships that passed in the night, lonely in the good and the bad times.

Elizabeth sat anxiously waiting for her mother to reply.

"Philip has found me a flat at the other side of the village. Richard will be able to continue at his school. I want as little interruption to his life as possible. He will be able to see John easily, and we will both be able to see you." Dot stopped momentarily then continued, "That is if you want to. Your father is going to share a house with an old friend who is on his own. He is moving out tomorrow. I think he will be all right there." Old habits die hard, and she could not help being concerned about John. He had been stunned when she told him that she was leaving, but he had quickly realised that he had brought it all on himself. He had pleaded her to stay promising to change completely, but it was all too late. However it worked out, she had made up her mind. John remembered how she had left home twice when she was little more than a child. He knew she would not alter her decision. He had lost her, and what was worse he knew it was his own fault.

"What about the house?" asked Elizabeth.

"It goes on sale next week. It gives me time to pack things up and leave the house swept and dusted."

Elizabeth was weak with shock. She looked at Tom. "I think I'd like to go home now and digest all this before I hear any more. I want to know how you arrived at this point, Mum, if you don't mind? I'll phone you later. I love you and I want you to be happy. It seems a giant hurdle to jump all on your own."

"That's just it, Elizabeth, I'm not on my own anymore. I have Philip." She suddenly looked happy and confident. "I'll tell you all about him as we go along. He is a good man. He cares for me. He is taking an enormous risk to be with me you know. He wants to meet you. If it's all right with you I'll arrange it as soon as possible." Elizabeth nodded. She hugged her mother tightly before they left.

"It's going to be fine, Mum. We'll help with the move." Dot heaved a sigh of relief; whatever difficulties she had to face, she had not lost her daughter.

"Take care of her, Tom."

"I always do," he replied.

"Yes, dear, I know," Dot answered, thinking, *And you always will.*

Dot felt drained when they left. There was so much to tell them about Philip himself, and the way their romance had slowly developed. Neither one of them had been looking for an affair. Dot, who had been far from happy married to

John, and often thought of life without him, had never considered another relationship. Richard's arrival had smothered her ideas of an independent life. Philip, who had been alone so long, had become more and more engrossed in his career in orthopaedic surgery, content to live his bachelor lifestyle, until Dorothy had re-entered his life, and then Elspeth had dramatically returned.

John and Richard had been out together to the pictures. They returned soon after Elizabeth and Tom's departure.

"The children have been here, you've just missed them."

"You told them I hope?"

"Of course."

"What did they say?"

"Not much, Elizabeth was very upset of course."

"She would be. What did Tom have to say?"

"Not a lot, he's very sensible. He'll look after Elizabeth."

"I hope you know what you are doing, Dot. Thirty years is a long time. Are you sure you want to throw away everything that we've worked for? You hardly know this fellow. It's not too late to change your mind you know." John was shell-shocked. He could not believe Dot was going. In his own selfish way he loved her dearly. She had been his life. However, he knew that he had treated her unfairly. He had not co-operated in her attempts to improve their lives. He wouldn't consider holidays for the children, or buying a car to take them out. He was satisfied with his visits to his local, meeting his pals, never considering his wife and children. Slowly he was waking up to what he had destroyed.

Dot made no reply. She was talked out. The previous days had been a nightmare. John had argued, pleaded, and begged. She had stood firm. There was no going back. However it turned out, this long episode in her life was over.

"I'm going for a walk, John. I won't be long. Will you get Richard to bed?" The boy was upstairs in his bedroom. He was ten years old, and had heard enough these last few days to make him feel very insecure. He didn't recognise the feeling, but it made him unhappy.

John moved out the next day. Richard was at school, Dot had promised to meet him at home time, and she went round to Elizabeth's to wait for John's call. He phoned when he was ready to go.

"My keys are in the garage, the usual place. I've found the phone number that you left for me. Mine is on the kitchen worktop. I'm going now." His voice was cold, but it trembled with emotion.

Dot shivered as she replied, "Thank you, John. I am sorry it ended like this, take care." She put the phone down quickly before he could say any more.

"Mum, are you all right?" Elizabeth peered anxiously into her mother's face.

"Yes, I'm fine. Just a bit shaky, it isn't every day you end your marriage." She looked sadly at her daughter. "I didn't want it be like this. I really tried to make it work. My heart aches for him, you know, if only he had been different."

"People don't change, Mum."

"I should never have married him. I suppose the attraction of a home of my own, a husband, and a family was just too much for me. It's my fault as much as his."

"I think we had better get over to the house, Mum. The removal van will be there in half an hour. Is everything ready?"

"Yes, and you are right, we'd better get going. The neighbours will be all agog."

They saw the last things onto the van, walked through the house to make sure nothing had been forgotten, and left without a backward glance. Dot felt nothing as she left. It was just a long chapter in her life and now a new one was to begin.

Elizabeth felt sad; to her the family was split apart and things would never be the same again. Johnnie's departure had been bad enough, but this was worse. *Don't be so selfish*, she thought. She ushered Dot into the car, Tom had used the train to travel to work. She started up the engine and moved off for the last time from her old home.

Dot heaved a sigh of relief. Whatever lay ahead would be worth it, and before long she would be with Philip, the wasted years forgotten.

The flat was only two miles away. It did not take long for the men to unload the van. When they left, mother and daughter looked around the place. The furniture looked lost in the huge rooms.

"Mum, this lounge is like a blinking ballroom!" exclaimed Elizabeth. Dot looked at her, and they began to laugh. They laughed until their sides ached.

"We'll have to sell entrance tickets at the door," Dot said and they started to laugh again. The stress of escaping from the old house and the twitching curtains was released by their laughter and they calmed down.

"It won't look so big when we unpack the boxes and hang the pictures."

"Tom's coming straight from work, he'll help put the beds up. Once they are made everything else can wait." They worked until it was time to collect Richard.

"I'm dreading this, Elizabeth, I don't know how he will react." Dorothy looked around the flat as they left. It looked a bit more like home now with the carpets down and a few familiar objects about the place. The two set off to collect Richard, each with their own thoughts as they travelled the short distance to school. Dot broke the silence.

"You know, Elizabeth, I used to laugh at you and Tom. I had no idea about how you two felt for each other. I am ashamed now of course. Here I am approaching fifty suddenly finding out about what you both shared. If your father had made the slightest attempt to make a go of our marriage, just tried to understand what I was telling him, I would not have left him."

Elizabeth touched her mother's hand. There was no need for more words. It was done and Elizabeth understood.

CHAPTER FORTY-ONE

Dot had been in a dilemma about telling Richard. Should she tell him before the break up, or on the actual day? Although only ten, he was already the world's greatest worrier. However she approached the subject it would be a terrible shock. Young as he was, it was going to be difficult for him to understand. He was close to his father who in his turn adored him. Elizabeth had not found it easy to come to terms with the situation, in spite of the fact that she knew how unhappy her mother was. Finally Dot decided to tell him on the day of the move. John was to phone him after school at the flat and take him out to the pictures. This they hoped would give him a feeling of continuity, and security. Dot was grateful for John's co-operation. There was so much good in the man, it was a great pity it had come to this. Still there was no going back; each of them was starting a new life.

Richard saw his mother first. He was less obvious in the horde of children racing to the gates. He also spotted Elizabeth and wondered why she was there.

"Hello, dear, we have a lift today, isn't that nice?" Dot felt her words were empty and fatuous in view of what she really had to say. Elizabeth looked at her encouragingly knowing that only her mother could tell him what was happening. Dot took a deep breath.

"Shall we go along the prom? I have something to tell you, Richard." She stopped, groping for words. "We aren't going home, at least not our old home. We have a new place, a flat with a big garden. There is a lovely room for you with loads of space for your records and player. All your things are there already, and you can arrange them as you like."

Richard looked wide-eyed at his mother.

"We are going there now? Is Dad coming?"

The last question was unexpected, and made things a little easier for Dot.

"That was what I was going to say next, Richard. Dad is going to live with Uncle George, you know, Dad used to work with him? He has a lovely big house, remember?"

"Yes." His head went down. "Will I see him again?"

"Of course, dear! He's seeing you tonight. He's taking you to the pictures. He'll ring when we get home and sort it out."

"Okay." The boy said no more, then, "What's for tea?"

Dot looked at Elizabeth, deciding at that moment she would say no more, hoping John would go along with her. She felt it best to give Richard a few days to accept the move before breaking the big news.

Elizabeth moved off, having played no part in the conversation.

Her brother was amazing. They climbed the outside staircase to the flat, and Dot let them in. Richard ran from room to room, whooping with delight.

"It's smashing, Mum, it's huge. I can see the sea from this window, which is my room?" He was flushed with excitement. The phone rang and Dot answered. Elizabeth showed Richard to his room, leaving Dot to talk to John privately. He was not happy that Richard hadn't been told everything about their split, but understood Dot's reason.

"I want him telling soon. I don't want him thinking I have abandoned him." His voice was like a stranger's. Dot could not blame him.

"Of course I'll tell him."

"I'll meet him at the cinema, six o'clock. I'll walk him home. Bye." Dot was shaking as she replaced the receiver. It was done, she had broken loose, and whatever the outcome there was no going back. She would say her good-byes to Elizabeth, how could she ever thank her, and wait for Philip to phone.

"I'll drop Richard off at the cinema, Mum." Elizabeth took her brother's hand and squeezed it tightly. "Come on, big boy, let's go."

The telephone rang at seven o'clock. The harsh bell of the old phone made Dot jump.

"Hello."

"It's me, Dorothy, are you all right?" Philip's voice sounded anxious.

"I'm fine, the move went well. Elizabeth was a great help and we have the place pretty straight."

"How did it go with Richard?"

"He took the move very well. He loves the flat. I told him that John and I were living apart, but I didn't mention you."

"I see." He sounded disappointed. "I suppose it was a bit much for him to take in all at once."

"I'm sorry for him, Philip. His young mind must be in a whirl, so much to take in all at once. I feel dreadful." She began to cry, worn out physically and mentally. She was also not a little frightened about what she had done.

"I'll come round shortly. It will be dark then, no one will see me."

Dot interrupted, "Dark, what do you mean? I thought all the sneaking around was over now, especially as Elspeth knows." She was angry and disappointed in Philip.

"I want to get in touch with the children, put them in the picture first."

"Why? They haven't even acknowledged your existence in all these years."

"I know, Dorothy, but it's something I feel I must do. Look, I'll sign off now, and get round as soon as I can. We can talk then, is that all right with you?"

"Yes." Dot was suddenly feeling insecure. "Bye." She replaced the receiver. Everything that had seemed so simple an hour ago began to feel anything but simple.

Richard arrived home from the pictures and went straight to bed. He was tired out. He clung to Dot as she kissed him goodnight.

"You won't leave me, Mum, will you?"

"Never, Richard, I promise you that. You are my special boy and I love you dearly." He smiled up at her and snuggled under the eiderdown falling asleep immediately.

Dot thought over Philip's visit. It had been brief, ending ten minutes before Richard's return. Dot didn't want him to meet Philip until she told him the whole story. Their conversation had surprised her. Instead of the wonderful warmth she had expected, snuggled together on the settee, Philip stood awkwardly like a schoolboy, searching for words.

"She's moved in, and the boys are on their way up presumably to talk me out of the divorce." Martin and David were the same age as Elizabeth and Johnny. Dot looked at him in disbelief.

"How did she get in? I wondered that the other day."

"She has kept the keys all these years. It's the sort of thing she would do. They have come in handy now, haven't they?"

Dot felt a trickle of fear like cold water down her back. What had she let herself in for? The boys would be on their mother's side naturally. Philip had a streak of weakness in him. She had seen it before as they crept around keeping their relationship secret.

"You aren't contemplating leaving me here in a flat I can't afford to run? I risked everything to be here to be with you, Philip." She could have said a lot more, but he looked so upset and vulnerable. There was a long uncomfortable silence. Dot walked over to the bay window. It was open, and the curtains moved slightly.

They need letting down, she thought, before turning her attention to the beautiful sunset. Philip moved up behind her.

"I won't let you down, Dorothy. I'll never do that. I'll explain to the boys as soon as they arrive that my mind is made up. I owe Elspeth nothing." He took her in his arms and kissed her gently. "You are so precious to me. Life would not be worth living if I lost you. I am going to leave the house immediately. I'll move in right away, instead of going through all the legal twaddle first, that's if you'll have me?" He suddenly looked anxious. "Would you mind? We'd be living in sin, you know?"

Dot turned away from the window, was he serious? She looked into his soft blue eyes, saying, "We haven't sinned up to now, Philip, all we've done is talk."

She laughed, her eyes crinkling up as the smile reached them. "I'll tell Richard tomorrow. He has taken enough on board for one day. Talk to your boys, at least they are adult, and must surely understand. Then move in as soon as you can. It's time people knew. I am not ashamed, are you?"

"No, I'm not, and you are right, it is time people knew. If they don't like it, that's tough. I think my divorce is going to be a long and bitter affair. It could take years and at our age we haven't years to waste." He looked down at her, his eyes moist. "What did I ever do to deserve you?" He kissed her again then said, "I'd better go, or Richard will be home. You must speak to him first. I hate leaving you." He held her tightly. "I won't be long."

As he left, Dot realised he hadn't looked round the flat at the result of Elizabeth's and her own efforts that day, or talked of Richard's delight at his room. There simply hadn't been time. At this point Richard arrived back from the pictures, a narrow miss. John had left him at the top of the road, sensitive enough not to invade Dot's new home.

* * *

Dot could not sleep. The hot nights of the Indian summer continued. The restless patients tossing around in their beds sedated by pills, some snoring, others coughing, didn't help Dot to find the peace that sleep often brought. The old lady in the next bed woke up and started shouting for a nurse, disturbing the whole ward.

"Press your bell, Betty." Dot told her, but she was ignored, as usual. Betty was a demanding woman who cared only for herself. She had no regard for the other patients.

"What is it, Betty?" The night nurse came hurrying in, trying her best to disguise her annoyance.

"I want the toilet." No please or thank you.

"You are a saint," said Dot.

"I wish they were all like you, Dottie."

Betty sorted out; the nurse asked Dot if she fancied a cup of tea.

"Wouldn't I just, thank you." The tea arrived and the nurse sat on the edge of Dot's bed. They often did this in the small hours of the morning.

"How's your daughter, Dottie?"

"She's fine, but all this is a bit much for her. She's working as well, you know."

"Daughters don't mind, they'll do anything for their mums." Nurse laughed quietly. "Mustn't wake Betty."

"Try and get some sleep, Dottie. It will help, you know."

"I know, dear, I'll try. I'll smother Betty if she wakes again."

"That would be nice. We could blame old Agnes over there. She's nearly as bad. We could get rid of the two of them then." She kissed Dot on the forehead.

"Sleep tight." Dot was alone again with her thoughts.

Richard was coming with Elizabeth tomorrow. He had been ill with flu for two weeks and they were all scared of their mother catching the virus. Unmarried, he still lived at home. He was going to be a great help when she got out of hospital. She remembered Philip's sons coming to the flat to see her when Philip was out. They cajoled and threatened, shouted and bullied her, until Richard came home from school. He walked in on them verbally abusing his mother.

"Leave my mother alone, go away."

Dorothy finally drifted off to sleep, her mind in the past as it often was these days.

* * *

"Leave my home, please. You were not invited here, and I won't have you upsetting my son." Martin and David looked at each other uncertainly. The arrival of the young boy had thrown them somewhat.

"Please go." Dorothy was angry and upset. "I can't believe that educated, successful career men could behave in such a manner. Your father will be horrified when I tell him."

"You won't have to tell me." Philip stood in the doorway. "I think I have heard enough." His face was pink with anger. He walked over to Dot and put his arms around her.

"This is Dorothy, the woman I am going to marry as soon as possible. I love her and that is all you need to be told. You know how your mother has behaved, leaving me ill and helpless, taking you to Rhodesia as boys, never to be seen until you were grown up. Do you call that a wife?"

Martin and David stood uncomfortably silent. They hardly knew their father, and his sudden appearance had left them speechless.

Martin looked at his younger brother. "We'd better go, David." David nodded and turned to go. Richard ran behind his mother as they left. The front door slammed, shaking the glass window.

"I'm sorry about all that, Richard. This is the last way I wanted us to meet. I am Philip as you have heard. I love your mother very much and we want to be together for the rest of our lives. She loves you just as much as she loves me, probably more." He smiled kindly at Richard, and took a clean handkerchief from his pocket to wipe the boy's tear-stained face. Suddenly Richard threw his arms round Philip.

"You will take care of her, won't you?"

"Of course, and you too, young man. I hope we can be the best of friends."

"I'd like that."

So Richard met Philip.

CHAPTER FORTY-TWO

Elizabeth met Philip shortly after her brother. Richard's instant acceptance of his future stepfather had been a relief to Dot. She arranged the meeting of the two dearest people in her life as soon as possible. They met for coffee the following Saturday in a local café. It was empty apart from themselves and the proprietor. Dot declined to join them, thinking that they could be more direct if she was absent.

"I like him, Mum." Elizabeth's voice was warm with approval. "He seems to be everything you said he is, open, kind and understanding. We didn't talk much. It was difficult for both of us I suppose, but he promised to look after you."

When Philip spoke of the meeting, he said, "I like your daughter, Dorothy. She obviously adores you and cares a great deal about your welfare. Both Elizabeth and Richard wanted assurance that I would take care of you. I found that very touching." Dorothy smiled happily at Philip, thinking that the two could have written their reports together, so similar were their words.

Archie was the next to meet Philip. Well into his seventies now, he had been shocked, although not surprised, at the news of Dot and John's marriage break-up. He had accepted Dot's invitation to stay for a while with pleasure and curiosity. Philip had moved in with Dot and Richard following the recent events, and the two were established as a couple by the time Archie visited. He too fell for Philip's gentle ways, and could see that his daughter was in good hands.

"I won't say I'm not sorry it came to this, Dot, but I can see why it did. John is a fool, but I was fond of him and he gave you three good kids."

"Yes, he did, Dad, but he left me to raise them. He didn't care if Elizabeth stayed on to sixth form or not, and he drove Johnnie away from home. I will say he was good with Richard, still is, for that matter. There were other things too, but they were purely between us."

"I know, love, you don't have to explain. It's your life. I may have done the same myself if I'd been born twenty years later. You would have had a better start in life, heaven only knows. Olivia was no mother to you, was she?"

"No, Dad, but that is history. While we are on the subject, please don't let her know where I am living."

"I wouldn't dream of it, Dot, I know what she is. A doctor in the family, she'd love that."

Dot often wondered just how much Archie knew about Olivia's philandering. She had made a play for John and even young Tom. She never knew why her father tolerated Olivia's behaviour, and could not bring herself to discuss the matter with her half-sisters.

Archie enjoyed his stay with Dot. He and Philip got on well, the latter learning much about Dot's early days, of which he knew very little.

"You haven't had much of a life, Dorothy," Philip said one evening when they were alone. Archie was back home and Richard in bed.

"Oh, I don't know, lots of it has been good. I wouldn't have missed out on the children for the world." She looked thoughtful, and then she said, "Woodleigh was the best time really. It was a new world for me. I learned so much, made good friends. I was carefree I suppose for the first time in my life. Then there was you; little did I know that we would be together one day."

"Are you happy?" Philip hugged her as he spoke.

"Of course I am."

"It's going to be ages before we can marry."

"I know that, Philip, but I can wait. At least we are together."

Philip felt a shiver run down his spine. Things were not going well with his divorce. Elspeth was firmly established in his house. She was running up bills all over the place, buying dresses and shoes. She was also entertaining on a lavish scale. She was poisoning the minds of mutual friends, telling tales about Philip and the slut of a nurse he was living with. Elspeth's usual comment to her friends and acquaintances was, "Did you know she was a personal maid to his mother before the war? The Hislops took her in virtually homeless, made her one of the family, and this is how she repays them. She tried to split us up when I went to stay at his home."

Philip was livid on hearing this and went to see Andrew Jenkins, his friend and solicitor.

"She can't be allowed to get away with this, Andrew. I won't have her hurting Dorothy like this."

"To say nothing of your career, Philip."

"I don't care about that." Philip was pink with anger.

"You have to be realistic about this, old man." Andrew's voice was soft and kind. "I know what all this is doing to you, but you have got to be careful. Elspeth is either being very clever, or she has a damn good divorce lawyer. She has managed to establish herself as the injured party. Your separation during the war is remembered by only a few. People forget, and she is telling them that she took the boys abroad for safety."

"What?" Philip was flabbergasted. "Nobody will believe that."

"She only has to convince the court."

Philip had told Dorothy nothing of this, but he felt that now he must. She listened in silence.

"According to Andrew it will take seven years for me to divorce Elspeth." He looked at Dot, full of despair. "Yours will be less as John isn't contesting, I think it's about three."

"Philip, calm down, please. Does it matter? We are here together, people have been hurt, and I'm sad about that, but the deed is done. It will be wonderful when we can marry, but it is obviously going to be a long time off." After a moment's thought she added, "Didn't you say something about divorce law reforms coming in shortly?"

"Yes, but that's nearly four years away."

"I realise that, but it is going to be easier, isn't it, and less messy?"

"Well, yes, two years for you and John on the basis of irretrievable breakdown of marriage and mutual agreement. Five years in my case because Elspeth will never agree."

"Well, why don't we wait until then, and do it the easier way? Speak to Andrew and see what he thinks. If he agrees, I'll get my name changed. It will be less embarrassing for us in a lot of ways, especially you with your professional status to protect."

"Don't you mind, Dorothy? You have done so much for me."

Dot did mind, but she could see it might make things easier in some ways. So the divorces were put on hold, and they settled down. Shortly it was as if they had been together all their lives.

Philip's boys had a go at breaking them up. They visited Philip unexpectedly. After a few scathing remarks about the flat, they started on their father.

"Mother's ill, Dad. She can't handle this separation. It's too bad of you to put her through this after all these years."

Philip snorted. "You are unbelievable. Your mother deserted me during the war, taking you with her, as you well know. She couldn't handle me being ill, so she walked. She has chosen to reappear because she suddenly realises she is in danger of losing something. Not me, but my possessions. Well, I can assure you that she will get all she is entitled to, that is if there is anything left. The way she is spending there will be nothing." Philip stopped for breath. He was shaking with anger and disappointment at his sons. Still, she was their mother, he supposed.

The boys looked sheepish and muttered something about going now, and left.

Dorothy had her share of harassment. If she and Elspeth ever crossed paths, Dot would be verbally abused. It was humiliating, but Dot learned to ignore these episodes. If they occurred at a social event, Elspeth's behaviour backfired on her, leaving her looking foolish and embarrassed.

Dorothy was growing as a person over this period. Life was not easy, particularly at first. Some of her old friends and neighbours took exception to her leaving John. They had no idea of her life with him. She had never told even her closest friends of her unhappiness. John, who was always the life and soul of any gatherings, was regarded as the injured party. Some even thought she was getting above herself living with a surgeon. She learned to live with the gossip and as time went by it became less.

She made new friends. Philip introduced her to a variety of people. They began to entertain, which she really enjoyed.

John, however, was not adjusting so easily. His world had fallen down around him and he simply did not know what to do.

"He calls on me every morning on the way to work." Elizabeth was distressed about her father. "He cries, Mum, it breaks my heart. I don't know what to say. How can I help him? I tell him he's still got us, we'll always be there for him, but we can't replace you, can we? George is very good to him, and he has his own sitting room and bedroom. At least he is comfortable."

Dot was upset. She felt so guilty about John, and she didn't want Elizabeth going through all this. Would she ever be able to relax and be truly happy?

"I'm sorry, Elizabeth, I don't know what to say. I didn't anticipate this. Your dad has been so matter of fact about everything up to now, and just gone along with things."

It took a long time, but things did get easier. John stopped dropping in after a while. He became used to his bachelor life, and began going out with his friends to the pub and occasionally a club.

"Don't worry about me, Elizabeth. I'm okay. There will never be another Dot, and I'm not interested in meeting anyone else, but I can still enjoy life, can't I?"

Elizabeth was relieved and told her mother who was pleased. A born bachelor, John now enjoyed a bachelor's life.

Then the little house was sold. It had been on the market for a long time. Mortgages were difficult to obtain at the time. The money was divided equally between Dot and John. It was a reasonable sum, even after the mortgage was cleared. This was when John went off the rails. He began to spend his windfall as fast as he could. He took to going out every night, gambling and clubbing with his friends. He enjoyed himself for a while and then it began to wear a bit thin and he settled down.

Dot was more prudent. She paid her share into a building society, having first treated herself to a carpet for the lounge. She often thought that if ever she needed proof of Philip's love it was to be seen in the flat. The furniture she had worked so hard for looked lost in the big rooms of their first place together. He had lived in luxury all his life, but seemed not to care about their lifestyle.

"One day, Dorothy, we'll have a place of our own. You will be able to furnish it yourself and we'll live happily ever after." Dorothy wanted to believe him, but doubted it would ever happen. There was still too much in the way.

* * *

Dorothy slept soundly that night. The consultant was due to give his final assessment on the morning round, and all being well she would go home the next day. The social workers had taken her to the flat the week before to see if she could cope. All the rugs had been removed to prevent her slipping and various aids installed to help her through her final recovery. Tom had put another banister rail in so she had one either side of the stairs.

"That's the most useful thing of all," she told Elizabeth when she next saw her. "I'll have those rugs down again as soon as I get home." Elizabeth sighed quietly to herself, thinking that there were going to be difficult times ahead. Her mother had become very stubborn during the seven weeks she had been in hospital. "I don't mean to be difficult, but they treat me like an imbecile."

"I know it's not easy, Mum, but it is all for your benefit, you know. You don't want to end up in here again, do you?"

"Indeed I don't."

"Well, then, go along with them, it won't be forever. We will dispose of the aids as you cease to need them." Dot cheered up at her daughter's positive attitude.

"We'll see." Then she added, "You are a good girl."

"I'll ask them to phone me after the consultant's round. If you can come home I'll bring your bag."

The day had come, Dot felt refreshed after her shower. The hairdresser had been the day before, and although not done to her liking, her hair felt clean. She sat in her chair by the outside door. The Indian summer was disappearing as October drew to a close. She waited quietly, praying that the answer would be positive and at last she could go home. There were those in the ward who would never go home, and she wept a tear for them.

The autumn weather, although cooling now, was nostalgic. Philip had been much on Dorothy's mind. It was their time of year. She saw Elizabeth enter the ward, and after their usual greetings and enquiries, she said, "I've been thinking about Philip this morning, remembering when he left me and went to stay with Robin Earnshaw."

"Whatever made you think of that? It was a lifetime ago. You should be thinking of going home soon, and how good that will be."

"Maybe that was what did it. Two months is a long time to be away. I remember Philip coming home one evening and telling me he had been asked to resign from his place on the hospital committee. A lot of the members objected to our situation, especially as I was a nurse and he was a consultant."

"Oh, Mum, medics are a stuffy lot and things were different then. Nobody got divorced, they just had affairs."

"I know all that, but your dad thought he had a chance to get us together again. I was so distraught that it almost happened. It was a second blow to him. He didn't deserve that."

"Mum, this is history, forget it. Look forward: you may be home tomorrow. I think I'd better close the door, the old girls will be complaining they are cold."

Dot laughed.

"You are quite right on both counts, I'm just being silly. It is nearly time for tea and the consultant hasn't been."

"Well, it will be tomorrow now, even if he says you can go home. I'll have a word with Sister on the way out. I'd better make a move anyway. You are nearly there now, Mum."

Elizabeth couldn't find Sister so she went on her way. She would phone in when she got home.

* * *

197

CHAPTER FORTY-THREE

The phone started ringing as Elizabeth arrived home. She dumped her load of shopping on the hall floor and picked up the receiver. Dot's voice shook as she started to speak.

"Elizabeth, he's gone!"

"Who's gone?"

"Philip. Can you come, I need you?"

"I'll be there in ten minutes, Mum. Unlock the outside door and I'll let myself in. Put the kettle on, I'm on my way."

Anything to keep her mother occupied until she got there. She didn't like the sound of her voice. She seemed on the verge of hysteria.

Elizabeth let herself in and found Dot sitting on the rug in front of the gas fire. The tea was ready for drinking.

"What ever has happened?"

"He came home for lunch in a terrible state. They have asked him to resign from his precious hospital committee. He's been under pressure from a lot of his cronies about living with me. It would be all right if we had kept quiet, but flaunting ourselves as a couple is beyond the pale. I had no idea he was going through all this. I have had a few unpleasant remarks and the occasional snub, but nothing too upsetting. Anyway, he's gone, taken all his things to stay with Robin while he sorts himself out." She halted, and then the tears came, quietly at first and then louder until they became a scream. Elizabeth was scared; she could not console her mother as she slipped into hysteria.

The doctor came quickly. He was a friend of Philip's and knew the history. He gave Dot an injection, and Elizabeth got her to bed.

"Is she going to be all right?" She was terrified. She had never seen her mother like this.

"She is on the verge of a breakdown, Elizabeth. Can you stay with her for a few days?"

"Of course, I'll do anything, my husband is on his way so I will have help."

"That's good. I will give you a prescription for her. It is a strong anti-depressant so we won't have her on it for long. I will come tomorrow, and I'll leave my home number in case you need me."

"How can I thank you? She had me really scared."

"She will be fine. Try not to worry, she is a brave woman and she has been through a lot lately." He gave Elizabeth a hug. "Things will work out, you'll see."

They went to the door together. She stood at the top of the steps and watched him go. Dot's cat seized the opportunity to slip inside. Elizabeth, feeling very lost at that moment, stroked him as he passed. As she turned to go in, Tom's car came up the drive, and she ran down the steps to meet him. It was the first time that Elizabeth felt the role reversal that is inevitable between parents and children, if all live long enough. She and Tom talked a while, and then she phoned Johnny and told him the news.

"I'll get home as soon as I can. I'll probably get a flight." Her younger brother seemed so mature, Elizabeth realised that the six years' age gap did not matter anymore. They were equally adult, and she liked the comforting feeling it gave her.

Dot responded to her medication, and always a fighter, she took hold of herself. Soon, she was nursing again. She never returned to the hospital where Philip worked. Her new post was private. It paid well and fitted in with Richard. She carried on, although she lost weight and looked drawn.

"I will have to find another flat, Elizabeth. I can't pay this rent. Fortunately it is paid quarterly in advance, so I've got a breathing space."

Johnny had to return to his job in Scotland about this time.

"I can't take any more leave, Elizabeth."

"Please don't worry. It's been marvellous having you here. You have been such a help, with Dad as well as Mum."

About this time, John came back on the scene. He wanted a reunion with Dot.

"I can put it all behind me, Dot, if you can."

She was stunned; this was the last thing she expected. She was very non-committal, not wanting to hurt him any more than she already had.

"How did you know about, Philip?" He could read nothing in her voice. It hardly sounded like his Dot. He still thought of her that way.

"You know the village, everyone knows everything almost before you know yourself." He paused, not quite sure how to handle the situation. "I hope it was all right my coming round, but I was worried about you." He stood looking at her with those beautiful grey eyes that had melted her heart so many years ago.

"Think about it, Dotty. We could buy another house, anywhere you like. We've plenty for a deposit now the house is sold. We could start again, a new life." He looked so eager that Dot could not bear to look at him.

"I can't consider a move like that, John. It is too soon. I feel as if Philip has died, worse than that. If he was dead it might be easier." She began to cry. John made a move to go.

"Can I come back in a couple of days, when you have had time to think?"

"All right, but don't get your hopes up." As she spoke she thought, *I shouldn't have said that.*

In spite of her doubts they did get as far as looking at a house that had come up for sale. It was not far away, and one that Dot had always liked. As they wandered through the empty rooms, dust dancing in the shafts of sunlight, Dot suddenly panicked. *What on earth am I doing?*

"I've got a headache, John, do you mind if we leave it for now?"

"No, love, of course not. Let's get you home." Elizabeth was waiting outside in her car.

"Any good?" Her mother shook her head and got in the car. Elizabeth looked into Dot's face as she spoke. Her eyes were lifeless; all the sparkling love of living had gone. Elizabeth knew then that they were only going through the motions. There could be no reunion, no fairy tale reconciliation. She ached for both her parents, but again she could not help.

Shortly after this episode, John's back gave way. He was a martyr to lumbago. He was at Dot's when it happened. He couldn't stand at all. He was devastated, just when he had a glimmer of hope; here he was on Dot's settee being nursed by her. He felt useless, frustrated, and angry.

Richard was confused.

"Is Dad coming to live with us, Mum?" She had no answer, and mumbled something about Dad needing looking after at the moment and left it at that.

After only a few days Dot felt all the reasons for her leaving John come flooding back. It was no use; she could not live with him. She would manage on her own. If she had considered it at all, it was for the wrong reasons. The thought of being alone had been terrifying, and John had appeared at her lowest point. She had grasped at straws. She was stronger now, and knew she must put him straight. It would be kinder not to let things drag on.

"I can't give you another go, John. It wouldn't work. It isn't fair on you to let you carry on dreaming of something that can't happen. It wasn't just Philip that made me leave you. I know that for sure. Forgive me, but I never encouraged you to come here."

John realised that it was useless trying any longer. When his back improved enough to cope, he left, returning to George, who welcomed him with open arms.

"I've missed you, mate, welcome home." John shook his hand and went to his room to unpack. He was surprised to find it felt like home, and he settled down, finally accepting that this was his life now, and he still had his kids after all.

Philip, meanwhile, had heard about John's attempt at reconciliation. Alan Morgan, Dot's family doctor and Philip's long-time friend, had let it slip.

"She took your departure very badly, Philip. She was on the edge of a breakdown. I shouldn't be telling you this, but I feel you should know. However, she came through, with the aid of medication, and the support of all her children. She is working for a private nursing agency, did you know?" Philip didn't know, and he hated not knowing. Life simply wasn't worthwhile living apart from her. He had known that as soon as he had left. When Alan told him about John's back and his stay with Dot, he suddenly came to his senses.

How could he have been so weak? He had let other people influence him and he had walked out on the best person in his life; after all they had gone through to be together.

That evening he went round to see her. He rang the bell, his hands shaking with nerves. Dot had just sat down after a long day and was nursing a mug of tea between her hands. She put the tea down, switched off the television, and went to the door, opening it cautiously, as she was not expecting anyone. She saw him standing on the outside landing, pale and anxious.

"I hope—"

"Philip—" They both spoke at once.

"Come in, it's freezing out there." She turned and walked through the hall to her own front door. She turned round, composed now. "You had better come in." Her voice was cool, disguising the turmoil inside her. She could not imagine why he had called.

"I resigned from the committee today. I told them my reasons in no uncertain terms. I am ashamed that I did not do it before. I owe you so many apologies for my weakness in listening to people who don't matter a damn. I love you so much. I have let you down appallingly, made you ill. I can't believe that I've broken so many promises. I miss you so much. My life is simply not worth living without you. Can you bring yourself to forgive me, to trust me after what I did to you?"

Dot walked over to the bay window, playing for time while she tried to gather her wits. She stood watching the sun set as she had so often done with him. She tried to form angry sentences to let him know how much he had hurt her. They would not come. Her love for him, the love she had tried so hard to stifle these last few weeks, came rushing to the surface. The anger and unbearable sadness drained from her.

"You are weak, Philip Hislop. You nearly lost me forever. I cannot go through this again, no matter what happens. You would destroy me." Her voice broke and she could speak no more.

"Does this mean you will have me back?" His voice shook with emotion. He waited for an answer. Dot turned away from the fading sunset to look at him. He too had lost weight, and his usually red cheeks were pale. He looked ill.

"What have you done to yourself, Philip, you look dreadful?"

"What have I done to you? How could I let this happen?"

"I don't know, Philip, I don't know, but if there is the slightest doubt in your mind that it could happen again, then let's say goodbye now, and be done with it." He looked shamefaced, standing motionless in front of her, wishing he could roll back time.

"I don't know how I can convince you that I know what a weak fool I have been. I ran away at the first big test; let you down like so many others in your life. I promise you that I will never fail you again. I love you more than life itself. I won't pressure you, much as I would like to. I am in your hands. I'll go now, and leave you to think about what I have said. Will you phone me when you have an answer?"

"Don't go, Philip, stay here with me where you belong. You can get your things from Robin tomorrow." She moved towards him and took him in her arms. They both wept. They held each other close. Their tears of remorse turned to joy in the comfort of their embrace. Dorothy buried her face in his rough tweed jacket and felt he was home to stay.

"Do you fancy a drink?" Philip nodded gratefully. He had never felt so much in need of a drink in his life. Dot let go of him, poured him a whisky, and excused herself while she rinsed her face and brushed her hair.

At that moment, Richard arrived home. He had been to the pictures with John. His father always walked him home, and he saw Philip's car in the drive.

"Looks as if Philip is back." The boy looked uncertainly at John, not knowing what he should say.

"In you go, son, you'll get cold. I'll see you next week." He left, knowing that this was final. His last chance had slipped through his fingers. Philip would not make the same mistake again.

Richard stood shyly in the lounge doorway. He looked at Philip uncertainly.

"Hello, young man, I've missed you!" Richard ran to Philip and put his arms around his waist.

"I'm glad you are back." His voice was muffled by Philip's jacket.

"I'm glad to be back," Philip said, wiping tears from his eyes as he spoke. "I promise I won't be leaving again."

Dot continued working with the agency. The money was useful and it gave her a feeling of security. She believed Philip was back for good. They slowly settled down again to what had become normal, and the niggling insecurities faded away. Their relationship became solid with the passage of time. They shared all the ups and downs that every couple experiences. Money was tight, because Elspeth was a terrible drain on Philip's income. She was deliberately trying to break him financially, spending wildly in his name. Philip tried to curb her spending every way possible, short of taking her to court. He could ill afford the publicity and subsequent scandal, and he did not want to alienate his boys any further. He lived in hope of reconciliation with them eventually, but Dot could not see that happening. They had too much of their mother in them.

One evening Philip settled down with Dot for a sherry before dinner.

"I've got something to put to you, Dorothy, and I'd like your honest opinion. It is something I have been thinking of for a long time, and an opportunity has come up." He stopped to light a cigarette. "I have been offered a part-time post in the new private hospital."

Dot was stunned, but after a moment's consideration said, "I think that is wonderful if it is what you want."

"I have considered it carefully, and I will still be able to do my National Health work. He stopped talking, and looked at her anxiously.

"You know very well, Philip, that I want what you want for yourself." Philip looked at her straight in the eye.

"I have to be honest, Dorothy. I have never really considered private work until recent times. I totally believe in the National Health Service, and have supported it from the beginning. However, things have changed, and I need the money. It will help me get out of the debt that Elspeth has got me in to since she re-appeared on the scene."

Philip took up his new post two months later. His hours fitted in with his other duties. Their spare time was spent together, and the outside world came to accept them in time.

They settled into their new life and waited patiently for the day they would be able to marry.

CHAPTER FORTY-FOUR

Dorothy sat at the kitchen table, her first cup of tea of the day steaming in front of her. The morning mail lay in a pile, mostly Philip's, who was bombarded with junk. She was staring at the one letter addressed to her. She opened it slowly, and then her divorce absolute fluttered slightly in her nervous fingers. She was free, it was all over, and she was mistress of her own life. It had been straightforward, as John had agreed to the divorce, and to her having custody of Richard, as long as Philip paid all the costs.

Philip would have agreed to almost anything to get Dorothy's divorce settled. He was still battling with Elspeth's spending. Although it had stopped now, after several legal warnings from Andrew, Philip was still left with debts to clear. His new post was helping his financial situation dramatically He comforted himself that he had time before his own divorce got under way to sort out his finances.

"I'm surprised I don't feel any different, Elizabeth." Dorothy phoned her daughter to tell her the news.

"I'm not, Mum. It's taken so long, and you and Philip are so settled. It seems as if you are married anyway."

"Not to Philip. He can't wait to make an honest woman out of me, bless him." He was of course relieved and delighted when he saw the letter that evening.

One hurdle behind them, life continued as it inevitably does, and the second divorce faded into the background. They grew closer, happier, and more content with their lives together. Richard became a teenager and began to spread his wings. Tom was promoted and he and Elizabeth bought a new house a few miles away. Philip's boys disappeared out of his life. He heard news of them occasionally through their friends' families.

Three more years were to pass before Philip held his decree absolute in his hands. He and Dot were married the following week.

* * *

The day had arrived. Dorothy was going home. Her bag was almost packed. She said her goodbyes to all her companions on the ward and sat by her bed, waiting for Elizabeth to arrive. The staff had all been so kind and they each in turn wished her well.

"We'll all miss you, Dorothy."

"I won't miss you." She laughed as she pushed the last few odds and ends into the bag. Finally she picked up the photograph of herself and Philip signing the register after their marriage.

* * *

It was the day of their wedding. A cold January wind bent the leafless trees, but the sky was blue, and no clouds threatened to spoil the occasion. Dorothy wore a woollen dress in a delicate shade of oyster with a matching coat. She never wore a hat, but had given in on this occasion, to Elizabeth's insistence.

"Mum, you have to wear a hat for your wedding." She was glad of it this morning as the wind howled in the chimney.

Philip had left earlier with Tom to arrive at the register office before the bride. They had decided to have a completely private ceremony, much to Elizabeth's surprise.

"Don't you want the whole world to know, after all you have gone through?"

"We aren't doing it for the whole world, Elizabeth. We are marrying for us, and you and Tom, who have stood by us from day one. The people who have snorted disapproval, gossiped, and tried to split us up mean nothing. They will find out in time, some will even come pussyfooting around, because knowing Philip can be useful to them. We are simply legalising our situation, whilst making a commitment to one another. After all these years it is hardly necessary." Dorothy looked serene and at peace with herself.

There was little planning to do. Richard was away at school now, Johnny up in Scotland still. They both knew, of course, but no one else did.

Elizabeth came into the room.

"Better put your hat on, Mum, it's time we were off." She fastened the spray of freesia into her mother's lapel, the delicate pinks complementing the oyster of her outfit. The taxi came up the drive on time, and with a final check on the flat the two went down the outside steps, heads down against the bitter wind.

Philip looked handsome in his new navy suit. Happiness shone from his face as he greeted Dorothy with a gentle kiss. Almost immediately they were called into the office. As the brief ceremony was about to take place, the door opened and in walked Johnny.

"I hope you don't mind, I know you wanted it keeping quiet." He rushed over to the couple standing ready for their marriage. Dorothy and Philip were overcome.

"Mind? Johnny, it's wonderful. It has made everything perfect."

The registrar coughed politely. He had another couple waiting.

"Sorry," said Philip, laughing as he spoke. Elizabeth patted the seat next to her, and her brother quickly sat down. They held hands as their mother took Philip for her husband.

Tom photographed them signing the register. Elizabeth wiped the tears from her eyes and prayed they would be granted many years together.

Tom drove them to their favourite restaurant for a celebration lunch. As they walked inside, Luigi, the headwaiter, came over to greet them. He spotted some confetti on their clothes, and looked questioningly at Philip. Bursting with pride, Philip could not resist.

"Yes, Luigi, she has made an honest man of me at last!"

"Congratulations, sir, I had no idea, we would have laid on something special had we known."

"All we want is our usual quiet table as arranged, thank you, Luigi. By the way, we are one more than expected."

"No problem, sir." The beaming waiter led them to their favourite corner, signalling for an extra seat and place setting as he went. Then sitting them down, he handed out the menus. He left momentarily, returning with a bottle of Bollinger!

"With my compliments, sir, and may I wish you both every happiness."

"How very kind, thank you, Luigi. You are the first to know."

"Not for long," laughed Dorothy.

"You know me too well, Mrs Hislop." Luigi poured the champagne and left them to their menus.

"Cheers," said Tom. "To Mr and Mrs Hislop."

The meal went well, and when the coffee was brought, Tom said a few words.

"I'm not one for speeches, as you know, but this is a very special day for all of us. Dorothy and Philip are beginning a new life together. We all wish them the happiness they have worked so hard for, and may they celebrate many anniversaries together. I give you Dorothy and Philip." The glasses clinked and Philip stood up. A shy man in spite of his position in life, he looked round the table, and began to speak.

"Thank you, Tom, and all of you, especially Elizabeth, who has been so supportive from the beginning. It is marvellous that Johnny arrived when he did. I really appreciate the effort it must have taken for you to get here in time. Looking at you all, not forgetting Richard, I salute my family. Together you have all made my life complete, especially Dorothy. She made me live again, remember how to fight again, and how to love, truly love, someone. To you all!"

Again the glasses clinked, Philip sat down and put his arm around his bride. She looked beautiful, as radiant as a young girl. She spoke quietly to Elizabeth at her other side. "Now I know what love is, Elizabeth. I believe I have found what you and Tom have. I used to laugh at you both, you know; you were so besotted with one another. I believe true love is a rare thing. You were lucky to meet one another so young, and had the sense to know what you had found. You have had a lifetime together. God bless you both."

* * *

It was a struggle up the staircase to Dot's first-floor flat. She managed, however, with an effort, and sank into the new, high-seated chair that Elizabeth and Tom had bought for her. This among other items had been made conditional for her return home. Elizabeth put the kettle on and returned to her mother. She found Dot placing the photograph of the signing of the register, on Philip's writing desk. Her thoughts were far away in time. *We had eighteen years together, Philip, before cancer answered the invitation of cigarettes and pipes. It was not long enough. I still miss you.* For some reason John came into her thoughts. He had died a year after Philip, suddenly in the night, of a heart attack. *I would have been a widow anyway. Poor John, he should have never have married.* She turned as Elizabeth entered the room. She gently touched Philip's image captured forever at their long-awaited marriage.

"Now we are both home again."

"Yes, you are, Mum, but you've never been apart, have you?"

Dorothy looked at her daughter and a smile passed between them.

"No, dear, you are quite right."

208

THE END

Printed in the United Kingdom
by Lightning Source UK Ltd.
116414UKS00001B/355-396